REDEMPTIVE BLOOD

A BLOOD WORLD NOVEL - BOOK 7

TAMARA ROSE BLODGETT

T . R O S E
P R E S S

VIP LIST

To be the first to hear about new releases and bargains—
from Tamara Rose Blodgett/Marata Eros—sign up below to
be on my VIP List. (I promise not to spam or share your email
with *anyone*!)

♥ SIGN UP TO BE ON THE:
MARATA EROS VIP LIST ♥
https://tinyurl.com/SubscribeMarataEros-News
♥ SIGN UP TO BE ON THE :
TAMARA ROSE BLODGETT VIP LIST ♥
https://tinyurl.com/SubscribeTRB-News

MUSIC

Music that inspired me during the writing of **REDEMPTIVE:**

"Into the Trees"

by
Zoë Keating

CHARACTER LIST

Trevor- Deflector

Northwestern Were Pack:
*Lawrence- Packmaster
*Emmanuel "Manny" - Beta to Lawrence
*Anthony "Tony" Daniel Laurent- Second to Lawrence
Adrianna "Adi"- Alpha female

Southeastern Were Pack:
David- Packmaster
Alan Greene- Alpha male
Lacey Greene – female Were and Alan's sister
Buck "Slash"- Alpha male
Karl Truman- former Homer detective
Ford- Alpha male/ FBI agent
Reagan - Moon Warrior, Lacey's daughter

Southeastern Vampire Kiss:
*Merlin- Coven leader
*William- new coven leader
Brynn- New leader of the Southeastern

Northwestern Vampire Kiss:
Gabriel- Coven Leader
Claire- William's cousin William-
Runner/shifter/Singer blood (now deceased)

Unseelie Sidhe fey:
Queen Darcel- Sidhe
Tharell- mixed Sidhe warrior
Cormack- Sidhe warrior

Domiatri "Domi"- Sidhe warrior
Rex- Sidhe
Kiel (*key-ale*)- dragon shifting Sidhe
Celesta- Sidhe warrior
Delilah - Vampire, third to Julia, Scott's half-sister

Rogue Reds:
Ezekiel "Zeke"

Rogue Alpha female Were:
Tessa

FEDS:
Tom Harriet
Tai (*tie*) Simon

Western Were Pack:
Tramack

[*the*] **Lanarre:**
Drek
Bowen
Tahlia
Neil

New Characters:
Jenni
Devin
Bray
Ella

A BLOOD OVERVIEW

Dear Readers,

Firstly, thanks so much for reading my work, for sticking beside me through so many books *and* for your patience while I write them 😊

The Blood Series has become a complicated work (keep your snickering to a minimum). Toward that end, I'd like to briefly re- cap the end of the last book, ENCHANT-MENT, which was released sixteen months before this one. A tiny refresher might help those of you who are fuzzy on the details of what the last installment wrapped up (and do nothing for those of you who write me saying you've re-read the entire series in anticipation of reading the new book)! *God love ya.*

REDEMPTIVE will be a spin-off of sorts. I envision the next few books to wrap each couple's story while filling in the "blanks" of others' as well, thereby deepening the knowledge base of the Singer world.

During the last installment, Julia and Scott enjoyed a handfasted Singer-style wedding, and they now make their way to the fey sithen in the hopes that group of supernaturals can relieve her of the demonic spore gifted upon her by Praile.

By the way, that evil asshat is still skulking around, horns and all, jonesing to make Lazarus miserable. Thank all that is holy that Tessa is One Tough Broad.

Can Laz be trusted? Because I left things in quite a little mess when the book ended. It appeared as though Laz and Praile were in cahoots with each other and were intent on tag teaming Tessa.

But then Drek shows up—he who hath stuck both feet in his mouth when Tahlia needed him most. Tahlia has assumed her bird form to escape his attentions, not even allowing herself to fully realize their potential as a royal Lanarre couple. And why should she? Drek tied her up and didn't give her a chance to fully explain things, while the grief over losing her guardians by Tony's (so glad that insufferable douche is dead) hand is still fresh.

Slash and Adi have plopped onto the lap of a benign witch. *Or so they think* . They're technically mated while trying to fly under the Lanarre radar since Slash so handily dispatched three Lanarres who thought they would get froggy and jump on Adi's lily pad. *Au contraire*, Adi managed an escape with Slash's help, but not before getting the bite on Jenni, the helpful nurse dying of terminal breast cancer.

Although Slash thwarted an attack on Adi, her Lanarre attacker fatally wounded this innocent human caught in the crossfire of Were against Were.

Now Jenni has become that which attacked—and ultimately saved—her.

Where can Jenni go? Who will teach her what it means to be Were. Is she cured? Is there a pack that would take her in or will the politics of the supernaturals deny her?

See where this is going, guys? I always make a tornado to sort and love the challenge of hammering out these characters' lives, developing devastatingly evil villains while the hope of love propels the entire tale forward at breakneck speed.

Hope you dig the ride.

- *Tamara*

February 2017

CHAPTER 1

JENNI

*J*enni heaves herself on her back, the dead leaves of the forest that borders the Port Townsend General Hospital offering a cushion and temporary respite.

She puts her forearm over her eyes. *What just happened to me?*

Hot tears of frustration and fear slide out of her eyes as she takes in the wet gloom of the forest she dragged herself into. She scans the forest, where the familiar smells surrounding the hospital are influenced by the deep-green blanket of wet vegetation so dense this close to the rain forest. Her scrubs are damp with moisture—and her own blood, from a wound that should have killed her.

Jenni shuts her eyes, remembering.

Today, she'd gone to work like any other day. Despite the knowledge of her impending death, Jenni is accomplished. She cares for others.

Creased and neglected, the papers that prove her

1

illness is terminal were left in her small condo, which was a stone's throw from PT General. Forgotten.

Like her future. It had once been so bright.

What had Lance told her before they broke up? Oh yeah, that they would live every remaining day to the fullest.

That was until her chemo and radiation failed to save her, and Jenni lost her hair.

Every strand.

Jenni got sick—and thin. Not the model thin so coveted by society, but with hipbones like tentpoles. Her every rib was countable, and the hollows that carved out her face made her resemble a skeleton.

Still, Jenni hoped, even as Lance grew more and more distant. Finally, he just stopped calling.

The cancer diagnosis was only slightly more awful than seeing him with his new girlfriend.

She looked healthy.

Jenni's shaky inhale is wet with the tears that come more freely now. She balls her hands into fists, angrily scrubbing her eyes of the sadness for a man less courageous than a hyena.

He laughed like one, too.

She guffaws, hiccupping through her tears, and makes a conscious effort to uncurl her fingers. In her entire short life, Jenni's never shirked a duty, responsibility, or anything that others put at her feet.

That's why she didn't back down when Adi revealed what she really was. Jenni still had a job to do, no matter how terrible the turn her life has taken.

Her fingers tremble as she explores her throat with

fingertips covered in her own blood. The skin beneath her touch tingles like a healing wound.

What did you do to me, Adi?

Jenni's mind whispers the answer before her next breath. *She saved me.*

Am I still sick?

A thin, rope-like twist of flesh is raw and throbbing underneath the brush of her fingers.

She drops her hand to feel the cool contact of decaying leaves.

The staff at PT General are going to wonder what the hell happened. *Where is Jenni? What about that mess in the underground parking?*

Jenni sits up, head spinning. She slaps her palms on the ground on either side to stabilize herself.

Her only goal when those creatures were going to town on one another was to get the hell out of there. She'll never get the image out of her mind. The half-were-wolves are an acid-etched memory inside her brain.

Jenni's sure that she witnessed the man who had crushed Adi's heart killing those who would harm her. The idea was confusing, but true.

Adi hadn't told Jenni his identity.

But Adi's eyes had told Jenni all she needed to know. She'd lived two lifetimes in her twenty-seven years. *Cancer that doesn't kill you ages you.*

Cancer that kills you ages you, too. Cancer blows.

Jenni understands a broken heart. Takes one to know one. She easily spotted the fissures in Adi like creases on a well-worn map.

Jenni shuts her eyes, scrutinizing her memory of Slash.

A mountain of a man, he burst through the solid-core steel door that opens from the underground part of the hospital to the subterranean parking lot Jenni escaped from.

The impact of the door being thrown open shredded the steel into curlicues. They scattered like metallic shavings, skittering to a stop where the border of the blood from her body pooled beneath her.

Jenni craned her neck, though her throat muscles and tendons spasmed painfully with the movement. Slash's eyes were a deep, slowly spinning emerald. A line of scar tissue bisecting his hard face became granite as he took in another man holding Adi.

In living color, their torment for each other was a movie playing out in front of Jenni's eyes.

Of course, Jenni knows they were not men. But werewolves.

She heard the conversation as though the words reached her through an underground tunnel filled with water.

Lanarre. Prosecution.

Slash didn't seem to care about the warnings from the others.

Jenny lay there and watched Adi defend herself against males who were far bigger than her. Claiming she was "in heat," they trailed Adi.

She'd wanted away so badly, she threw herself into a highway with cars traveling in excess of sixty miles per hour.

Even with the remnants of dead humans coating her body, they scented Adi. What degree of smelling sensitivity would these dudes need to have if they could find her through a body bag of human gore?

Acute, that's what.

Jenni understands she's procrastinating, that the edges of shock have worn off during the couple of hours since the battle.

I need to get out of here. To regroup.

Jenni stands, gripping a nearby tree trunk. She clings to it, pressing her forehead against the rough bark, and just that little bit of physical exertion is enough to leave her weak.

The depths of the forest have grown murky. Night's coming. *Great. Just what I need.*

Jenni rolls her face against the tree trunk and swipes a hand through her straw-like hair, plucking a leaf out of the disaster. Clinging to the trunk, its sharp bark biting at her flesh, she takes stock of her options.

She shouldn't have lived. Adi bit her on the throat, and she can still feel the heat like liquid fire pouring from the entry wound.

Jenni will never forget those spinning silver eyes. Never.

Adi injected Jenni with something vital. In fact, if Jenni concentrates, she can feel an echo of Adi.

Like a locator.

Jenni, get a grip. You don't *know* this girl. She's somebody that coated her face with dead people like war paint.

The facts are: She's a werewolf. I wasn't long for this world. She gave me a stay of execution.

Or so she assumes. Jenni allows several deep breaths

to steady her. She's a classically trained nurse—who doesn't believe in myth.

In school, Jenni was one of those girls with her nose stuck in a book. Math and science were her favorite subjects, and when she splinted a bird's broken wing, she understood what her role was in this life.

Doctoring was her calling. Too bad life wasn't going to give her time to fulfill that destiny.

Now *this* is her destiny.

Her chilled fingers touch the marred flesh of her throat again, as if the two were magnets drawn together at the spot where this new life began. And her touch finds smooth skin where a scar like a whip of rope crossed her neck a half hour before.

Jenni's gasp is loud in the forest, startling the small creatures nearby.

The grievous wound vanished completely.

She's lost blood—and seen things she shouldn't have: events that didn't seem real and creatures in half-human, half-wolf form with talons at the tips of their fingers and bright glowing eyes that appeared to spin depending on their range of emotions.

Her gaze spears the woods, finding the small gap between the trees and the softly lit streetlamps that surround the hospital.

Can I drive?

Jenni takes a step away from the tree. Her body begins to shake with a hunger she's never known before.

A random thought surfaces in her mind: *I need meat.*

Her mouth runs with saliva, and she licks her lips.

Jenni thinks if she doesn't get food in the next ten seconds, her body will start to consume itself.

She hesitates, looking at the distance between the edge of the forest and the parking garage where her car is.

Maybe *that's* possible. Her scientific brain whirs into action. If what she suspects is true, and with her healed throat, she's inclined to believe what she can see and touch. *I'm becoming a werewolf.*

If such a thing were possible, the metabolic shift would be enormous. In theory, such a change would reshape her body, necessitating an extreme amount of fuel. Maybe her desire for red meat isn't a craving—but a God-given need for a specific kind of gas for this new body.

She removes her hands from the tree trunk and takes a few steps. Then noises reach her, and she spots strobes of blood red and cool blue color pulsing icily across the parking lot.

Cops exit their cars. Jenni counts three, and her heartbeat ticks faster.

Shit.

Her nostrils flare, and she smells something else. A lone growl whispers past the lips of a working police dog. She can see the hackles of his mottled tan-and-black coat rise at the ridge of his back.

The dog knows where she is. Her eyebrows fold together. A canine is also likely to know *what* she is.

Jenni turns her head, cocking her ear at the tight group of police. Even in her numb state, she hears what they say without too much trouble.

"We've got enough blood on the ground for a typical

gang encounter, but not a single weapon—powered or otherwise—can be found."

Jenni steps nearer to the fringes of the thick trees that tease the asphalt of the parking lot and ducks behind a tree whose roots lift the lip of the hard black edge of the parking lot.

She narrows her eyes, taking in the scene, swiping away sweat that has begun to run from her temple to chin. Jenni fights holding her breath as she listens.

The older cop, fingers wrapping his chin, nods. "The staff have been tallied. The only person missing is Jennifer French. Nurse." The cop removes a small notepad from his front pocket, running a blunt finger down the page he flips to.

Jenni's fingers clench into fists, instantly stilling when she hears her name.

The other cop, whose hair is blond enough to show well in the twilight, hikes his chin. "One of the doctor's is hot to find the patient who was under French's care, now MIA. Adrianna?"

Jenni closes her eyes. *Dammit, left my notes there. In my own defense, I didn't know I'd witness three murders and one decapitation, in addition to becoming a supernatural creature.*

Jenni bites the inside of her cheek to keep from laughing. This is *not* the time. But sometimes, the urge to laugh grips her at the most inopportune times.

"Think it's weird the doc doesn't care as much about his staff as he does this mystery patient."

The older cop shrugs, lifting his fingers to scratch his scalp beneath the bill of his hat. "Doesn't matter. Equal status. Two women missing. Buckets of blood and brain matter all over the place. Some serious killing went on, and forensics will have a helluva time mucking through that mess." He jerks a thumb at the yawning entrance to the garage behind them.

"You think the nurse—"

The older cop drops his hands to his sides, clearly frustrated. "Don't speculate, son. Not going to help her get found."

Can't stick around for this. They'll definitely ask questions Jenni doesn't have the answer for. Then her answers will get her locked up.

Forever.

Nobody's going to believe the story she gives them. Better to wait until things settle before getting her car.

She pats down the pocket of her scrubs as a brutal cramp assaults her stomach. Twenty dollars.

Enough change for burgers.

Longingly, Jenni peers in the dark hole of the underground garage. Bright-yellow crime scene tape bisects the entrance.

Damn.

The dog inside the police cruiser lifts its nose, running it along the edge of the partially ajar window.

It growls, and Jenni's insides tense, making her gnawing hunger worse.

The young cop gives the dog a hard look.

"Butch, what is it fella?" He walks over to the cruiser and sticks his hand through the window to scratch the German shepherd behind the ear.

The dog whines, pointing its snout in Jenni's direction.

Jenni sinks deeper into the gloom, her stomach

loosing an ear-splitting growl. She can't remember the last time she was this hungry.

Her sharp mind supplies the instantaneous answer: *BC.*

And no, that's not "before Christ." *Her* BC stands for something completely different. Before cancer.

The young cop's hand goes to his holster, his alert gaze moving to where she stands, though Jenni's sure he can't see her.

She doesn't think too long about why she can see him like it's daylight instead of early evening.

His weak human eyes can't see me. The same eyes I had early this morning.

"Butch isn't jumpy," the young cop states thoughtfully, his gaze continuing to roam the thick trees.

Old Cop heaves a shoulder, letting it drop abruptly. "Never used the dogs."

The young cop doesn't look back at his partner, his blond head poised forward like a duck. "They can sense things we can't."

Jenni's palms dampen. *I bet.*

The silence feels loud to her. Or maybe it's because all she hears without them speaking is the blood rushing in her ears.

Jenni creeps backward. Pain stabs her gut, and she stifles a scream, wrapping her belly with her arms as a small whimper escapes.

The dog barks, a sharp pressing word of greeting that Jenni instinctively understands.

Thanks, Butch.

His tail begins to *thunk* inside the car.

Jenni backs up faster, trips over a bare tree root, and falls on her ass with a crash that seems to echo in the still woods.

Shit. The transference of sound is exactly perfect for them to hear her klutz move, and Jenni leaps back up.

The gun has cleared the young cop's holster now. Alert eyes on the woods, he releases the handle of the car. Butch smoothly leaps out of his prison within the cruiser.

He comes straight for Jenni.

She pivots hard, and her only thought before she takes off running is: *Food.*

There's a primal sense of time running out. The transition Adi set into motion needs something as a catalyst to solidify the morphing of what Jenni's becoming. After facing her own death for so long, the gift of life, even though it might be a terrifyingly different one, is one she doesn't want to lose.

Nobody gets a second chance—especially girls with terminal cancer.

Jenni runs, surprised by how fast and strong her body is. She easily avoids every branch and leaps over half-caved-in decaying logs that were clearcut a hundred years before she was born.

The scenery flanking Jenni blurs in wet emerald glory, nighttime breathing its dark coldness through the dense copse of trees.

Butch is far behind, losing her.

Jenni can hear his heartbeat and scent his need to find her. She also knows where every living thing is within the woods that she's sprinting through.

Her nose tells her everything.

When she can no longer hear her pursuers, Jenni slows then eventually stops. Bending over, she plants her palms on her knees, panting, feeling the grit of filth and stiff, caked blood on her scrub pants. The pain from her hunger scores her body like razor blades, and she sucks in a gasp.

She straightens, walking toward the busy road buzzing with traffic.

Then the golden arches come into view.

Jenni feels how weak her smile is, ignoring the tears of relief that spread like a river on her cheeks. Doesn't matter. She struggles to the shoulder of a road she's traveled on a million times by car.

Agony stabs deeply, and she slaps a hand over her mouth, lurching forward. She staggers across the road and navigates the last twenty paces to the restaurant. She tears open the metal door. The force makes the glass shiver within the aluminum frame.

Jenni doesn't care about anything but food. Her vision is closing at the periphery, feathering to grayish black at the edges.

A girl with hair dyed the same shade as Jenni's takes one look at her and takes a half step back from the register.

Jenni doesn't have the benefit of a mirror, and there are no shits given at the moment. She sways where she stands.

She needs a burger.

Right now.

"Hi," the girl begins with a comedic hesitation that

would make Jenni laugh under other circumstances. Not today. "Welcome to Mc—"

"I need eight hamburgers."

Cheese. Jenni licks dry lips. "I mean cheeseburgers."

The girl blinks, and Jenni's eyes take in the garish violet eyeshadow and liquid black eyeliner circling the girl's eyes like a cat's.

She latches on to that sight, clutching the cheap laminate countertop and trying to stay upright.

"And a cup of water. Large."

The girl's hands shake as she taps in the order to the register. "That'll be…"

Slapping the twenty on the counter, Jenni stumbles, managing to revolve herself in a stiff semi-turn, and takes the first seat that presents itself.

"Don't you want your change?" the girl asks.

"No," Jenni whispers, flopping in the molded plastic booth and folding her arms, making a cradle for her head.

It seems like hours before the food comes, but the girl who took Jenni's order sidles up beside her, sliding the tray of steaming burgers next to her head.

"Looks like you're hungry."

Jenni rolls her eyes up to look at the smudged goth makeup. Past the makeup, past everything, the girl's gaze is compassionate.

"Thank you," Jenni manages to rasp.

Then she digs in.

CHAPTER 2

ADI

*W*ater runs out of Adi's open mouth. Blissfully hot, fresh, cleansing water.

The cramped shower space barely allows turning, and she thinks how much the tight quarters will blow for her new mate. Slash is tough, but catching that soap on the way down might be a little *tough*.

Adi smirks.

If someone would have told her yesterday—while she was running from Slash and his misunderstood treatment of her, from their mating, from his rough conduct—that she would be taking a shower in a witch's house in bum-fucked Egypt—she would have laughed.

But, here she is, in a forest supposedly filled with trolls. Now, Adi's not prejudiced. Live and let live is a totally solid plan. But trolls? Adi's not sure about the truth there.

She's not sure about a *lot* of things.

Adi soaps her body. The light scent of rose soap

mingles with the steam from the shower as she thinks about the last forty-eight hours of her chaotic life.

Slash is standing guard while she does her damnedest to clean human death from her body and make sense of her hair.

Adi gives up, rinsing the rats nest attached to her scalp and praying for a comb.

Della may or may not have one. Adi's not sure what toiletries her unicorn backpack still has.

She presses her palm against the molded fiberglass shower wall, warm water dripping between her breasts. The image of bright-blue shampoo running out of the bottle when she ran from the Lanarre has her breath quickening. *Definitely the shampoo's gone.* Everything's so muddled. She's lucky she thought to take the pack.

Adi cranks the faucet to off. The showerhead drips loudly inside the chipped and split porcelain-enameled cast iron basin. The drops echo within the confines of the tiny bathroom.

Adi shivers.

Slipping carefully out of the shower stall, she folds the wonky glass door back to the closed position and plucks a worn towel from the commode top where she left it earlier.

Drying off her feet, she works upward slowly. When she gets to her crotch, she winces and, instead of rubbing, dabs the area, which is still sore from what Slash and she shared only a day ago. Her smile is crooked. Obviously, she's gonna hurt—losing her virginity and shit. Adi gnaws on her bottom lip and finishes drying herself off.

Adi would give anything to have some private time to exhaust the issues between her and Slash.

But there hasn't been time.

Jenni tried to get her out of the hospital, then the fucking Lanarre showed up and were rude bastards. Just thinking about those cocky butt munches makes her eyes go wolfen.

Tossing the towel over the top of the shower door to dry out the damp material, she turns, plucking panties, yoga pants, a thin *T* and socks off the top of the commode lid. No bra. All she has is a cami with a shelf bra. Adi pulls the lightweight material over her head then tightens the straps, hiking the girls up so they don't misbehave—the bane of any gal with a bustline. Adi takes a steadying breath and opens the bathroom door. The entire bathroom is so small, a person can hardly get dressed, and the shower's a joke, but Adi's grateful to be clean. That whole human roadkill paste was getting kind of ripe.

Steam pours out of the space as Adi exits, cautiously peering through the vapor of heat. She's certain she can sense Slash's presence nearby.

The opaque white barrier between them evaporates, revealing Slash, hard and tense like always.

He comes to stand before her, looming large.

"Better?" he asks, and Adi reads everything in his one question: *Are you all right? Are we?*

She gives a quick dip of her chin, and Slash's shoulders ease from the stiff posture they'd been held in.

Adi's attention shifts to the woman who took them in.

Della smiles back guilelessly.

Her shock of white hair has been poorly tamed into a

knot at her nape, where several stiff, curly strands escape like lightning strikes. Long skirts rustle softly as she stands beside Slash, who towers alongside her.

Della whacks him suddenly in the thigh with the decorative cane she's holding in her right hand.

Without even flinching, Slash turns slowly to face Della, building thunder contorting his features.

She puts her hands on wide hips. "Get over there and allay her fears, Red." Della purses her lips.

Slash's lips curl up. "If you could cease and desist from beating me for a minute, I might do that."

"Humph." She leans on her cane and juts her chin in Adi's direction.

"Are you afraid?" Slash asks in a low voice as his deep and penetrating gaze holds hers prisoner. Not everything is right between them, but his ability to protect her from whatever threatens, isn't in question.

Adi's heartbeats stack as she lies, though she knows Slash can scent it. "No."

Their eyes clash, and she painfully swallows under that probing stare.

Slash nods, appearing to take her at her word, and passes within inches of her.

His fingertips brush her hip. "My turn."

Adi's eyes shift to his for a split-second, seeing the clear warning there. Della's hospitality might involve things they don't want, that brief look says.

She frowns, not sure they're safe.

Not sure about anything.

That seems like the theme since she left the Northwestern.

"Sit, my dear." Della blinks rapidly and slowly lowers her girth into a tattered couch. Upholstery that sported fat cabbage-style roses long ago looks vaguely like a watercolor painting on cloth, weathered from age and use.

Adi walks reluctantly toward the sofa and sits at the opposite end. Her backpack—the one with the sparkly unicorns now partially decimated by road scrub—sits on the floor at the foot of the couch. She touches it briefly like a talisman, noting the weight with a hooked index finger, then lets the beat-up bag drop the inch she lifted it.

"I'm not a robber." The corners of Della's mouth turn down as the soft pattering sound of water reaches them from the closed bathroom door.

The awkward quiet comes to life around them. Adi can hear a clock in a faraway corner tick. Gooseflesh rises at the only sound between them.

Their eyes meet, and Adi notes Della's are like pale pool water, the kind that the human kids splash and play in on hot summer days.

"I don't have much," Adi finally admits, trying to explain her territorial behavior. "When the Lanarre found me in the forest, I had all my toiletries spread out by the riverbed, and all I could do was toss the pack on my back and run."

Della leans back, scrutinizing Adi so hard, she fights squirming.

Adi's all about generosity. Taking that shower and having a safe spot to kick back for the night makes her dizzy with gratefulness. But... she feels an assessment here that makes her uneasy. Being an alpha female Were gives Adi her instincts—ones she doesn't ignore easily. She suddenly wonders if Slash feels this way, and glances at the closed bathroom door.

"Why did you run from the Lanarre?"

Jarred from her thoughts, Adi shifts restlessly. "I-I'm in heat," she confesses. Adi owes the witch that. Besides, with her powers, Della might have already guessed the issue.

"Ah," Della says, folding her gnarled hands together, her features alight with interest. "So the Lanarre happened upon you and laid chase."

Adi nods, clenching her own hands, brow furrowing.

Here it comes.

"Why was your mate not there?" Her white brows arch. "Those Were would not have touched you had he been there. Once claimed, you are off limits, as the humans say." She sniffs derisively.

The state of being human is frowned on by all super-naturals.

Adi studies her knotted hands, clenched so tightly they're bleeding to white. "We got in a fight."

Della chuckles, and Adi scowls at her.

"That doesn't seem possible."

Well, it was. Slash had acted like a numero uno dick. Just thinking about it makes Adi pissed all over again.

Adi meets Della's eyes. "There was a pack of mutts from the Western den who ran across us after..." Adi stares at her lap. TMI-much.

"I understand," Della says smoothly, releasing Adi from having to explain.

Adi tucks her chin and takes a deep, fortifying breath.

"Anyways, they started trying to get at me, real rogue types—"

"Though they were from a pack?"

Adi nods, going on without mentioning the *L* word. "Yeah. Clowns." She swipes a wet strand of hair that's come out from the towel wrapped around her head like a turban. "So Slash wasn't gonna stand for that and tried to beat them down. I did, too," she whispers. Adi's exhale is like a deflated balloon. "But they hurt Slash bad—paralyzed him. And I was hurt, but I could move."

Not that it helped me.

The silence is heavy between them again.

"But Slash could not?" The wrinkles on Della's face converge into lines of concern.

"No. He was down for the count." Adi feels suddenly weary and puts her head in her hands. She's tired of her crazy life, worn down from the heat bullshit, and exhausted from running. She wants some fucking peace.

"He told you what he needed to so that you'd be safe."

Adi's face whips up, and her hands drop to the tops of her thighs. Her sigh is tired, like the rest of her. "Probably."

Della's face perks with a wicked grin. "Definitely. Male Reds are renowned for the protectiveness of their females."

"I know," Adi says, propping her face into her hands again. "I just think his delivery sucks."

Della holds up a weathered hand; her veins are like blue lace under her thin skin.

I wonder how old she is?

The water stops, and Adi turns to look at the closed door again, relief flooding her.

"No matter what he said, he did it for your benefit, Adrianna."

"Adi," she states automatically and turns back to look at Della.

She smiles again. "Adi."

Adi's mesmerized by her teeth. They look sharp.

Slash opens the door, and steam pours out.

"Why I bother with feeding the woodstove is beyond me!" Della plants her hands on the couch and heaves herself up. She trudges to the wood stove and bends over the cast iron belly to adjust the damper. "There. You two have put more hot air inside my house than I've had in a coon's age."

Slash glances at Adi, obviously assessing her temper.

Smart man.

She folds her arms, leaning back, not wanting to admit she feels safer simply because he's within sight or that she needs his presence. A small part of her still wants Slash to suffer for making her sick with what she thought was his rejection.

Sometimes being in love sucks donkey dicks.

Adi's exhale is a puff of irritation. She's agitated that Della saw the core of her anger with Slash and that her emotions are so transparent. She's mad that Slash is two hundred plus years older than her. Like the male can help *that.*

And she's in heat. Which means he will need to sate her. Only his seed on a more or less continuous basis will ease her during her heat. Even as she sits there, Adi can feel her need building. Slash's nostrils flare, and her core plumps with the gesture.

Adi wants to cry; she hates being that obvious. The fresh hurt from Slash's abandonment still echoes in the chambers of her heart.

Then Della turns. "I don't have many guests, especially your kind."

Your kind. Adi can feel Slash's frown without looking in his direction.

"Why don't you sleep on it, and when the sun rises, everything will be righted. No decision made on the chasm of exhaustion is a good one." Her face grows serious. Her watery blue eyes appear to glow in the soft lighting of lamps scattered in dim corners. "And the trolls be about. They are most active at night."

Adi gives a small shudder. Trolls sound creepy.

Slash strolls across the scarred wide-plank wood floorboards and stands in front of Adi.

I won't look at him.

But her face rises against her will, her sex throbbing for one thing. She makes a mute plea with her eyes, and he shakes his head, denying what she begs him with her gaze.

Can we just talk?

No, his face clearly says in silent reply. They'll be doing way more than conversation. He holds out his hand to her, and she slides her own inside his, defeated by her own biology.

The sheer size of his hand engulfs hers as he gently pulls her off the couch.

"The wards will hold. No troll is brazen enough to cross." Della's chin kicks up.

Slash gives Della an assessing look and finally says, "Thank you for your kindness, Della."

Her smile is thin. "I'm not kind. Just practical." She cackles like a true witch, and the fine hairs at Adi's nape rise.

But the next moment, she melts against Slash's strong chest, and he hooks a heavy arm around her, pulling her close. Warmth and security surrounds her, and instantly, Adi's breathing slows to a purr of contentment.

Slash stares at Della for a heartbeat more, then Della turns toward a long corridor in the opposite direction, giving them her back.

Adi scoops up her pack and follows.

Slash's arm remains around her.

* * *

"THE DUST IS FREE," Della quips, moving swiftly ahead and plumping pillows on a small double-sized bed covered by a wedding ring-style quilt.

A small nightstand of dark polished wood stands at one side of the bed with a Kelly-green Depression-era knob at the center of a tiny drawer directly beneath the top. Adi recognizes the style instantly because Susan from the pack was a big antique collector.

A knot forms in her throat, and sudden tears threaten. Her emotions are so right *there*. She hates it.

Slash grips her shoulders, turning her to face him, and his scent engulfs Adi. Need spears her harder.

"What is it?"

His dark eyes pierce her emotions and thoughts. The scar pulls tight in his stern face as his lips mark a flat line across his face.

"Homesick," she manages to croak.

"He is your home now, Adi." Della's wisdom swings wide, sweeping over her like a meat cleaver in a field of daisies.

The stem of her metaphorical flower sways backward from the flashing metal, and she gives Della a sharp look. Adi doesn't want to hear people's thoughts about what she should think—or how she should feel.

They can all get fucked.

Even this witch that offered them temporary sanctuary. She opens her mouth to say so, and shame fills her at the compassion she finds in Della's open face.

I'm being a dumb bitch. Adi covers her face and listens as the rustle of Della's skirts gradually quieting as she crosses the room, leaving Adi and Slash alone.

"Is it the heat?" Slash asks beside her temple in slow quiet words, and she leans her face against the roughness of his, feeling stubble and his ragged scar against her own unmarred skin.

"Yes. No—I don't know."

She presses her forehead against the hard planes of his chest.

"Things are unsettled now, Adrianna."

Adi laughs. She can't help it. She steps away, though Slash's hands remain on her shoulders. "Are you kidding me? Unsettled? *Unhinged* is more like it. I killed that nurse, Jenni. I gave her a death sentence."

Slash tightens his hold, giving Adi a small shake. "No, you gave a precious gift to a human female—your essence. Only an alpha can make another Were." His eyes are unwavering on her face as though he's memorizing every feature. "I smelled her disease. As a human, she was *already* dying. As a Were, she lives."

Adi searches his face. "I know it was against our laws."

Slash's smile is amused, lightening the moment. "As though that matters. I think we've broken every Lycan law ever made."

Adi's eyes grow wet, burning with tears she doesn't shed. "Jenni was only human, but she saved me. She *tried* to save me."

Slash nods. "She gave us time. Without her, I might have—" Slash scrubs a hand over his skull trim. "I might have not gotten to you in time."

They exchange a significant look.

Slash cups her chin gently. "I cannot stand the thought of what they would have done to my mate."

Adi grips his thick forearms as Slash pulls her against him.

"Help me," Adi begs, tears beginning to pull at the corners of her eyes. "I hurt."

"Let me service you, Adrianna. It is my role. My pleasure. My duty."

Adi raises her head, silent tears streaming. "How can I say no, you sweet-talker."

But his face remains solemn as he tenderly brushes the wetness away with a swish of his thumb.

Adi gulps back her stress and tension. This is the male she gave herself to, the male she's loved since she was a whelp. No matter what Slash felt he had to do to protect her—and that she hated how he did it—Slash was motivated to save her from more harm.

She replies using the ancient words, "Ease me, mate of my heart. Curator of my soul."

Slash's smile is for Adi. And her alone.

CHAPTER 3

TESSA

*T*hat *horned fucker*, Tessa thinks a second time. She doesn't bother ruminating on Laz pairing up with Praile. It's too painful.

Besides, she needs to survive.

Just as Tessa's gearing up to get a beatdown or worse, the Lanarre prince who's betrothed to Tahlia bursts through the thick log door inside the cottage. He morphs to wolfen as he flows through the threshold. His stature gains inches before her eyes. A dusting of inky hair tipped with silver springs over the surface of his skin, spreading like a slick mat of black as it shivers to life over his flesh.

Drek crouches, arms spread like whips of muscular rope, tips his head back, and roars.

A bird in the distance caws. Tessa recognizes the sound of Tahlia in bird form.

No time to worry over being saved by the cavalry.

Or if there'll even *be* one.

Tessa sinks low.

Praile comes for her with eyes so black, she can't make

out the pupil. His horns seem to have lengthened, and he dips his chin, tail rising behind the deep-red hair of his head.

The end of his tail takes her breath. The sight of the perfect circle the size of her head, broken only by short ebony spikes of a smooth bonelike material freezes her.

Then Praile swings the fleshy weapon high above them all, a toothy black smile on his face.

Tessa's paralysis breaks, and a sound of pure distress escapes Tessa as she crouches even lower, her eyes meeting Laz's.

Betrayal fills Tessa to her toenails.

But confusion strikes her as Laz's gaze pegs her own, his eyes flipping from black to pale blue smoke.

At first, Laz is running her down with Praile. In the next moment, a slashing blur of red smoke swipes the flail-like end of Praile's tail, the very weapon that was readying to bash her head in. The ball of spiked flesh falls to the wooden floor, severed from the stem of his tail.

Tessa's so stunned she falls on her ass, the painful impact jarring her teeth together.

A fountain of black blood spurts from the tip of his amputated tail.

Gasping, she whirls, scrabbling against the slick, wide boards. Gaining purchase, she doesn't look left, right, or behind her.

She runs.

Something grabs her braid, jerking then winding hard.

Tessa screams, reaching backward. Talons spring from the tips of her fingers, and her next scream is the agony of a change too fast for her body.

28

Slicing the arms that grip her, she spins in midair, unwinding her braid as she does. Bounding from the tips of her toes, Tessa widens her arms and plunges her hands into the torso of...

Praile.

He grins inches away from her face. "A little skewer never hurt a demon, bitch."

Her eyes flick behind him, and the tail begins to mend itself. A pulsating, bulbous coating of flesh has already sealed the wound, restructuring the end of his tail.

Tessa's scalp throbs from the grip he still manages to maintain. Praile's dark blood flows over them both, covering her wrists, giving the illusion her hands have been amputated.

She clenches her teeth. "How about a scramble, fire dick?"

Praile's dark eyes widen as steam escapes every open, soft part of his body. *Yeah, even that one.*

Tessa gives a vicious twist of her wrists, and Praile's skin splits like a ripe fruit, opening to dump his guts from his body.

Deep-black entrails fall like snakes, spilling into a steaming, intertwined mess at their feet.

Tessa tries to jerk her hands out of his body—and can't. Panic chokes her.

Praile's forked tongue hisses. The tips are gray, and the appendage looks like a decaying piece of meat. The center is so black it's nearly colorless.

Tessa bends her body backward in an extreme arc, and Praile takes a step forward, grabbing her forearms and jerking her against his chest.

She is tall, but Praile is much taller. Her eyes meet his throat, and she feels her pupils dilate.

"I will fuck you until you have no cunt left, Were."

Rotten-smelling steam fills the short space between them.

Oh Moon. Tiny bumps pour over her skin, damming against where Praile's fingers tighten mercilessly against her flesh, causing her bones to ache.

Drek howls behind them, and out of her periphery, the soft blur of Laz appears like crimson water flowing through the air.

Just as her hope flees, Tessa turns to Laz desperately, like a flower to the sun.

Help me, she pleads.

Tessa shakes off her fear, scrambling backward as her feet lose purchase on a floor slick with Praile's guts.

She begins to fall, taking Praile with her.

He takes advantage of her tumble, and before he lands, Praile jerks her hands from him, whipping her arms away from her body.

Tessa lands hard on her back, the air whooshing out of her.

Clamping her wrists and pressing them against the wet floor, he kicks her legs wide with a force so hard, he bruises the inside of her thighs.

"Laz!" Tessa shrieks in a high-pitched keen full of desperation.

"Yes! Laz!" Praile taunts from above her.

Tessa moans as he presses deeper between her legs. Only her thin yoga pants keep him from stabbing inside her.

Tessa struggles, her hope draining away by the second. She's never dealt with a supernatural this strong and relentless.

Tessa throws her head forward, smashing her forehead into Praile's.

He laughs while her ears ring.

Then she feels his erection. "No," she whispers, tears of frustration stinging her eyes.

"Yes," Praile hisses with soft menace, flicking his tongue against her throat like a sick wet slap of flesh.

Squirming, she attempts to position herself in an effort to nail him where it counts.

"No you don't, Were mutt."

He heaves himself forward, spearing at the crotch of her yoga pants like a branding fire poker.

"Lazarus!" she yells again—hearing the commotion behind her, but not caring. She's having all she can do, staving off her imminent rape by a demon.

Tessa goes limp.

Praile smells instant victory and moves closer to her, his throat above her mouth.

Tessa grunts as the quarter-change leaves her and the wolfen form moves through her body like liquid fire.

Hurts.

Her body morphs beneath Praile, but he's so intent on stabbing her with his dick that he doesn't notice.

Then Tessa tears out his throat. She closes her eyes as scalding blood drenches her face. He's rolled off her, and Laz stands directly above them both, blood covering him from throat to feet as if a can of paint was thrown on him.

Only his pale eyes are stranded within his face as though he wears a raccoon's mask.

Holding back a scream to keep blood out of her mouth, Tessa crawls away from Praile and turns. Blinking his reeking blood from her eyes, she sees the pale glimmer of spine through the hole she made in his throat.

Heal *that*, fucker.

With a shaky breath, Tessa stands. She wipes her mouth dry with her sleeve.

Laz lifts his foot high and brings it down on Praile's head with a well-executed stomp.

His foot lands again and again.

Laz doesn't stop when the flesh of his instep is shredded by black skull fragments.

He doesn't stop when whatever Praile was is nothing but demonic soup on the floor, coloring the cracks in the floorboards like dirty soot.

"Laz," Tessa calls, voice hoarse.

She steps closer, but Laz isn't listening, his tail is thwacking what's left of Praile like a huge meat tenderizer.

The sounds of the unusually-shaped tail end striking Praile's body are thick and wet. Meaty.

"Stop," Tessa says, daring to inch closer.

A thick layer of steam, tinged red, surrounds Laz. "Die," Laz hisses, and his forked tongue makes short work of the word, causing the single syllable to echo with final perfection.

Tessa touches Laz's arm, and he whirls. Eyes like shining oil eat at her, and Tessa gasps, suffocating in the heat emanating from his body.

"Don't hurt me," she whispers, putting up shaking hands before him as her body melts back to quarter-change, and heaves an exhausted sigh.

Those flat black eyes that, a moment before, regarded her with cold indecision now dull to smoky gray.

Then the crisp light blue she knows is Laz without killing intent washes the irises clean of evil.

The vapor surrounding him disappears like morning mist conceding the day.

Laz comes at her faster than Tessa can retreat. Her rapid changes have made her slow and clumsy.

If he tries to kill her, there's nothing she can do. Tessa is spent. Praile almost raped her. Deep down, she knows Praile would have enjoyed raping her to death.

She's never ridden the knife's edge as closely as she just did in her long life.

But Laz doesn't kill her.

He hauls her against him, their heartbeats finding a familiar pattern of unity.

Laz strokes hair that's more loose mane than braid. The blood they wear makes them stick together.

Tessa doesn't mind.

Because one touch from Laz is like a thousand tongues of licking fire and a salve to the problem of her being in heat.

Laz tips her head back, looking deeply into her eyes. "Did you doubt me?"

She shakes her head, biting her bottom lip to guarantee her silence.

His eyes search her face. "Yes, you did."

Tessa nods and tries to smile. Instead, a sob breaks the

seal of her lips. Delayed shock robs her of her quarter-change, and she diminishes within Laz's embrace.

He easily compensates, holding her smaller human form tighter.

"You are my Redemptive. Praile would know exactly what to say to cast doubt. We had discussed that plan."

Her eyes move to his. "Then why...?"

Laz's smile joins his eyes within the sea of blood that coats his body.

Tessa swallows against her rising gorge.

"It *is* rare. Praile was taking an educated guess. He could not know that you really *were* my Redemptive." He cocks his head, appearing to consider. "It's a legend. As I said before, a Redemptive blood is so rare, many demonic who possess mixed blood, especially in the Hades realm, do not think it's truly possible."

A loud groan comes from behind them.

Laz turns, never taking his hands off Tessa, and they survey Drek.

"Oh no," Tessa says, making a move as if to go toward Drek.

Laz holds her. "He's of no consequence. The Lanarre prince attempted to stop me from getting to you."

"But, oh my Moon, we'll be outlaws. You don't kill Lanarre royalty and live to tell about it, Laz."

He shrugs. "I thought their, whatever you call it—welcoming committee—left something to be desired."

"Ah—no. He probably heard me freaking out, spotted a couple of demonics, and tried to lend a hand."

Laz gives a speculative glance toward the Lanarre bleeding out at their feet. He frowns. "Or talon," he muses.

"That's not funny, Laz."

"Not at all," Tahlia says from the door.

Tessa's face whips in the direction of the broken wood that used to be the door to the cottage.

"Tahlia," Tessa says in a relieved breath.

Tahlia covers her face, quiet crying breaking through her fingers.

"Come 'ere, baby."

Tahlia runs to Tessa, and Laz makes room for the women to embrace.

They break away after a few seconds and look at Drek.

"What should we do?" Tahlia asks in a voice that's breathy from her tears.

Tessa turns to Tahlia. "If he dies, they'll hunt us. There won't be an explanation true enough that will stop our deaths." Tessa gives a significant look to Laz, who stares back imperiously.

The demonic must not be much for worrying. *I bet he'd be scared out of his shorts if Lucifer himself put in an appearance.* Tessa snorts, and Laz raises a pale-red eyebrow obscured by drying blood.

"Never mind," she mutters.

Wrapping an arm around Tahlia, who gives Tessa's body a once-over as if she's thinking, *Really?*

Tessa's eyes sweep down her form. She's soaked with Praile's blood.

"Sorry."

Tahlia giggles. "It's okay, Tessa."

Their eyes go to Drek.

"Let him die. They won't know how it all happened."

Tahlia gives him such a scathing look of disdain that

he scowls at her. "Are you kidding, demonic?" She jerks her face back. "You smell like a demon. The wounds you inflicted on the prince can't be scrubbed away. It's like a fingerprint of your wrongdoing."

Laz looks at Drek's body and sighs. "Fine." He walks to Drek then sinks to his haunches. Laz extends his fingertip out from his body as though unwilling to do what comes next.

He presses the tip of his finger between Drek's eyes.

The Lanarre prince gasps, taking in a shaking inhale so long that Tessa's not sure when it's going to end.

Then it does, and his wolfen eyes pop open. Slowing spinning discs of mercury revolve, regarding them all.

"Now you heal me, after rendering me useless?"

Laz nods without answering.

Healthy color pulses from where Laz touches Drek, moving outward like ripples in a disturbed lake. Drek's eyes flow to Tessa—then Tahlia.

"Tahlia."

Their eyes meet, and she retreats into the shadows near the door.

"Don't go."

She shakes her head, then with a cry that is halfway between a startled bird's cry and a human female's wail of anguish, she disappears in an explosion of white feathers.

Drek's howl of despair chills Tessa's flesh.

CHAPTER 4

JENNI

"*Hey.*" Jenni stirs, cracking an eyelid, and meets violet eyeshadow surrounding kind muddy-brown eyes. A dot of ketchup is smeared on her turned yellow collar.

The nametag reads "Devin."

Jenni lifts her head, trying to orient herself. Her fuzzy surroundings come into focus slowly, so slowly. Square tiles from the 1980s in rust-brown with black grout form a grid underneath where she's sitting.

Jenni glances down. Wrappers from the cheeseburgers she ate litter a table with faux wood graining.

Night is a solid black pressure against the glass of industrial-style windows encased in beige aluminum frames.

"What?" she croaks in delayed reply. Clearing her throat, she continues, "How long was I sleeping?" Her eyes scan the empty restaurant. Somewhere in the back, a fry timer shrills then quits mid-shriek.

It's just her and a rough-around-the-edges girl named

Devin. She extracts her cell phone. The thumb she uses to swipe for the time has the barest amount of chipped black polish still clinging to the nail.

"Almost two. Shift's over. Gotta book." She stretches her arms toward the ceiling, snapping gum like machine-gun fire. Devin lands on her heels, stifling a loud yawn.

Jenni's mesmerized, as if she's in a fog from which she can't escape.

Devin hikes her chin, rolling the blue wad between her teeth. "I let ya sleep. Seemed like you needed it."

Jenni jumps a foot when Devin snaps another bubble. She juts out a hip. "Listen, I need to get home. You got a place to go?"

Snap.

Jenni flinches then slowly nods. Licking her lips, she gazes into the empty cup of water from her earlier cheeseburger gorge.

Devin shoots the same thumb she used on her cell toward the soda fountain. "Have a pop. Free."

She eyeballs Jenni's empty cup.

Can werewolves have pop? Better not chance that particular bag of worms.

"I think I'm good with water, but thank you." Jenni hastily inserts her manners then licks her parched lips again.

"Need a ride?"

Jenni peers around the bright-blue bubble obscuring Devin's face, meeting eyes that are now bloodshot.

Jenni caves, nodding. If she can get back to her car at the hospital parking garage, she can get the hell out of here.

"Yes. Ah, do you know where PT General is?"

"Hospital?" Devin narrows her eyes on Jenni's scrubs. "Is that blood?" she asks with more caution then Jenni wants to hear.

She bites back a sigh. "Yes."

"How'd that get on you? Seems like a ton." *Snap.*

Oh boy.

"Had an emergency gunshot patient today." A very small white lie. Or a big, fat whopper. Depends on perspective.

"Ah-huh." Devin's expression clearly paints a picture of how weird it would be that Jenni came to a fast food-restaurant, consumed eight cheeseburgers while her scrub uniform was full of dried blood and dirt from the forest, *then* decided to take a nap.

So normal. "It's been a tough day."

Gum snaps. Her overly plucked eyebrows lift. "Whatever. I don't judge."

Jenni can see that. She can also see that even if Devin has a tough exterior, she's giving Jenni a good turn. "Yes, thank you. If you could drop me by the hospital, I can get my car and get home. I'm beat."

Understatement of the universe.

"'Kay, Dale's in the back." She turns, and Jenni eyes catch on long, sleek and ebony cone-shaped gauges stabbing through her earlobes.

They look painful.

Devin turns back to her. "He's closing, I'll let us out and lock up, then we'll get outta here." She smiles at Jenni. A flash of metal winks from her tongue.

Perfect. Jenni stands and collects all her wrappers. She

gets rid of her trash and walks to the pop fountain. Water sloshes inside the paper cup as she snaps the plastic lid on the top and stabs the perforated center with her straw. Jenni takes a long, soothing gulp.

Better. She wipes her mouth with the back of her hand.

"Need to grab my shit," Devin comments, rounding the counter and digging into an unseen spot beneath a row of three cash registers.

"Okay," Jenni says, only half-listening.

I'd sell my own mother for a shower. Of course, she would have to be alive. A pang of sorrow touches Jenni like a ghostly hand then lifts. The grief of their car wreck from last year still lingers.

No time for self-pity, grief, or any other luxury emotions. Jenni knows her parents would be devastated to know she was dying. It's sort of a mercy they're not here to witness that.

Jenni abruptly stops, hand cooling on the bare metal bar that crosses the center of the glass door leading out of the fast food joint.

She's not sure she *will* die now. Adi did more than change her. *Maybe she cured me*

... Only one way to find out.

"Ready," Devin says at Jenni's elbow, and she jumps. She gives a nervous laugh. "Chill, it's only me."

Jenni pushes open the door. Fresh air smacks her to full wakefulness, and she instantly feels better—more alert. Something about being out in the open eases a tension she didn't even realize was running through her since the moment she woke up.

She glances behind her. The inside of that building felt

almost claustrophobic. Jenni stops outside the door while Devin locks it behind them.

"Why are you being so nice?" Jenni asks Devin in a soft voice.

Devin shrugs, hopping off the curb of the sidewalk that hugs the perimeter of the building.

The golden arches dim to a ghostly phosphorescence, and Jenni turns to look at the darkened building. Guess Dale shut off the lights. The soft all-night fluorescent security bulbs throw off an ambient glow that casts dark, long shadows into the empty parking lot.

"Just paying it forward."

Jenni stops, forgetting the question she asked. Oh yeah —*why was she being nice?* "Paying what forward?"

Devin turns, giving her a puzzled glance. "Didn't see the movie?"

Jenni shakes her head. Between nursing school, her job, the cancer diagnosis, *and* Lance—she just hasn't used her discretionary time for anything but sleeping. Jenni was just starting to get out of that cycle and concentrate on her end-of-life matters... then the werewolf thing happened.

Werewolf thing.

"Some little kid does the right thing and dies for it. Principled little dude." Devin's voice holds a wistful note.

"Did someone do something good for you?"

Devin nods, and Jenni takes in the sheen covering suddenly moist eyes. "Yeah. So you get a vibe for somebody, know when they're a good person, if they're down on their luck. It doesn't cost nothin' to just, ya know, be good back."

41

Seems simple. Jenni is reminded of how *she* helped Adi.

Then Adi made her into a werewolf.

Jury's out on if that was *paying it forward* or not.

A sudden sense tickles Jenni's nose, and she halts only steps from the curb. Her gaze sweeps the parking lot.

Footsteps approach from the left and Jenni's head snaps in that direction.

Devin's busy digging in a black metal-studded purse for her keys and doesn't see who appears. "Need to clean this shit mess up," she mutters as she scours the interior of her handbag.

A big guy, maybe six feet two or so, moves out of the shadows and into the weak light. He's got a couple of buddies with him.

Instantly, Jenni is on alert. Nothing good happens at this time of night.

"Hey. D."

Devin's head jerks up from her search.

"Hey, Bray." Devin's voice is devoid of enthusiasm. In fact, Jenni's keen hearing picks up on tension.

Who's Bray?

The three move around the corner of the building, coming closer.

Jenni's senses light off, tingling. A brilliant intuition surfaces, pressing her to leave. Now.

Jenni's always been led by Science and the tangible, not emotion and instinct. Maybe that's all changing.

"Whatchya doin' here skulkin' around?" Devin asks, dropping her hand from her purse and hanging the bag back on her shoulder.

"Hey, baby," Bray spreads his arms from his body as though he's harmless and moves nearer still.

Small wounds from a needle are scattered across his skin like measles.

Great, a junky. Jenni's no fool. She uses a needle dozens of times in a shift to help others.

She knows when an amateur is shooting up.

"Don't be that way. Just need a little bump."

Devin shakes her head, backing up. "I don't do that shit no more."

Bray takes Jenni in for the first time, and his nostrils flare. "Who's your friend?" His eyes glitter with menace that Jenni can easily make out.

Devin gives a nervous eye flick at her. "Jenni," she says to Bray, probably hoping to diffuse the situation. Devin's eyes dance around the three men.

"Well, Jenni can get lost. I just need those keys for McDonald's, and we can take whatever cash stash is there, and we'll be on our way. Easy-peasy, baby."

Fuck.

"No, Bray." Devin shakes her head, whipping dyed-black hair hard from side to side. "I got this job, and I want to *keep* it. I'm not letting you rob my work. Besides, Dale's closing. He's already gone. Place is locked."

An image of her keys comes to mind.

Dale is *not* gone. It's as easy to know as feeling her heartbeat inside her body. Jenni knows because… she can smell his deodorant through the closed steel door at the back entrance.

She blinks.

As though an awareness light switch has been flipped,

Jenni realizes her sense of smell detects a trace of heroin still in Bray's veins.

Her heart thumps hard in her throat, and Jenni turns to look at the other two.

Meth.

Coke.

It's a full meal deal with these three winners.

Some innate sense, buried during the last thirty minutes she's been awake, swirls to the surface of her thoughts. Burying intellect. Eschewing her rationale.

A low growl seeps from between her lips, she can't smell what lays beneath the layers of drugs, but it scares her.

Four gazes turn to look at Jenni.

Bray's eyes widen. "Holy shit—check out that bitch's eyes."

Jenni stares at Bray as though she could burn holes through him from her will alone.

Devin's eyes are round as she stares at Jenni, the irises pure white, chasing the red of tiredness away with this new fright.

Jenni's pretty sure she doesn't look very normal right now. But since the drug kingpins have turned up like shitty pennies, she'll just *be herself.*

Jenni's parents were older when she was born. Doctors said they couldn't conceive, and the instant that statement was made—*pow*—Jenni came into being. She has a few antiquated expressions in her verbal arsenal.

She uses one now. "Why don't you guys make your-selves scarce." Jenni lifts her upper lip, instinctively baring her teeth.

Devin gasps, backing away.

The smell of her fear is like a brushfire in Jenni's nostrils.

Bray takes a step forward like he means business, curling his fingers into fists at his side. "Fuck you, cunt."

Ah, so original.

Jenni looks at the other two. It's dark, but her new eyes have no trouble seeing all three perfectly.

"Devin."

Devin whips her head to Jenni.

"Come stand by me."

"No offense, Jenni—but you're trippin'."

Jenni nods. If she looks anything like Adi did in the hospital, she can understand why her appearance might give Devin pause.

She laughs suddenly at how the tables have turned.

Bray straightens. "Something funny, *bitch*?" He enunciates the last word through his teeth.

Devin throws Jenni a rabbit-caught-in-a-snare look, and a tear causes a crack through the foundation on her face like a carved line. "Please, Bray, just go." Devin lifts her hand, palm toward the night sky, beseeching. "I don't wanna lose this job. I *need* it."

Bray the Magnificent thumbs his chest. "All you need is your man. Now dump this job. What do ya make?" His face aligns into a disbelieving expression. "Eight bucks an hour?" Bray snorts, realizes the movement picked up snot from the ruining of his body through his drug habits. He plugs one nostril, shooting a stream of noxious mucus an impressive five feet through the other. It hits the pavement with a wet splat.

Devin makes a noise of disgust, backing up a step and scrunching her nose. "Gross," she mutters.

Jenni remains unaffected; she cleans bodily fluids for a living. Bray can bring it, and she won't be fazed. What Jenni really wants is a shower, her own bed, and the hell out of this tight spot. Not in that order. And she might be kind of hungry again.

It's been a long damn day.

Devin retreats another step closer to Jenni. "I don't want to be your mule for drugs. I'm not gonna do them anymore. I just want to work my shift and mind my own bizz."

Bray smiles, and the sense of impending dread rises from deep within Jenni.

She knows before they do that they'll move, and she's just *there.* Without thought or plan.

Bray has rushed Devin and put his hand on the strap of her purse.

She doesn't think Bray understands that Jenni's a threat.

Jenni didn't really know, either.

His eyes widen. Up close, Jenni's threat assessment skills come to life as she determines the scent symphony lying beneath the drugs.

Bray is sterile, hasn't eaten in half a day, is dehydrated, and has the beginning of a sinus infection. An almost-imperceptible odor runs underneath the rest that she can't identify, and he has a stubborn patch of dried cum clinging to the base of his penis.

All of this from her nose.

Jenni doesn't dig deeper or try to find out more info or

contemplate why she knows what she does. Her skill set encompasses a thorough knowledge of the human body.

She laces her hands and pounds her combined uni-fist on the arm that holds Devin's purse strap.

The hammer of her hands moves through Bray's forearm like a butter knife, making a clean break.

He bellows like a stuck pig, pinwheeling backward and falling on his ass.

Jenni's heightened vision lands on the break.

Jagged bones erupt from the skin. The radius bone connecting the wrist and hand dangles from a still-attached tendon.

Jenni grunts. *Maybe not so clean.*

Devin stares at Bray for a few seconds, her face paling, then pivots to the right and begins heaving her guts onto the asphalt.

Oh.

"Bitch!" one of the guys to Jenni's left bellows.

The other one wraps his beefy arms around Jenni from behind, lifting her off the ground. He tightens his arms like bands around her torso.

Squeezing, squeezing.

Instinct consumes her as her mind shuts off.

Something painful bursts from her fingertips. Stars explode at the edges of her vision. Lightheadedness sweeps through her.

Jenni raises her hands.

Small knives of bone protrude from the tips of her fingers like a nail job gone bad. *Look, I'm Wolverine.* Jenni snickers, realizing she's on the brink of losing consciousness, with shock closing in fast.

The other loser charges like a bull. Head down, he never looks up. Never thinks of an alternative that doesn't involve beating the shit out of her.

With the symphony of Devin barfing in the background and Bray writhing on the ground, Jenni gives a sloppy sweep of her hand at the oncoming druggie.

Ragged stripes of parted flesh cross his chest.

Slices of white soon fill with red.

He stands, staring at his chest as if he's seen a phantom. "What. The. Fuck!" he screeches.

Jenni's vision is going gray, and the guy who's holding her starts to shake her back and forth, like a dog worrying a bone.

"Die, bitch!"

"No!" Devin screams, lurching shakily in their direction.

"My chest!" the one who Jenni sliced screams, backing away. His palms come away slick with his own blood.

He's losing a lot, Jenni notes dimly.

Devin sweeps in. The vomit lacing the corners of her mouth smells stale as she bashes the one who holds Jenni on the head with her purse.

"Ah!" he roars, loosening his hold.

She does it again. Lipstick flies out of the handbag and loose change pings on the ground—along with the keys that Bray was so interested in.

Dickhead drops Jenni, attempting to scramble toward the keys.

Jenni turns smoothly, hitting him in the chest with her palm, intending to shove him off balance.

Instead, he flies ten feet before landing on a bed of

late-blooming rhododendrons in the small triangle of landscaping that holds the To-Go audio order board.

He crashes into the electronic sign, folding it in the middle with a groan of metal and crash of glass breaking.

"Watch out!" Devin screams.

Jenni spins, dropping low as arms covered in blood converge where she just was.

Like a determined zombie, the guy she slashed with her new claws lumbers forward, stooping awkwardly to get to her.

Jenni plants her hands on the pebbled asphalt, kicking out wildly with her right foot.

He flies backward, tumbling into a moaning Bray, who clutches his arm, shouting in agony as the other guy barrels into the wounded appendage.

"Jenni," Devin says from above her, shock causing her skin to look like a sheet of paper.

"Yup," Jenni answers, breaths sawing out of her.

"What—what are you?"

She looks up at Devin and gives the best answer she can: "Not exactly sure, but exploring that right now doesn't sound like a good call."

Devin nods vigorously. "I'll…" She looks around at the beaten guys and covers her face with her hands.

Jenni staggers to a standing position, surveys the group hugging the ground, and grabs Devin's hand, towing her carefully around the pile of puke. On the way to the only beat-up car in the parking area, Jenni stops to pick up the stuff that fell from Devin's purse.

When they get to the car, Jenni plucks the keys from Devin's unresisting hand and unlocks the door.

Devin sniffs, wiping streaming eyes.

"I'll drive," Jenni announces.

"Okay." Devin's voice shakes.

They get in. Jenni starts the car and takes off, leaving the drug trio for the cops she'll call when the car's out of sight.

CHAPTER 5

SLASH

*S*lash cradles his mate's face, trying to force her to look at him—take from him.

Adrianna is unbelievably stubborn. One of many things Slash admires about her is some of what frustrates him, as well.

"Let me ease you, Adrianna."

She shakes her head, tears easing out of the corners of her eyes. Adrianna is a tough Alpha female Were.

She is also an infant in Were years, going through her heat too young, with circumstances of stress and her first sexual encounter preceding where they find themselves right now.

And Slash is not wholly comfortable with any of it.

Della has not shown them violence. In fact, she has—for a witch, and for what he knows of their kind—been downright hospitable.

His nose doesn't smell violence. But his instincts are lit up like a firefly in June. Slash always trusts his feelings. A human male would be full of bravado. Slash doesn't *feel* things—he *thinks*.

And that's where humanity has lost its footing. In their arrogance, humans have decided that instincts shouldn't be followed.

Slash knows differently. Instincts have kept him alive for nearly three hundred years. During battle. During ascensions. During his mating with Adrianna.

A human male would have gone soft with Adrianna. Would have comforted her instead of getting her out of harm's way.

Not Slash. He knew the move was paramount to get his mate away from where males without ethics might return for easy pickings.

He uses that same instinct now. A deep and abiding foreboding has set up residence inside him. Slash will not ignore the internal warning. Every fiber of his being is pushing him to resolve this issue of Adrianna's heat. It's as though a clock has begun endlessly ticking.

If they need to run without notice, they will not be able to stop so Slash can breed Adrianna. And the pain of her heat will go on unabated, rendering her absolutely immobile.

Slash must protect her.

"I don't want to here, Slash." Adrianna bites her lip, her face wet with tears, nervously looking around the loaned bedroom.

"You're not thinking straight. If we breed, this indecision and emotion will end."

Her face tips up to his, bright hazel eyes regarding him. "Promise?"

Slash shakes his head, lowering his forehead to hers, where he presses their flesh together. "No."

Her brow furrows. "What?"

"I can't lie. Until your heat is gone—utterly vanished— we must breed."

He feels the warmth of her skin as a deep flush takes hold. "Don't be ashamed. I am your mate—your life partner, Adrianna."

"I can't help it. We're in this witch's house, and I've... you're the only male I've ever been with, and look what happened."

Slash can't help the low growl that escapes his lips.

Adrianna breaks contact, leaning back to see him better. "Why are you growling?"

He pulls her roughly forward again, cupping the back of her skull. "Because no other male will ever *know* you."

The corners of Adrianna's mouth curl.

Slash's hands creep to the bottom of her buttocks, cupping her tightly. He hoists her easily, and her legs lock around his waist.

"Don't make noise, and I will take you tenderly, my mate."

A single tear slips out of her eye, and she nods, swiping the wet drop away.

Slash grins suddenly, and Adrianna reaches for his lips, lightly brushing over the curved expression and the ball of scar tissue at the rise of his cupid's bow.

He kisses her fingers. "You smell of soap and me," he growls, gently nipping the tips of her fingers.

Their eyes lock, and the next moment, he's spun her, pressing her back gently against the wall.

"Slash," she chokes, head rolling against the wall as she gasps, "I'm a little sore."

"I will treat you like glass." He doesn't waste time. Tearing his loose athletic pants to his ankles, he grasps Adrianna's ass cheeks hard, tilting her pelvis and spreading her with his hands.

Her feminine fragrance hits him like a bullet, and his cock goes hard.

Slash groans as he sights how wet she is for him, how pink and tender. How willing.

"Adrianna," Slash whispers and rubs the tip of himself over her wet folds, lavishing precise attention on the bundle of nerves located above her entrance.

"Ah!" she sighs softly. Grabbing the back of his head, she crushes him against her.

"I will go slow," Slash promises, worried about making the second time better. He is dying to take her hard, as a mate should, yet he loathes the idea of hurting her. She is open to him, but new to mating.

He throbs, but stills, offering only light friction, spreading her wetness while stimulating her clit with his tip.

"Don't," she murmurs. "Once you enter me, please take me. Don't be a pussycat."

A huge insult to a male Were.

Slash smirks, inching the head of him inside her tight, wet entrance.

He withdraws, and he can feel Adrianna's frown before he plunges partway inside her heat. Waiting, he allows her to adjust to his size.

"I forgot how big you are," she says, her voice strained.

Slash's smile widens. "That's why I told you I'd move slow. No matter how much you spur me on, female, my body knows what yours needs, and I won't give you more than you can accept, Adrianna."

"You sure talk a lot."

Slash moves more deeply, and she moans, a sound that is music to his ears. He adjusts his hold, hiking her up higher and spreading her wider.

"I'm in your hands, stud," Adrianna says, giving him all her trust. All her body. Her love.

Slash moves to the end of her, and they pulse together. Adrianna's body begs for his seed, and Slash holds back when he's never wanted to pour it forth more.

"Slow, Adrianna," Slash says through gritted teeth. His mate is tight and slick. Her womb is an open invitation for what he can give her.

But Slash wants her pleasure as well as the salve of his seed to sate her heat.

He can do both. *I will do both.*

Withdrawing, he rocks back inside her, deeply seating himself for a painful second of wanting to release. In and out, he thrusts inside Adrianna, and her body begs him for his seed with each deep rock of himself inside her.

Slash clenches his teeth, working her clit with his thumb, fighting the silken feel of Adrianna's tight, drenched flesh like a well-made glove around his cock.

Slash increases the tempo of his thumb on her sensitive nub.

"Please," Adrianna begs as he hits high and deep, her back sliding along the wall as he plunges.

Slash presses his head against the wall, laying soft

kisses against her throat as he moves over and over that spot inside her.

Her body tenses, back arching. "Yes!"

Adrianna's screamed orgasm is muffled against his neck as his next rock forward is the cooling seed her heat so desperately needs.

He pours everything he has inside his mate, jerking her hips against him, joining their bodies so tightly that there is no escaping the moment, smothering her womb with his release.

Adrianna's body milks him of every drop, eventually falling limp against him. She sighs, her head dipping forward against his shoulder.

Their heartbeats sync, and Slash straightens, still within her, and shuffles to the bed.

He gently lowers Adrianna, his half-hard erection falling away from her entrance.

Adrianna's eyes widen on his semi-hardness. "What?" she gives a little laugh.

Slash gives a rueful shake of his head. "Until your heat is gone, there is no down time."

"Again?" Adrianna asks with a poorly stifled yawn.

Slash nods, gently swimming between her legs. He lays a kiss on her inner thigh, his cock going full tilt with the mingled scent of them both so close to his nose.

He rubs his face against the tender skin at the inside of her thigh and places a gentle kiss on her hot center.

"Slash," Adrianna whispers. "Do you think Della heard us?"

He smiles against her thigh. "I do not care. If she

doesn't understand mates breed, then I have no hope for her."

"Moon!" Adrianna's breath catches as Slash tongues her from entrance to clit.

"Your seed..."

"Tastes spectacular with your drenched parts."

"Drenched parts?" She gasps as he does it again.

And again.

Adrianna moves underneath him, and he flattens her knees wide, licking her until everything is gone.

"There is not enough of my seed inside you." Slash can't wipe the smile from his lips, pressing kisses against her softness.

"I feel better," she says then moans as he inserts the tip of his tongue inside her.

"Slash—please."

"Please what?" he whispers, the scar tissue next to his mouth painfully tight.

That's what happens when he can't stop smiling. An unusual event. Before Adrianna came into his life.

"Stop."

He instantly halts, but keeps his warm breathing at her parted, sensitive flesh.

"Why?"

"Shouldn't we? I don't know..." she says, struggling to close her legs.

Slash easily keeps her where she lays.

"No, I want to pleasure my mate and come inside you again. That will assure me as a male Were, you are well and truly sated. That I have cooled the fire of your heat."

"I don't know about this heat thing."

The silence lengthens as Slash's powerful hands hold her thighs and his hot breaths bathe her entrance.

"But I love the feel of your mouth on me," Adrianna admits, and Slash can sense her embarrassment. Her restrained pleasure.

He purses his lips around her clit and gives a final sucking pull with his mouth.

Adrianna comes off the bed, back arched in frozen spasm. Her gorgeous breasts fall away from the center of her chest, nipples pebbling in the coolness of the room.

She collapses back on the bed, and he reaches up to pluck a nipple as he works her slick clit within his mouth.

He closes his teeth around the flesh without biting, and she trembles.

Slash inserts two fingers deep inside his mate, and her tight walls pulse around him as the orgasm breaks from her mouth in a series of choking gasps.

His Adrianna tries for quiet, and it's adorable.

Slash badly wants her composure to shatter but knows they have an audience of sorts.

Instead, he covers her mouth with the hand that was just playing with her nipple and breaks the seal of his lips on her clit.

Withdrawing his fingers from her, he replaces them with his huge erection, plunging inside her wetness as far as he can go.

Her eyes widen, her nostrils flaring as she sucks breath and he covers her mouth.

"Make all the noise you want."

Slash feels her smile and thrusts hard, not worried about his size or speed anymore. He is a male who has properly prepared and pleasured his female, and she can now take what he offers.

Slash pumps in and out, the muscles of his buttocks coiling and uncoiling as he stabs forward, his tip meeting her end.

He feels another spasm and lifts his hand right before her scream so Adrianna can take breath.

He catches her wail of pleasure in his palm, and she bucks as his own release shoots out of him in hot, wet jets.

Slash feels the build of a second course following the first, and he slowly lifts his palm, the throbbing of his essence sinking deep once again.

Adrianna captures his hand with hers, clinging to him. Gradually lowering his hand to her face, she kisses the center of his palm softly.

"I love you," she whispers. "No matter what happens, I love you."

Slash knows he's always loved her. No matter how much he tried to deny it or talk himself out of her. That Adrianna was too young or that he was too ugly to deserve her.

In the end, they were meant for each other.

"I love you more than the moon," Slash says in a voice so quiet that it's breath and words.

"No Were loves anything more than the moon."

Slash just smiles.

There's no need to defend that which is so deeply felt.

CHAPTER 6

LAZ

*L*az scowls. "What is the meaning of all this?"

His Redemptive, gorgeous even with a thick coat of Praile's blood still covering her body, folds her arms, giving Laz a look he's grown accustomed to in their short acquaintance—irritation.

"What is the *meaning*?" Tessa asks, incredulity saturating her question. Sweeping her palm at Drek, knees planted on the blood-soaked ground where Praile's decimated corpse fills the cracks between the floorboards, she spins to face Laz.

Laz cups his chin. Apparently, she is still irate over the Praile incident. However, Laz is unfazed. He did not get where he is within the ranks of the high demonic by losing his composure. And he's not self-deceiving. Laz understands perfectly that if Praile had truly suspected him, the outcome would have been much different. Laz might have been the one soaking the floorboards instead of Praile, leaving his Redemptive at the mercy of the merciless.

Thank everything dark that Tessa was not Praile's plaything.

Laz suppresses a shudder at the unbidden thought. "Yes. The Lanarre princess has flown the coop, as the humans say. I have healed Drek of the wounds he procured because he *kept* me from my Redemptive. Why would this concern us? I healed him only because you asked it of me. Drek is of no consequence."

Tessa blinks.

Laz scrubs a hand over his face, suddenly tired. "I am demonic. The Lanarre do not concern me. What does concern me is the health of my Redemptive." Laz gives Tessa a lingering look then continues smoothly. "Now, I have righted this"—Laz spins his hand casually in the broad direction of the Lanarre prince—"issue." He raises his eyebrows.

"What?" Tessa says, but more softly this time.

"Let us leave before the remainder of the Lanarre awaken and see the mess that we made, the state of their prince, and have a meltdown."

The corners of Tessa's lips twitch. "'Meltdown'?"

Laz's return smile is unhurried. "Yes. I know quite a bit of human vernacular, but I must think before employing it."

"I see that." Tessa laughs.

Laz holds out his hand, and she steps forward, wiping tacky blood off on her black lightweight pants then slipping her palm inside his.

A tingling current runs through their casual contact, and they exchange a look. Tessa's expression holds surprise; Laz's does not.

They turn, and Drek is staring at them. Laz believes he barely took the Lanarre prince in the short battle to get to Tessa. If it had not been for his demonic speed, all would have been lost. A male standing nearly six and a half feet in human form is something far more dangerous in the half form of wolfen.

Drek's light-gold eyes regard him. "I thank you for the healing, demonic."

"Lazarus," he seethes, loathing being addressed by his species when his name is known.

Drek's square jaw hikes. "Yes—Lazarus." Folding his muscular arms, he winces, clearly still in the process of knitting the damage from their fight. "However, you attacked a Lanarre prince who was trying to assist a female Were."

Laz shrugs. "She is my Redemptive. Praile, a high demonic and second only to the Master, was assaulting her. *You* wasted valuable time asserting your assumed dominance. When all the while, Praile was attempting to rape my female."

Laz pulls Tessa in tightly against his body, ignoring the blood. Normally, blood and demons go hand-in-hand. How many had Lazarus tortured during his duties in Hades?

Many.

How many did he heal then re-torture? Legion.

Those days are behind him now. With his Redemptive warm against his body, and these Lanarre soon to be a distant and distasteful memory, Laz can begin a new journey.

A new life.

"I did not know you were helping. It looked as though you were part of the attack."

It would look thus from the outside.

"Please, Drek." Tessa's voice is soft, which makes Laz's prick hard. *Of course.*

The timing could not be more inopportune. But that is the flummox of the demonic. Controlled by fate, master-minded by biology, he is meant to be with her.

Laz turns to gaze down at her beautiful face. Blood or not, Tessa calls to him.

"Who you're really concerned about is Tahlia. Admit that."

Drek's powerful jaw flexes, a flutter appearing like an errant heartbeat at the edge. "And she has changed into bird form and flown away. Unprotected."

Tessa's fingers flex. "While that bitch of a cousin Tanya is here, trying for a throne that doesn't belong to her."

"What can you tell me about Tahlia?" Drek leans forward, expression troubled.

Tessa lifts a shoulder. "Nothing. I mean, I don't want to stay here as prisoner while I explain how you fucked up."

Laz gives a dark chuckle.

Drek scowls. "I do concede, things could have been handled better in my absence."

"Handled better?" Tessa scoffs. "You don't 'handle' a female of her caliber—or any female, for that matter. You said so yourself that Tahlia is Lanarre royalty and so *much* above every other female."

Laz easily detects the sarcasm in Tessa's voice, but believes Drek is too self-absorbed to notice. He bides his time, waiting for the prince to dig a deeper grave. Hours ago, Laz might not have thought that possible, but a demonic can always reassess.

"True," he replies, "but all female Were are precious."

Tessa laughs as though she can't help it. "Now *that's* the only smart thing you've said so far."

The prince's lips thin while his expression grows pained. "Why do I displease you so much, Tessa?"

"That you have to ask is the biggest problem."

They stare at each other for a moment.

Laz breaks the silent stand-off. "About us taking our leave, Lanarre prince…"

Drek turns his attention to Laz. "If I secure safe passage, would you stay and discuss Tahlia?"

Laz squeezes Tessa's hip in an effort to keep her silent if only for a moment.

"Passage by blood oath?" she asks.

Laz narrows his eyes at her, his attempt at subtly unsuccessful. "I do not like oaths. By anyone." Two spots on his scalp itch as though horns could grow.

Without looking in Laz's direction, Tessa answers him: "It's sacred among the Were. No Lycan would dare break blood oath."

He threads fingers through his short hair; the ghostly feeling of horns remains. "Why?"

Strands of Tessa's black hair whip the bare skin of his arms as she turns to regard him. His flesh heats where the silken tendrils met his skin.

"Because if an oathbreaker commits that breach of trust, at the next full moon, the Moon herself takes the blood of the oathbreaker."

Laz feels his lips curl. "A bloodletting by the Moon herself. I like that outcome very much."

"It is the most serious promise between us." Tessa's smile is small.

"Yes," Drek says in slow consideration. "I will."

* * *

LAZ SOAPS HIMSELF TWICE.

That's what it takes to rid himself of Praile's stench.

Now that he and Tessa have made an agreement with Drek, they are no longer prisoner here.

The Were are still snoozing off Praile's demonic thrall, and the two of them can finally wash the blood of battle from their bodies.

Laz would take Tessa the way a Redemptive should be claimed if she would let him. He could ease her need—or "heat," as the Lycan name her body's biological directive to breed.

He exhales wearily as the water running over him finally runs clear.

Praile is gone. Yet the worry of a new order takes seed inside Laz's mind. The absence of communion with their Dark Ruler will not go unnoticed, and another high demon will be sent to investigate.

Lazarus's absence will be noted, as well.

Lucifer will see to why that is. A void in the high demonic ranks casts a ripple like a stone in water.

Laz has been privy to many tales of different supernaturals over his lifetime.

Fey.

Blood Singers.

Lycan.

Vampire.

And among them all, there are many branches of subspecies, and within those ranks, each species distinguishes one from the other.

Laz is learning.

Not because he cares. But because the more he knows, the safer he and his Redemptive are.

Praile used a Were with demonic blood to do his bidding, killing many of the Singers who possessed the blood of the angelic. Tony Laurent—Laz remembers the sadistic Were easily. Sometimes, those who possess only a small amount of demonic blood are nevertheless ruled by it. Genetics among supernaturals are a strange thing. And no path of blood can be wholly predicted in its manifestation.

Laz has spoken of it with no one, but his healing ability is troubling. Demonic do not possess that ability. However, there are many supernaturals who do.

The Angelic possess the strongest ability to heal, and his mind trembles around the possibility.

Few from Below have healing talent of any kind. But none have voiced that Laz might have the blood of the heavenly running in his veins. How would Laz stand the hot dark place he once called home if that were the case?

Unless...

"Laz," Tessa calls.

Laz's train of thought fades, and he shuts off the water. Lifting his fingers, he inspects each pruney digit.

He feels the presence of Tessa and slowly spins to face

her. Only the solid panel of glass is between them. Rivulets of chilling water cascade from his wet hair, down his naked torso, splattering at his feet against the cold tumbled-marble tiles.

Their eyes meet, and Tessa's need slams into him, slaughtering the lighthearted banter he'd planned. Instead, her nearness causes a mammoth erection to form. Hot and painful, the tip of him touches the hard, cold glass.

Laz doesn't even flinch.

Nothing but the heat of her flesh wrapped around him will cool the rage of his arousal.

Her fingertips press against the clear wall separating them. "What's happening?" Her pale-gray eyes seek an answer on his face, from his lips.

"It's the need," Laz says in such a thick voice, he must clear his throat before he speaks again. "Only my Redemptive can soothe me."

Laz palms his cock, leaning his forehead against the cold glass and warming it with his heated flesh.

Her eyes dip to the heavy arousal between his legs. "I can't, Laz. If I mate you, we'll have… there's a chance we'll have…"

Offspring, Laz finishes for her inside his head.

He drops his hand and yanks open the shower door. Stepping out of the basin, he grabs Tessa by the shoulders. "There's a chance we'll have what we were meant to."

Tessa's wearing clean clothes.

Laz shreds them with a nail gone black with his intent. The material comes away from her body, fluttering to the ground between them.

Tessa gasps. "No, Laz."

He flattens his palms, fanning them down her back and spreading his fingers at the base of her spine, kneading the flesh there.

She groans, and he stiffens against her.

"I am demonic. I will never cause harm to my Redemptive." Steam gives away his passion, rising from his mouth as he speaks, leaking out of his ears and nose. His vision goes to opaque tinged with red, and he knows his eyes have become gray with the momentum of his desire.

Tessa clings to the back of his neck. "I can't stand this. Normally, during heat, I would go into hiding, lock myself away in an abandoned house, a cave—anything until my cycle passes."

Laz presses her against his naked body, seating his hard prick between them and dumping his forehead to hers. "And now?"

"I'm desperate."

Laz tenses, looking deeply into her eyes, feeling the frown form between his brows. "So you would mate anyone?"

Tessa's exhale is irritated, and she shakes her head. "No. That's not what I meant. But I always knew if I mated someone, it would be for love—not to just relieve my physical needs. I've had sex, but I'm not easy."

Her lips quirk.

Laz breathes his fiery breath around her sensitive neck, and the skin turns pink wherever it lands.

Tessa shivers, her small smile slipping away.

"You don't love me?" Laz asks, a hint of humor threading his voice.

"I care, but I'm so in lust, I can hardly think." Tessa pants as Laz's hands move up and down her body, and he can scent the unique fragrance of the female meant for him and only him.

Laz leans his face lower until his fingers sink into her still-damp hair, and he uses his thumbs to pry her jaw up, meeting eyes that are such a light gray they're a hint of the storm that Laz feels brewing deep within himself.

Their lips couldn't fit a hair between them, so tightly are they mirrored.

"I have no choice. I knew you were my Redemptive when I first laid eyes on you. But you will not know me as I know you. It isn't the way the connection works."

Tessa searches his eyes. "Then what about giving in to this temptation and later regretting it? Letting it bite me in the ass later? Because—let me tell you, Laz—my luck sucks."

Laz smiles, and with a jerk, he crushes her body against his own, kissing her with fierce abandon, his forked tongue hot and seeking at the seam of her lips.

He eats the groan she makes as their tongues twine, catching her head in his hand as she tips her face up.

Her bare throat begs for his touch, and he gives it, licking and lightly nipping the flesh she presents.

"Do you feel lucky right now, Tessa?"

Her eyes hood, and she gives a vague nod, her fingers convulsively squeezing his ass.

"Then let me love you enough for both of us."

Tessa sighs. "I can't fight you, Laz. I've lived my entire life running, being tough—hunted."

"Don't run anymore. Let me care for you. Those who would hunt you will die."

Laz feels his eyes darken with the instinct to protect her. He waits with held breath, his cock a throbbing nightmare, every nerve ending alive to meld with Tessa.

When he hears her softly spoken yes, Laz falls on her like a starved thing.

A needy thing.

CHAPTER 7

JENNI

*J*enni creeps along at about ten miles an hour. Spotting the yellow crime scene tape, she moves on down the road.

"What are you doing?" Devin asks, twisting her torso to face her.

She spares Devin a glance before shifting her eyes once again to the damp street ahead.

"I'm going to park at the curb and get to my car—see if I can drive it home."

"Okay."

Jenni looks at Devin more closely.

Her pale skin has a waxy, clammy sheen. Slight tremors cause her hands to quake as she pushes her hair out of her face. The light catches her cone-shaped ebony gauge perfectly, giving the effect of a stabbing at her ear. A bursting heartbeat jumps erratically at the hollow of her throat.

Dammit. Shock at oh-shit o'clock, and with a fun time

had by all at the burger place, Devin's in no shape to drive herself home.

I owe her. Kind of. Jenni understands that bozo Bray and company would have made an appearance regardless of her presence. It was chance. She gets that. But maybe Devin would have been a few seconds earlier—already in her car or driving by then if Jenni wasn't there, needing help.

Jenni didn't kill anyone. But they would talk. No woman by herself could dispatch three men without specialized skills.

Or maybe they won't say anything? Possibly, those turds attempting to hold up a defenseless admitted former drug addict at her legit place of work wouldn't be something they would want to pass on to the authorities.

Well... let me help that along.

"Can I use your cell?" Jenni asks, quickly patting down her stiff scrubs with one hand and finding no cell phone.

She slides up next to a curb about a block past the turn-in for PT General. Letting the engine run, she puts the gearshift into park.

Jenni never keeps a cell on her person until she's leaving her work after a shift. Can't be communicating with people while you're taking care of patients. It's a distraction. And messing with her cell would be counter-productive and make patients feel less human when their caretaker is dismissing them for a snapchat.

Jenni knows most hospital employees don't hold to that standard. But facing death has made her introspective in a way that others haven't needed to be. Jenni *has* felt dismissed. She felt like less than nothing when she received her terminal diagnosis.

When people find out you're going to die, suddenly, they don't see you. Don't call. Like Lance.

Of course everyone seemed genuinely distressed—at first. Then she became just a number. Waiting to die.

Now she might live. But not as she was before.

Jenni puts her hands on her head, squeezing her skull as though she could press hard enough to push the thoughts out of her head.

"Here—hey, are you okay?" Devin's lip trembles as she holds out her cell, and a lone tear runs out of her eye, marking a fresh track in her makeup.

"Yeah." Jenni tries on a smile, and it feels like a hard slash of plastic on her face. She grabs at the cell and looks down at the fingerprint-laden crystal display.

"Oh, sorry—wait." Devin presses her thumb onto the button. The black screen disappears, and a photo appears of a small child.

Ignoring the little girl for the moment, Jenni swipes to the keypad and taps 911.

Ringing, ringing. "9-1-1, what is your emergency?"

Jenni sucks an inhale. "There's been an attempted robbery. Three men, probably drug users, tried to hurt a McDonald's employee to grab cash."

One second's pause then, "Location?"

Jenni recites the general area. Everyone would know the place.

"What is your name?"

Jenni swipes the phone to *off*.

"They'll trace that to me, ya know."

They exchange a loaded glance. "You didn't do anything wrong. You didn't perpetuate any crime."

Devin's eyes fill with tears. "I just got my kid back. I don't want to lose this job. It took everything I had to win Ella back."

Jenni blinks. "You have a kid? My God, what are you? Twelve?"

Devin gives a nervous laugh. "No, twenty-two. But Ella is four."

Wow, I feel old, but there's only a six-year difference in our ages. "Is she Bray's?"

Devin nods, tears beginning to overflow. "He doesn't know. In those days, Bray was blasted out of his mind half the time—we both were. I started to get clean, didn't know I was knocked up at first. Thought the withdrawals were just lasting forever." Her smile is rueful, tired.

"Like three months' worth?" Jenni asks.

Devin's smile fades. "Yeah." She breathes out slowly. "Then it occurred to me I hadn't had to deal with my monthlies for a while." The hands she was wringing break apart, and she lifts them slightly then lets them fall on her lap again, defeated.

Jenni's head falls back against the head rest. "What a mess."

"Yeah," Devin agrees. She looks at Jenni, swiping her wet face, a furrow between her brows. "Are you gonna figure out your car?"

Jenni nods, but her head is spinning. She can't stay at her job at PT General.

Werewolves need not apply.

Her house is worthless, too. Her small condo is all hers, thanks to her parents' life insurance policy.

Jenni's idea is a seamless one. *Pay it forward,* Devin had said.

Okay. "You have a place to live?"

Devin's chin lifts. "Yeah, I got an apartment. Me and Ella, we do okay."

Poor thing. An image of that fuckwit Bray rises to the surface of Jenni's brain. There's something about him, something she can't quite put her finger on. She shakes off her misgivings. "I'm sure you do. But how long will it take before Bray comes calling."

Devin bites her lip then releases it. Jenni watches fresh color bloom where the flesh was pinched. "He hasn't come around in a long time. I didn't even know he knew where I work."

Jenni's so tired, it feels like the beach has just landed inside her eyes. She wants to rub her grainy, itchy eyeballs out of her face. And she's grimy. God.

An exhausted sigh slips out. "Why don't we grab Ella, and you can come to my place?"

Devin lifts an eyebrow. "I don't know you, and no offense, something weird as fuck is going on with ya." Her eyebrows shoot up.

Jenni nods. Devin's not exactly enlightening her of the new *situation.*

"Yeah." She adjusts her position in the driver's seat of Devin's small car, "I'm aware. If you just wait here, I'll go to my car and grab my purse and keys, get back here, and we can go get your girl and go to my house."

"Why?" Devin asks. "Because this is—this messes with my kid's head."

"No." Jenni shakes her head. "What'll mess with Ella's head is Bray showing up, whacked out of his mind, and maybe hurting you guys."

Devin's hands fly to her mouth, and her eyes are wide.

"Come on, you *had* to have thought of that possible scenario already." Jenni searches her face and comes up with... *no*. Devin clearly hadn't ever really thought Bray making an appearance was a possibility—until tonight, when he and his posse of asshats jumped out like jacks-in-the-box.

Jenni attempts an explanation. "I feel like me being at your work caused you to be late. That if I hadn't been there, you'd have already been gone when Bray arrived."

Devin's eyebrows pop, her lips flattening. "Okay, what happened is so many levels of fucked up, but you're *not* to blame. Nope." Devin holds up her hands stubbornly. "Bray's a nut job. He doesn't need any help with that part. You being there"—Devin shrugs, chin trembling as more tears begin to fall—"he would've just shown up eventually. I'm glad you were there." Her soft brown eyes are intense when they meet Jenni's, and her jaw clenches as she angrily flings tears with her shaking fingers. "You-you *saved* me. Bray and his dudes"—she spits the word—"they would have done bad stuff to me *and* robbed my work."

All of that sounds spot-on to Jenni.

"So let me pay it forward, Devin." Jenni latches on to Devin's gaze. "Let me get my stuff and take you to my place. Protect you and Ella."

Devin looks at her and doesn't ask Jenni how she'd

protect them. After all, she was in that parking lot and watched Jenni lay out three large men.

She licks her lips, all traces of her blackish-purple lipstick gone. "But what about you?"

It's Jenni's turn to look at her hands. "I'm going to have to go. Find other people like me."

She looks at Devin. Part of her face obscured by a streetlamp; the other half is cast in deep shadow.

Seconds tick by, and the silence is loud inside the vehicle.

"Will you wait?"

Devin nods, and Jenni takes her at her word, sliding out of the car and shutting the door softly before she loses her courage. With a last glance over her shoulder, Jenni jogs toward the underground parking garage. She isn't out of breath when she arrives.

Not even a little.

Yesterday, she was as weak as a kitten, still recovering from the chemo and radiation, unable to believe that the treatment had made her sicker than the disease that was killing her.

Now she feels invincible.

It's a heady feeling. It's also terrifying. Jenni doesn't have answers. She has a bunch of questions. And she knows exactly who could help her.

But Adi's not here right now, and Jenni lassoed an innocent young woman into the chaotic weirdness her life has become in a matter of hours.

Instinctively, Jenni lifts her chin, flaring her nostrils. The move is as automatic as breathing.

Her chin drops. Eyes piercing the gloom surrounding

her, Jenni scents no one. And something deep within tells her she would if they were near. Her acute senses discern the smell of death, disease, illness from the bowels of the hospital, and the products used to treat and disinfect all that. But it's a vague mix of scents. Broad. Unimportant.

What's real is her own scent, disease still threading through the unique signature, which Jenni tracks directly to her car.

* * *

JENNI TRIES THE HANDLE. Her VW rabbit came with her parents' death, along with all the rest of their possessions. It'd been her mom's grocery getter.

Locked. *Of course it is.* Jenni's hot with security, unless she's busting out werewolves from the hospital via the morgue.

Shit.

She sees her purse and coat right inside. Scanning the murk of the parking garage, making certain she remains unobserved, Jenni sinks to her haunches, feeling around under the wheel well. Seeking the magnetic box that holds her spare key fob, Jenni's fingertips stumble over the rectangle of cold metal, and she tugs hard, loosening the connection of magnet to steel. The top of her hand hits the car with the force of the pull, and she yelps.

"Ouch!" Jenni hisses, cradling her hand. She sucks the blood that wells to the surface of her skin. *Just what I need.*

She stands, hand throbbing, and pushes the automatic button on the archaic fob, and the locks bounce to attention inside the interior of the car.

Jenni opens the door and reaches inside. Hauling out her colorful paisley Vera Bradley purse, she slings it over her shoulder to diagonally cross her body.

She hates the idea of getting blood on it and sighs. Rooting around in the compartmentalized depths, she extracts her cell phone and immediately presses her thumb to the button for security. The display lights and she sees the power stands at only eight percent.

Of course, there are no texts.

Lance of Pud Wackers Unite no longer phones, and her friends have all distanced themselves—too unsure what to say or do when their friend is dying.

So they don't do or say anything.

Grief, regret, and sadness try to have their way with her, and she beats the shit out of those three like she's done a number of times before.

Taking a deep breath, Jenni checks the time: 3:08 a.m. She lets the phone drop back inside the purse then zips it closed. She gives in to her fatigue, rubbing her eyes.

Grabbing her lightweight hoodie, she closes the door and locks it. A shrill beep sounds.

Dammit. She meant to hit the manual locks.

Her eyes sweep the concrete floors and find where she was bleeding out. She slowly walks to the spot.

The dull rust of blood is a loose circular stain, with a semi-clean spot at the middle. The blood smells fresh to her new senses. Diseased.

Jenni holds her inhale then lets it shudder out. Raising her eyebrows, she wonders if Adi and the others could smell that she was dying. If the hours-old blood is any indication, they definitely could.

She swallows hard, allowing her eyes to drift from where she lay dying, to the area where the steel door used to be, now boarded up with a sheet of plywood.

Remnants of the violence that took place here is proof that it happened.

It happened to *her*. Jenni doesn't realize she's crying until the tears obscure her vision.

I need to get out of here.

She turns her head, glancing at the yellow crime scene tape, and wonders where the bodies of those werewolves went. Surely that would be a little *much* for the cops to discover?

What did Adi call them when she and Slash were talking?

Lanarre.

Adi talked about retribution for their deaths. Does that mean they'll be looking for Jenni, too? If they were, would they know that Jenni was just caught in the crossfire of some weird paranormal snafu?

Jenni cups her elbows, nervously eyeing every surface. The cops *must* know she's missing—she heard them discussing her.

That Adi is missing as well.

Maybe blame has already been assigned. And maybe offering her place to Devin is putting the young woman and her daughter in more danger than they were already in with Bray sniffing around.

Jenni presses her palms to the sides of her skull. She's too tired to mentally power through this. She needs a shower, fresh clothes, food—yet again—and a bed.

Jenni trudges up the slight incline leading to the

outside parking lot and stoops underneath the tape. She lets the slick plastic drop, and it makes a soft sound as it flutters behind her.

"Stop where you are, miss."

Jenni's face whips toward the voice. Scents assail her. The last one is a scent of danger. Gun oil. The thing she's becoming lifts within her body like an imposter of someone else inside her body.

Police.

Jenni takes in the familiar uniform. It's not rocket science that Jenni understands she has to get the hell out of here.

Right now.

She wraps the arms of the hoodie around her waist.

"Are you Jennifer French?"

Jenni doesn't answer.

She runs.

CHAPTER 8

ADI

*S*lash's hand hasn't stopped moving up and down her naked hip to where Adi's waist narrows in almost an hour.

Back and forth, the light touch of his fingers strokes her side. Hands she has watched kill, maim, and crush are so tender on her flesh. If Adi were to close her eyes, his touch would be like a breeze instead of the flesh and blood of her mate.

Her mate.

Adi still can't fully believe that at her young age, she is mated. For life. A little thrill shivers through her.

With Slash.

He presses his nose against her neck, scenting deeply of her. "What are you thinking?" He licks the side of her neck, ending with a kiss.

So much shit... That's what she's thinking. Adi looks away, flustered. "Ah, I'm thinking I'm lucky. Lucky to be with you."

Slash rubs the stubble of his jaw against her neck, tickling her, and Adi giggles, lightly pressing her hands to the sides of his face.

"I am the fortunate one." His dark eyes hold her still, searching her face. "I hurt you." Slash covers her chest where her heart lays beneath the skin.

Adi drops her hands from his face. "Yeah."

Curling a finger under her chin, he props her face up, perfectly aligning her vision with his.

Soft light from a tiny lamp on the nightstand illuminates his imperfect profile. The scar appears fresh—and raw—in this lighting. But Adi knows that what scarred him happened a long time ago, when their enemies used weapons of silver to permanently maim or worse.

"I would do it again."

Now it's Adi's turn to try and uncover the meaning of his words.

"Any measure, no matter how harsh, is not harsh enough if there is threat to my mate."

She nods slowly. "But since your *delivery* sucked so bad, maybe you can you just explain stuff better in the future?"

Slash bursts out laughing, hauling her underneath him. He pins her with his much larger and more powerful body. "I adore you."

Adi's still kind of pissed. She can admit it. "I thought, after we shared something so personal, that you were dumping me or something. It sorta felt like you were scooping my guts out... with a soup spoon."

A ripple of pain flows over his hard features, making the scar tissue flatten as he manages his emotions.

Adi wonders if a lifetime of keeping his feelings contained has taken its toll.

"I believed that if I were to take time to explain my thought process, you wouldn't leave and seek safety."

Adi begins to look away, and he captures her face again, shifting his weight so he doesn't crush her.

"And I didn't heal the paralysis from that fucking Were from the Western until an hour after you'd already left the Singer stronghold."

Adi can also admit she wouldn't have left Slash there without his legs working. She knew it. He knew it.

"Would you have left me, heart of my heart." Slash smooths his palms along the side of her head and forces her face still, gazing deeply into her eyes.

She shakes her head inside his hold. "No fucking way. I would've fought those dickheads off with my bare hands." Adi clenches her hands into fists, just thinking about it.

Slash slowly nods. "Then a harshness was required that I would never willingly do otherwise. Do you see that?"

Tears slip out of her eyes, and Slash thumbs them away.

"Why didn't you get with a bitch that was a wallflower type?" Even Adi hears her stubbornness.

Slash chuckles softly then breathes a gentle kiss against her mouth. Adi closes her eyes to feel it better, depriving her sense of sight to hold on to the sensation.

"Because the female that I love is right here."

Adi opens her eyes. "Took you long enough."

His smile widens, and the knot of scar tissue at his

upper lip stretches with the movement. "I could not mate a whelp. As it is, you are a baby."

She reaches up, stroking his strong jaw, and his eyes close with a rapturous expression.

I do that. I make Slash feel again.

"I don't feel like a baby," she says in a voice gone low with need.

Slash's ebony eyes snap open, so intense and dark that she drowns inside their depths. "No, you don't."

His tone of voice has her breath catching.

"You can't want to again?"

Slash cocks his head. "Are you denying me, mate?" There's a hint of humor in his words.

Adi shakes his head. "I feel a lot better—tons. But how long will it last? Heat? How many times will we have to mate to make me feel okay?"

"As many times as it takes."

Slash grins.

So does Adi.

* * *

"IT'S criminal I can still walk." Adi gives Slash a significant glance.

He swats her butt.

Adi gives him a look that stops him in his tracks.

"Female, you will be the end of me."

She shakes her head. "I think for an old guy, you do okay." She pops her hip to the side and cups her breasts like a hand bra.

His eyes follow her hands, landing on her naked flesh.

Slash leaps at her, and she yelps, jumping away, hand to chest. "Slash!" she hisses in a whisper.

He wraps his arms around her, and with them both standing, her head only reaches between his pecs.

"I hate being short," she grumbles at his muscular chest.

Slash tips her chin up. "You are female."

"I'm small even for a female."

He slowly turns her until the back of her is against his front. Folding his forearm around her chest, he holds her tightly. "You fit against me as though made for my body, Adrianna."

"Why does everything you say sound so sexy?"

She can hear the smile in his words. "I'm not making an effort."

Adi lifts his heavy arm from her chest and turns to look at him, cocking an eyebrow. "Not *trying*. Horsepucky, Slash, you're a breathing, walking sex machine."

"Hmmm, maybe for you, Adrianna."

She pushes him in the chest, and his smile widens. "Seriously?"

He nods.

"Huh, you're entirely too pleased with yourself, ya big lug."

His lips curl. "Yes, yes, I am. And what do I have not to be pleased about? Tell me that, my mate. I have you. We are safe, sated, fed, and rested. We can leave this place and make our way south."

Adi feels a churn begin in her gut. "Are you thinking we should go back to the Northwestern Pack? I don't know if I can." Her eyes flick to his, unable to contain her anxiety. "And you're a Red."

Slash places his palms on the wall, caging her. "No one is more aware of my rogue status. I kept it well hidden. But now I am here. You are my mate. Those who ruled the Northwestern are no more, correct?" His scarred eyebrow rises, and Adi recognizes in that moment, Slash no longer hides his face from her.

"Yes," Adi replies in a whisper, thinking of her brother and Manny. Those two, she grieves for. Not Lawrence, who never did anything but place females to be battled over. She shivers, remembering Tony, who turned out to be part demonic. *No surprise there.* He was a douche canoe waiting for a lake.

"What?" Slash asks, scrutinizing her face.

Her bark of laughter is short. And pained. "I'm glad Tony's gone, is all."

He immediately grins. "Yes, and in spectacular fashion."

"Deserved it, the prick."

Slash says nothing. No need.

Everybody thought Tony Laurent was King Dick.

Adi bites her lip then releases it. "I don't know who's at the Northwestern anymore. I miss Susan."

Slash is silent, letting her talk.

"But I'd love to see the rest of the pack again. I'm not a Singer. I got caught up in their mess, and now I just want to belong again to a pack, be with other Were."

"They might not accept me," Slash says in his neutral way.

"Screw them. We're mated. You can't undo that."

Slash shakes his head. "No, we cannot." He runs a finger down her cheek, and Adi leans into the caress with a shiver of pleasure. "And I don't want to. But as you know, there can only be one Red per pack. If another Red were there—too many Reds in one place isn't good. And the Lanarre will scent us if we stay in this region."

Adi slides her arms around his bare, hard waist. "Why did you kill the Lanarre, Slash? Why?"

"Because they wanted to breed my mate."

She leans back, studying his expression. "They'll hunt you. Us."

Slash nods. "They might. However, they have plenty to do. With the possibility of Tessa and Tahlia at the Hoh." Slash's inhale is deep, broadening his chest even more.

Adi places a hand in the center of all that muscle, feeling his strong steady heartbeat. Slash's exhale is rough as he captures her hand, holding her fingers tightly.

"Well, I guess our options are taking our chances at the Northwestern and hope another Red hasn't sought pack membership, or hang around here until the Lanarre come for us."

"We're not staying."

Adi nods. She doesn't want to stay, either, though Della's been cool. For a witch.

They'll just take off and move south.

Nobody is going to know what happened up here unless they confess. And they won't.

Ever.

* * *

ADI THINKS she's died and gone to heaven. Buttery flavor explodes inside her mouth as crumbs tumble from her lips.

So good. Adi gives an internal groan of acute satisfaction.

Della's face lights with a broad smile. "Do you like those?"

"*Like?* Pfft—love!" Adi chimes, licking sticky honey off each finger.

Slash folds his muscular arms, giving her a look of indulgent tolerance. "What?" she asks, reaching for her third biscuit. "I'm starved."

"I would never have my mate without food," Slash comments in a droll voice, directing a secret smirk at Della.

They can bite me.

Adi grins, stuffing half a muffin into her mouth. Having sex with Slash and eating this huge breakfast has made her feel invincible.

Having sex with Slash. Her grin broadens wider, if that's even possible.

"What are you smiling about?"

A fine blush broils over her cheeks, and Adi's suddenly very interested in finishing the eggs and cheese left on her plate.

Slash gives a satisfied chuckle.

"Terrific grub, Della." A wistful pang hits Adi. Della's cooking reminds her of Susan. *She's probably on my mind a lot because we're heading there today.*

Adi blinks, momentarily dizzy, and she glances at Slash, who's speaking quietly with Della.

She sets down her fork and takes a swig of OJ. Bright citrus flavors cover her tongue as chilled juice flows down her throat, hitting the warm load of food she put in her stomach.

Another wave of dizziness strikes, and she makes a small noise of distress.

Slash is suddenly beside her, taking her hands in his.

"What is it?" His dark eyes are rimmed with green, and Adi knows his beast swims below the surface like a shadow beneath water.

Adi puts a shaky hand on her forehead, and her palm comes away clammy. "I don't know, I was okay—hungry —then I got dizzy all of the sudden."

Maybe it's the heat. Adi clings to Slash. "I'll be okay, probably a lot going down. What with leaving and everything."

"Nobody's going anywhere," Della says.

Slash's face whips to the witch.

Too late.

The shotgun kicks, and buckshot hits Slash in his flank as he shields Adi's body with his own.

Adi screams, trying to stand, and the edges of her vision go black.

"What the fuck?" Adi roars, trying to help Slash.

"No—" he gasps.

Adi tries to sight in on him, but she can't see.

I'm fucking passing out.

Holes ooze with blood, and dawning realization slams into Adi.

Della's the enemy.

She and Slash mated in this house. Slept here. Showered.

Ate.

Adi gazes at her nearly empty plate as Della props the shotgun against the pot-bellied wood stove. "You forced my hand, young wolf," she says, bustling to where Adi stands.

Adi tries to push out her talons but falls on her ass instead. Next to Slash.

"Adi!" He attempts rolling onto his hands and knees.

Why isn't Slash healing this? Adi asks herself. Her mouth tries to form a question but she's been struck stupid and slow.

"Silver!" he bellows.

Oh no.

Della reaches them.

Adi swings out with her arm, and the witch casually bats her hand away. Her palm smacks the edge of the end table, and Adi yelps, pain chasing the lethargy back.

The witch poisoned her.

Slash slices through Della's heavy skirts, missing her leg by a millimeter.

"No ya don't, Red." Her fist strikes him in the head, and Slash's skull hits the floor with a resounding thud.

"Slash!" Adi's scream fills the cottage.

He's out cold. *How can a witch do that to a Red Were?*

Adi's tears burn down her face, and she crawls to her beloved mate. "Slash…"

"He'll be dead soon, young wolf."

Della flips Adi over easily. And she stares up at the old woman who is no longer old, but as young as Adi. "He did what I wanted. He pricked you, and now you carry his whelp. And that whelp will lift my curse."

Moon. Adi's head swims.

"The trolls?" Adi asks senselessly, trying to crawl away as Della inches closer.

The smile on Della's young face is cruel. "Guardians of the innocent."

"They would have *helped* us?" Tears run freely now as snot fills her nose and her stomach heaves.

Slash is going to die.

Adi's heartbeats fill her, blood coursing like a river inside her eardrums.

Della wants their baby.

Adi wants Slash. But he's full of silver buckshot while an insane witch has poisoned her.

Moon help us.

CHAPTER 9

TESSA

"*I*s the door locked?" she asks breathlessly, eyes scanning the solid wood.

Laz gently fans her ebony locks of hair from beneath her, spreading the wavy tendrils far and wide on the large bed.

"If they wish to come in, there is no stopping it."

But Tessa craves the illusion of security—and privacy. It's hard to focus with Laz's nudity literally in her face.

Her eyes run down his body. He's a beautifully sculpted male, hard and ready. A flash of her heat has Tessa clenching her teeth in pain, and she knows that a Were male would be the ideal choice to relieve the agony by breeding her.

In fact, she's not entirely certain that the seed from *any* male will do.

What Tessa *does* know is she wants Laz. If she were honest with herself, she's wanted him nearly the instant she bumped into him in the butler's pantry at Region One.

Tessa didn't run from Tramack for twenty years so she

could exchange one Were for another. And Lazarus is no Were.

Tessa chooses who she will eventually mate—and breed—with.

Her core pulses for a male, true—Tessa can't help the biology that brings heat for Lycan females. But the benefit of choice in this instance is a heady one.

Laz's nostrils flare, and using his knees, he walks deeper between her spread legs. He spared her panties when he tore off her other clothes.

Literally. Tore them off. *Now where will I get new ones?*

Her thoughts scatter as Laz's fingertips trail along the sensitive skin of her inner thighs. A riot of gooseflesh flows like a river after his touch, squelching thoughts of her wardrobe.

Tessa sits up, wrapping her arms around his naked form, dangerously close to the tip of an impressive erection.

Laz releases his next inhale in a raw eruption of oxygen, laying his large palm at the base of her skull.

She burns for this male. Every deep and penetrable part of her wants Lazarus. Tessa can scent his maleness, along with an alien note of fragrance that is utterly foreign to her, and yet as familiar as home.

Tessa clutches him, and Laz draws in another shaky breath as her fingertips bite into the muscles of his hard ass.

She turns her face and slowly, so slowly—flicks her tongue out, tasting him for the first time.

His dick kicks beneath her wet touch, and Laz sinks

his fingers into her hair, pulling her head back until her throat is a long, taut line of flesh exposed before him.

Vulnerable.

A female Were would show her throat only to a male she trusted with her life.

It's at that moment that Tessa knows.

He might be a devil, but Laz is the other piece of her. The part that she's been unwittingly running toward all this time. Lazarus is why no Were ever seemed right, why she let her heat ride her unmercifully while she hid in the dark. Sure, Tessa had sex before. But sex outside of heat is not meaningful. It's simple relief from basic needs.

Laz hisses. "Do not—or I will go against your mouth instead of inside you, female."

Tessa tries to swallow but can't. She reaches for that quivering staff of hot flesh and wraps her slender fingers around his thick girth tinted a light red like the rest of him.

Perfect. Straight. Hard.

Laz groans, breaking her desperate hold on him and bends over her, tightening his grip on her hair.

She gasps, pain mixing with anticipation. His eyes move to charcoal, then he's kissing her like he'll eat her from the inside out.

Tessa thought he would bruise her lips with the need that darkened his gaze. But Laz surprises her with a gentle sweep of his fevered flesh against her mouth.

She opens her lips, and his tongue slides between them, caressing and plunging.

Tessa wants what he does with his mouth—from his cock.

She whimpers, pain and pleasure saturating her sex with want, and Laz scoops her roughly against him.

Her breasts are crushed against his hard chest, and she has trouble breathing. Tessa's not sure if it's because Laz is so close, or because he holds her so tightly.

She loves it.

He speaks quietly against her temple, "When I had you in that closet at the Singer compound for only a kiss—I knew."

"I did, too," Tessa admits breathlessly. "I've never felt like I do for you about anyone."

"But you could stop feeling that." Laz lifts her, seating her above his erection, and she wraps his waist with her legs. Only the thin, lacy material of her panties separates their flesh from joining as she so desperately wants.

"I don't feel like I could," Tessa says, clinging to his broad shoulders as she rolls her lips along his muscular chest, capturing his nipple in her mouth.

She lightly nips the hard flesh with her teeth, and Laz groans.

Laz throws his head back, hanging on to her ass. "You could, ah—*Tessa*—my cock weeps for you. Stop that nibbling."

"Okay." She releases his nipple with a pop and a quick flick of her tongue. She looks at him through her eyelashes as he dips his chin to regard her.

Swirling blackness drowns the color of his irises to dark coins inside his face.

Tessa should be afraid.

Laz's skin has gone from pale to light red, and his eyes

are devoid of color. Metallic black bumps of bone break the smooth light-blond hair that covers his head.

Horns.

But Laz's hands are tender on her. Every fingerprint on her skin is a branding of fire from his touch.

"You'll feel hot inside me," she whispers, stroking his length. The girth doesn't allow her fingers to meet.

"Let's see."

Cradling her butt with one arm, he jerks the side of her panties, tearing the fragile fabric, and flings them to the ground. Laz brushes his tip against her entrance.

They groan together at the contact, and a wave of scorching heat sweeps her body, causing her hips to hike in shameless greed for what he offers.

"Please," she begs, "I can't stand the heat…"

"The need," Laz says as though he understands.

He begins to enter her, using her hips like handles and holding her body above his seeking, hard length.

Slowly, he lowers her, impaling her on his tip.

Laz is not hot as she'd anticipated but… "Perfect." Tessa arches, widening her legs further.

His palm slides up her back. Her spine is slick with sweat while his other palm holds her ass against him. Laz pushes more of him inside, and Tessa's body begins to resist all that male flesh piercing her so thoroughly, stretching her tightness.

Laz slows, and Tessa feels their heartbeats unite.

She opens her eyes and finds his have gone to glacial blue.

Laying her on the bed, he keeps her hips high while her head is against the soft mattress.

"Do I hurt you?" he asks softly at the exact moment his thumb presses against the juicy bundle of nerves between her slick folds.

"No," Tessa breathes, rolling her face to the side and trying to ram her hips down on Laz.

"Not yet, Redemptive." The word slides over her, soothing her, making her more drenched for him.

A little more of him slides inside, slowly stretching Tessa, making her feel—and want—every fat, long inch.

As he moves in and out, a great pressure begins to build deep inside her.

"Please—harder," Tessa begs, her heat swamping her sex, igniting her core like a brushfire.

"Patience," Laz says in a tight voice, but he's killing her with his thumb swirling on her wetness, and a tingling begins at her raw nerve endings.

With a last push, Laz brings himself to the end of her, where they throb together, joined tight.

"Yes." Tessa's breath eases out of her from want, from her heat.

Kissing her womb, Laz slowly withdraws.

When he pushes back inside, Tessa throws her head back in a silent scream of pleasure, so full of his length that she can't take another breath.

Laz chuckles then swings his hips as he rocks into her deeply again.

Tessa whimpers before she explodes around him, pulsing with so much force, he fights to stay within her depths. When her body's clenching finally subsides, she says, "My turn," and sits upright with him still inside.

Laz captures her around the waist, instinctively

knowing what she wants, and he lies back with her riding him.

"I'm going to do *you* now." The hint of a growl edges her words.

Laz smolders up at her, steam pouring out of him. The fragrance of him is like the smell of the best food on the planet.

"What is that?" Tessa asks, breathing deeply of him, but Laz doesn't reply.

His hips begin a deep, punishing rhythm beneath her. Tessa throws her head back, meeting every upward thrust.

Before she can guess at the wonderful scent Laz is producing, he's rocking inside her so hard that another orgasm begins to build.

Tessa's beast surfaces, roiling beneath her skin, begging for Laz's seed to cool her heat.

Tessa realizes she *wants* to be pregnant with Laz's child. This is why she couldn't use another male during her heat.

Her body is made for this moment.

When she comes again, Laz is helpless beneath her, going rigid as she milks him of his own release.

The jets of his essence cool her heat, and she collapses on top of him. Their labored breathing is the only sound in the room.

His delicious scent lingers.

Laz and Tessa lay together for several minutes. Finally, he gently rolls her off him and tucks her against his side. Giving her his full attention while he moves a stray hair from her face, Laz says quietly, "I have planted my seed deep."

Tessa wants to laugh at his ancient language. She's been in the world of humans far too long, thinking and speaking with their slang and words. But something in the way he says the words has her sitting up on her elbow.

"Ah, yeah—I feel really good now." Thank Moon, because she was desperate and needy. Stressed. Tessa's still horribly anxious, but at least she doesn't have the heat riding her.

Laz brought her some fucking peace. And that emotion's been hard won over the past two decades she spent running from Tramack.

Laz strokes her face, running his hand down her long black hair. "Sated, Tessa?"

A slow exhale slides out as a tight knot in her stomach loosens. Whether the orgasms or Laz's nearness are the cause, she's not sure. But neither could have hurt. She gives him a small, spent smile. "Yes. This is the first time I've allowed myself to be bred during heat," she admits softly.

Lazarus's smile is wide, and she stares at how white his teeth are against a bright-red tongue. A tongue that was everywhere on her body.

"Me, too."

Tessa jerks up into a sitting position. "What?"

Laz gives a lazy nod, flopping back against the soft sheets and pillows. "The demonic have a *need*, as well."

"Heat?" Tessa nearly yells, her heart beginning to race.

He presses a fingertip to lips that are plump from his kisses, tracing the swell of her full bottom lip.

Laz lifts a heavy shoulder. "Of a sort. But I'm male. With the right female, I will release a pheromone, a very specific one. It calls my breeding seed to the surface, and only a sterile female will not give me what my body requires."

"What is that?" Tessa asks, though she's certain she knows. His answer is more a confirmation than anything.

"Offspring."

CHAPTER 10

DARK MASTER

*W*ater like heated oil coats every surface of rough tumbled charcoal-colored boulders. They fit together perfectly, lining the walls of the subterranean environment of Hades's interconnecting and well-traveled corridors.

Dark Master is of course, as always, in his element. Perfectly suited to the smoldering atmosphere, he is unable, and uninterested, in going Above. Visiting the realm of humanity and supernaturals who live Between is about as interesting as uttering a prayer to He whom they shall never mention.

That is why he instructed Praile, his most trusted servant, to move Between in his stead. Praile was unusually keen for the half-breed high demon, Lazarus, accompanying him.

The Dark Master snorts, loosing plumes of steam. Lazarus's loathsome looks notwithstanding, he possesses a certain charm.

And the healing skills! Dark Master folds his hands,

careful not to shred his deep-red skin with his own ebony razor-sharp talons. Lazarus was nearly indispensable to the sort of torture Hades perpetuates.

He knots his hands carefully behind his back and dips his chin. Dark Master has not heard from Praile in almost two Between days.

Given the circumstances of the objective—to infect or kill the Rare One—Dark Master's directive might have been a challenge to accomplish, even for Praile. Though Devil knows, he is as vile a servant of Hades as any.

He allows a small smile to curl his lips as steam briefly obscures his vision. With an impatient palm, Dark Master sweeps away the hot vapors that always seep from his orifices, continuing his trek down the corridor toward the rooms that hold his most important work.

The rooms where he perfects his art.

He moves swiftly for one who walks over crushed hot coals. They burn the flesh of the lesser demonic. Pieces of their charred bits fit between the embers of the ever-burning coals.

Stalactites, fissured and deep crimson, glow—perfectly illuminating his path. The tips continually drip their burning deposits from the ceiling of rock in the high caves of Hades, growing the cone-shaped formations that Dark Master weaves between as he strides toward his destination with his usual purpose. Slowly melting lava-like crust oozes down the sides of the narrow spires, creating a layer of molten crust at the base of each stalagmite as it meets its mate from the ceiling. In some cases, the stalactite and stalagmite touch, their middles pinched like a wasp's, the two seeming to reach for each other.

Dark Master typically admires the beauty of his realm.

But not this day—for this day marks the third day of time Between in which Praile has not communed with him.

Disquiet has settled over his realm. Not the kind of daily evil that Dark Master thrives on, but the sort that tells him in a deep and instinctive way that something has not gone as planned.

Something from Above.

Dark Master shivers. A perfect balance of good and evil shall be maintained. It is the order of things. As it has always been. As it will be forevermore.

His evil heart yearns for more blackness, spreading like a slick of oil over Between. However, he knows there are too many of the angelic Above to allow for that.

Dark Master grins. Steam rises in a great plume directly in front of him. He strives daily for that evil to propagate. *One can hope.* After all, Dark Master *is* immortal. He has all the time in the realm to execute his purpose.

He comes to a stop in front of a door of forged iron, contemplating. If one of the fey from Between were to make it to the demonic realm—though that would be unlikely—iron is like a sickness to the fey. Thus, all the doors are fashioned with it.

Dark Master has always ruled this realm. As the one who shall not be spoken of has ruled Above.

In all the days of eternal fire and suffering, he has seen only a handful of those from Between traverse this realm.

And it has come to his attention that the Rare One, or her future offspring, could be such a being—a being of mass destruction. A being capable of ruining all the terrible and beautiful accomplishments Dark Master has already seen to fruition and is committed to continuing.

He sent Praile to end this Rare One, this perfect specimen who represents hope for so many Between—and those from Above.

Dark Master carefully clenches his fingers into a fist. He would see her body come to ash.

Praile enlisted the help of a Lycan who possessed enough blood of the high demonic to be used.

Dark Master has a brief pang of sadness, touching his talons to his chest wherein a black heart beats. Tony Laurent was such a loss. *To have so little of the demonic blood, yet be so supremely and naturally evil?* He shakes his head, despairing.

A waste. What a demonic Laurent would have been if more of their precious dark blood ran in his veins.

Brushing off his uncharacteristic feelings of regret, Dark Master pushes the door wide with a fingertip, the metal briefly singeing his flesh.

The whirls of his fingerprints steam, flattening to what a human of Between might interpret as a second-degree burn, only to be absorbed and healed in seconds.

Dark Master is one with this environment.

He does not close the door. Even the lowly demons who toil and enjoy only the small fleshy tortures allowed to them will be rewarded with the sounds of his torture.

For he is master of that, as well. And he is inclined to share his spoils. It is a boon for morale.

A staked prisoner is splayed atop a stone that is slightly elevated at one end. The rough square holds the antiquated blood of the legion of dead who now inhabit the fine cracks.

The age of the rock is undetermined.

Dark Master does not remember a time when his stone torture tableaus were not in use. It's as though they always existed. Their thickness—somewhat less than two feet, but not more than three—serves his intention perfectly.

His eyes run over the prisoner.

Dark Master is happy when blue veins like thin lace rise to the surface of this one's flesh in throbbing, painful response to his presence.

Excellent.

The prisoner wails, whipping his head from side to side. It is a misery for a being of the angelic to reside in Hades. In truth, though Dark Master would never tell it, the male Singer is exceedingly resilient.

In theory, he *should* be dead already. That makes Dark Master ecstatic.

"Release me, Lucifer!"

"No," Dark Master replies, frowning at the use of his ancient name. The name he held before the Fall. *Dark Master* is more becoming.

The fool baits me.

He strolls casually to the tableau, and the high demonic who have restrained this prisoner of Between back away, their battle tails tucked tightly between their legs as their deadly toenails click against the rock floor in cautious retreat, eyes downcast.

They are naked, as is custom Below.

Dark Master hisses his displeasure, a forked tongue

lancing his lip as he does. The flesh splits, repairs instantly, and splits again.

The high demonic subjugate themselves before him. Their heavy cocks brush the hot stone floor as their forearms hold their faces off the burning surface.

Their whimpers of pain are amusing, but Dark Master doesn't take time to relish their fear and agony as he usually does and instead releases them from their prone position.

As the pair stands, the skin at the undersides of their forearms, their knees, and the tips of their toes blisters. Turning red, they heal as he watches.

The tips of their dicks bleed in color to a deep red that is nearly black from the oozing melting they endured because they disobeyed him.

"My instructions were clear." His voice trembles, sounding of thunder and burning words.

The high demonic swallow their fear simultaneously, and one has the balls to actually speak. "We could not— his blood is too tempting to be kept in his body, Master."

"That is for *me* to decide!" he roars, spittle flying from his mouth. A few droplets land at the feet of the angelic.

A single liquid gem falls at the male's ankle. The droplet reacts like acid, sizzling as it begins to burn a hole to the bone.

The prisoner's screams are music of the sweetest variety to Dark Master. He sighs at the sound, delighted beyond measure. Lifting a hand, he lets it float as though he's conducting a symphony.

The high demonic bow their heads, too, afraid to defend their insolence.

Dark Master watches the angelic's blue blood soak the stone. Like a soothing river of ice, it crystalizes everything it touches.

He dips his finger in the blood, and the angelic male Singer attempts to jerk away. Dark master lifts his digit, watching as the blood coating the tip of his finger eats away at his talon like acid.

When the knife-like talon disintegrates, the azure blood begins on the skin at his fingertip. Like a glittering, flesh eating worm, the angelic blood would quickly consume his body.

Everything from Above is powerful—even more so in the realm Below.

That fact angers Dark Master.

He turns to his two disobedient servants, wishing so badly for Praile that he feels as though a physical burden has been placed atop his chest, emptying his lungs of oxygen.

"Do you see what one drop of the angelic blood can do?" his voice shakes the interior of his torture room.

A place he retreats for solace has been violated because these two thought to play grab ass while in his service.

They back away, and Dark Master presses forward.

"Do you prize what dangles between your legs?" His voice is filled with his anger, and literal vapor of fire licks from the seam of his lips.

They cover their pricks.

Dark Master moves rapidly. To human eyes, the motion would be nothing more than a streak of crimson steam. In the next moment, he stands before them.

"You thought to bleed the angelic? Even now, his blood

poisons our realm." His black eyes, rimmed in red, sear them in place. "You do not bleed one who has substance from Above."

Dark Master takes his left hand and gently cradles the head of the high demonic who is closest, careful not to get caught up in the ebony horn that is nearly at this demon's temple.

Spreading his arm wide, he takes his right hand and repeats the tender cradle at the right side of the other demonic's head.

They mewl like a pair of kittens inside a sack, awaiting drowning. Their pathetic eyes widen—one's black, the other's pure red.

He slams their skulls together.

The shards of bone pierce his skin. But that does not matter. Dark Master has minutes, not hours, to undo the damage wrought by his disobedient servants.

Their bodies drop, and with a quickness born of his station, Dark Master stabs his wounded finger inside the guts of the dying high demonic. One distended eye rolls toward him, his body desperately trying to heal the wounds.

He screams, high and piteous.

The lower demonic stop their petty tortures at the sound of one of their own dying.

Silence infiltrates the normal chorus of begging, screaming, and shrieking of the realm Below.

Grabbing an ankle of the high demonic, Dark Master easily drags the two at either side of the stone tableau.

The holy blood of the angelic drips onto their writhing

bodies. One demon bucks hard when the drops land on his exposed torso.

Dark Master chuckles. The demon can't decide if he has sufficient hands to hold in his brains while also trying to escape the acidic blood of the torture victim above him. The entertainment value of that indecision?

Priceless.

Dark Master arrested the advance of the angelic blood's destruction. The tip of his finger heals as the destroyed talon begins to grow back. He raises his hand, inspecting the mess of his finger.

He glances below him, effectively transferring his wounded digit to the high demonic who dies.

His body is now shrouded in frozen agony. The normally deep blood-red tones of the high demonic pale to those from Above.

It is rumored that if a demonic suffers too much blood transference from an angelic, it can turn them.

Like the vampires from Between, the demonic would become that which he despised.

Dark Master ignores his dying charge, stepping over bodies that undulate like frantic snakes.

He leans in to more closely observe the face beneath him. Crystalline eyes in the perfect sky blue of heaven gaze back at him defiantly.

The angelic are truly ugly. No horns. Pale skin. Light eyes—many have blond or red hair.

"I do not have my right hand beside me." Dark Master chuckles. "However, you will have to do." Dipping his hand inside the slowly oozing stalagmite, Dark Master coats every bit of his flesh with the realm of Hades.

"I will tell you nothing. Do what you wish. I am a Blood Singer, and clearly, my blood is like poison."

Dark Master pierces the male's eyeball, tired of looking at the watery perfection.

The male from Between arcs his back, screaming shrilly. One after another, after another.

A low demonic cheer rises in the background. Dark Master ignores their praise.

He needs no accolade.

Dark Master dips his hand in the soothing heat of Hades, coating the flesh to withstand the blood of the angelic.

He stops his torture only when the male passes out.

Dark Master does not take sustenance. He does not need to feed. His work edifies him.

In the end, when the Singer awakens. He talks.

He talks and talks.

Until he has no mouth left from which to speak.

CHAPTER 11

JENNI

*J*enni feels that other part of her being like an echo inside her, leading her flying footsteps as though there were an internal map.

"Halt!" the cop behind her yells.

Scenery flows past her like water; streetlamps are blurred beacons of light that barely illuminate Jenni's racing footfalls.

Still, her sight is bright, sharp, and perfect.

Jenni's purse smacks her hip with every beat of her feet on the pavement like a frenetic drumbeat.

Rat-tat-tat!

Blood courses in her ears, and she can't hear anything but the rush of her breaths.

Not even when Devin steps out of the car, eyes wide.

A bullet whizzes past Jenni's head—a warning shot.

Devin screams.

Jenni doesn't think. She leaps.

Her legs move like she's on a bicycle midair. She comes down hard, landing smoothly in a crouch. She slaps her palms on the asphalt and stands, scooping Devin around the legs and tossing her into a classic fireman's hold.

Jenni executes the impossible move as though performing a choreographed routine.

She flies forward, one arm wrapped around the back of Devin's thighs while her legs carry her easily and swiftly into the heavy forest that blankets the Olympic Peninsula.

"Hang on!" Jenni screams and jumps, clearing a small ravine in that same leg-pumping, adrenaline-fueled maneuver. She nails the difficult landing, and Devin grunts as she nearly slips on the slick leaves, but with a grace she's never known, Jenni rights herself and gets moving again.

Thumping footfalls chase after her, more bullets whistle harmlessly past her head, behind her.

They're either the shittiest shots she's ever witnessed, or she's avoiding the bullets with her new senses.

The cops, men who should easily overtake a sick woman carrying another over her shoulder, are not fast enough to catch Jenni.

Their yells and commands fade behind her.

Jenni tries to focus on one thing.

Her condo.

But now she knows there will be police there, hunting for her.

And she must be their prime suspect—the dying nurse who killed enough people to leave a bloodbath behind.

Yeah, that's so *me.*

"Jenni!" Devin yells, and Jenni slows to a jog, sides heaving.

She sets Devin down.

The young woman turns, slapping her palm against a tree trunk, bends at the waist and vomits.

Jenni wants to cry.

With a shaky hand, Devin wipes strings of puke from her mouth. "What the *fuck*?"

"I'm sorry," Jenni says.

Devin's petite jaw slides back and forth as she loads up her mouth with saliva and spits the entire load to the ground. "Gross—shit." She gives Jenni an incredulous stare. "Why are the cops shooting at you?" She feels her side. "I think you bruised my ribs!"

"How come you threw up?" Jenni asks.

Devin rolls her eyes. "Because it's three-thirty in the middle of the freaking night, I got assaulted by my ex, met a—whatever the hell ya are, and just got chased and shot at by Port Townsend's finest. I'm fucking dandy!"

"Please don't yell," Jenni says quietly, scanning their surroundings nervously.

"Right," Devin replies, folding her arms and nodding vigorously, "because the cops might come and *kill* our asses."

Jenni winces. Agonizing gnawing begins in her stomach again. She supposes all the physical theatrics come at a price. She puts a hand against her belly and can't help the small groan that escapes.

Devin's face crumples, searching Jenni's body for signs of the problem. "What? Are ya sick?"

Jenni shakes her head. "I don't think so—not anymore."

"Just tell me what the fuck is going on, and don't hide shit. I've had enough of that to last me a lifetime."

"We're going to have to go to your place. I think the cops are probably at my condo."

Devin laughs. "No shit? I had that figured out when I got a load of the crime scene tape." She snorts then her face flashes to serious. "I need to get to Ella. I got a neighbor lady who sticks around my place until I come home. Best I can do." She blows a stubborn piece of fried hair out of her face and wrinkles her nose at her own breath. "And I'd give anything for a toothbrush."

"I need to eat," Jenni admits, her stomach folding in on itself.

"What? Again?" Devin's eyebrows hike.

"Yeah," Jenni answers, dejected. "How far do you think your place is from here?"

Devin looks around the woods. "You can thank your lucky stars I grew up here. I know every square inch of PT." She drops her arms and points to a vague circle of light shining through the dense forest.

"My apartment complex is a dump—built in the 1970s. But there's no crime, and the spaces are bigger from then. And I like the way the forest is right behind us." Devin sounds like she's trying to convince herself. But Jenni doesn't care at the moment.

Thank God there's a stopping point.

Jenni begins to walk toward the patch of illumination ahead, and Devin follows. "Listen, I know I said I was trying to help you back there... but I gotta be honest. I got a kid and that—I can't risk Ella for whatever strange shit you've got goin' on."

Jenni stops, looks up at a sky unsullied by light pollution, and exhales. The noise of the air rushing out of her sounds as defeated as she feels.

"I get it. I totally do. Can I just get some food, grab a shower, and sleep on your couch? I'll figure my own life out. I'll leave money."

Devin folds her arms, tensing. "I don't need no charity."

Jenni turns, looking at Devin closely. "I'm not giving charity. I need someplace to be for a few hours. My life is a disaster. I'll go away tomorrow."

Devin walks closer, takes Jenni's hands, surprising her.

She's brave. Jenni can smell her fear. It's a yummy scent, which makes Jenni feel ashamed.

"I don't want to kick you out, Jenni. I mean—you took care of Bray—boy, did ya. But I got Ella, and I don't know what kind of trouble you're in. And nurses make a lot of money, right?"

Jenni holds Devin's gaze. "Yeah."

She knows that she'd be perceived as rich in Devin's eyes. And to the rest of the world—she is. Who owns their own place at almost twenty-eight? Nobody. Of course, almost anyone, if they had the choice, would have their parents back instead of money.

"Just stay the night, take what you need, then go, 'kay?"

Jenni shoulders slump, and tears clog her throat before she looks away.

"Cops will get who you are soon enough," Jenni says as they continue walking.

A branch snaps back, striking Jenni in the neck. She hisses at the biting contact. Lifting her hand, she touches the cut at her neck, and her fingers come away stained with blood. *Nice one.*

Devin breaks out of the woods first, turning. "Yeah. My car being at the hospital, you tossing me over your shoulder and *sprinting* into the woods? Surprised they're not already here." She shakes her head.

"Yeah," Jenni whispers. Folding her arms, she cups her elbows, scanning the backyard of the dated apartment complex as the lawn rolls into the dormant blackberry bushes that border the forest, a few rotting berries still clinging to the prickly canes.

All at once, everything overwhelms her. The hunger, the uncertainty—the danger she might have inadvertently put Devin and her daughter in.

Jenni bursts into tears in the middle of a lawn at a rundown apartment building of a girl she's known less than a few hours.

"Hey," Devin says softly and takes her hand again, towing Jenny to the bottom of a flight of steps.

Each pebbled tread is suspended in metal, and they climb as a sobbing Jenni stumbles after her.

They reach a cheap door marked Number *212*.

Devin unlocks and opens the door. A bleary-eyed older gal looks up from a book, sees them, and hoists herself off the couch.

"Devin, what's happened?" She glances between them.

"Darlene, meet Jenni—Jenni, Darlene."

Jenni nods, tears still streaming down her face. It's like she's made of water or something.

"Oh dear, what's ever the matter?" the old lady asks.

It's too much, too near to what Jenni's own mother

would've asked if she were alive. She sinks where she stands, and Devin closes the door softly. "Listen, Darlene —I need to get my friend cleaned up and fed. It's been a long night—"

"I'll say," Darlene says, lips thinning into a single line as her eyes clearly take in the scene of Jenni on the floor and Devin smelling like vomit.

"Is Ella okay?" Devin asks, clearly trying to distract the older woman.

Darlene nods, brows puckering. "Yes, she's just fine."

"Can I pay you tomorrow?" Devin asks.

Darlene's brow quirks, appearing offended. "You know I only take payment because you force me. I'd watch that darling child for nothing."

Devin nods and touches her shoulder. "I know, Dar. I just—I need a little bit of time. Bray came by work tonight, and there was a showdown..."

"Oh dear." Darlene covers her mouth, eyes widening. She looks first at Jenni, then at Devin, then at Jenni again. "Were you part of this scuffle?"

Devin sighs, wrapping an arm around the older woman. She begins herding her to the door. "Jenni helped me, Dar. I'll fill you in when you come back on Thursday, 'kay?"

Darlene nods, wary eyes shifting to Jenni.

She knows something's up with me.

Devin practically tosses her out the door, closes it, and slides the bolt. She turns and leans against the door. "I love her but, damn. Nosey as hell."

Devin breezes past where Jenni sits on the worn carpet. "I'm gonna check on Boo then be right back."

Jenni gives a distant nod. Probably her stomach is digesting her spine at this point. She's so beyond hunger that the drywall covering the dingy apartment walls is beginning to look appetizing.

Damn, damn, damn. Jenni feels the tears drying on her face in a sticky mess. She's spent.

Devin breezes back in. "My little angel is knocked out." She smiles, and Jenni is taken aback by the expression. The change in her features removes all the hard edges, and the young woman Devin must be looks back at her.

"What?" she asks self-consciously, patting down her hair.

"Nothing," Jenni blinks, refraining from rubbing her eyes. "Do you have any food?" she asks in a meek voice.

Devin's face lights with surprise. "Hell yeah. Got an entire bucket of KFC."

Jenni salivates. She uses the corner of a beat-up coffee table as a handhold and stands awkwardly, giving Devin critical scrutiny.

"What?" she asks again.

"You're skin and bones."

Devin shrugs. "Look who's talking." She grins.

Jenni doesn't. Everybody is unhealthy skinny after treatment. Hell, Jenni didn't even have hair left when they were done, and her tits are nonexistent. At least her hair grew back, but the color was so light, Jenni dyed it black.

It looks awful, but at least she's *got* hair now. Girls never know how much their femaleness is tied to hair until they're bald.

Devin scrunches her brows, apparently seeing something on Jenni's face. "Are you okay?"

Jenni shakes her head, breathing deeply. "I'm really not, but you know how everything looks so bad in the middle of the night without sleep?"

Devin gives a wan smile. "Totally."

"Well, if I can eat, shower, and sleep—I might feel human again."

Of course, as soon as she says it, Jenni knows that's bullshit. She's not human.

Not anymore.

* * *

SOMETHING SOFT BRUSHES Jenni's nose.

She lifts a hand without opening her eyes, and moves it out of the way with a lazy swat of fingers. A soft exhale, on the verge of being a snore, eases out of the tight recesses of Jenni's chest as she begins to relax again into sleep.

She's just starting to doze again when the second light touch occurs.

Jenni's eyes snap open.

A pair of eerily familiar brown eyes gaze back. But they're not Devin's. They belong to a very pretty little girl with eyelashes so long, they nearly touch her light-colored eyebrows.

Jenni blinks.

The girl is holding a Barbie doll, if Jenni's any judge of little girl toys. The long hair from said Barbie is brushing across Jenni's face, tickling her nose.

"Hi. I'm Ella. Wanna play with my Disney princess?"

"Ella!" Devin calls from the other room.

Jenni licks her lips. "Sure," she replies, but the word sounds like a poor imitation of a croaking frog.

Ella climbs up on top of Jenni, where she's been lying on the couch, and sits on her stomach.

That same stomach was distended from all the drumsticks she sucked down in the middle of the night but is now as flat as a pancake again. Does this mean she has to eat constantly?

Jenni grins.

Does this mean I get to eat constantly?

Finally, a perk.

"Whatcha smiling about?" Ella asks, beginning to groom the Barbie's hair with a small glittery-pink comb.

"No dieting," Jenni quips and moves to sit up, almost toppling Ella.

She grabs the girl, easily hefting her along with herself —one armed. Jenni decides she could totally get used to the strength she's gained. In fact, Jenni doesn't think werewolf status could have been gifted to a more grateful subject.

Ella laughs as they clumsily readjust on the couch.

"You're funny." Ella touches a stray hair that crosses Jenni's nose.

Jenni smiles and finally introduces herself. "I'm Jenni."

"Mama's friend?" The little girl's pale-blond brows scrunch as she tries to figure out relationships of random chicks who just appear overnight.

Jenni nods, deciding that's easier. After last night, they're certainly acquainted.

"Ella!" Devin calls out, more loudly this time.

"Better scoot."

Ella gives her a sly smile. "Maybe Mama will forget 'bout cleaning up my messes."

Jenni shakes her head. "My mom never did."

"Never?" Her large brown eyes widen.

She grins at Ella, patting her golden head. "Never."

Ella grumps, "Better go."

"Good thinking."

Ella hops off, grabbing the doll and brush from the floor where they fell during her graceless dismount off Jenni's stomach—which growls again.

What a pain in the ass.

Her eyes travel to the fridge. Suddenly, Jenni remembers her purse. Spying it in a pile on the coffee table, along with her deep-red Old Navy hoodie, she stands.

She feels light-headed, sits again, then stands. *Better.*

Scooping the purse off the scarred surface, she roots for all the cash she has in the world. Two twenties and one ten.

She finds a *Mama's mood is good* magnet on the fridge and centers the bills beneath it, firmly attaching the money to the fridge.

She opens the freezer and looks inside as icy air bites at a face still warm and fuzzy from sleeping so hard.

Jenni rubs her eyes, peering inside the cold box of the freezer, and sees a pint of Ben and Jerry's. She reaches for it then eyeballs the one that's hiding behind it. She rolls her bottom lip between her teeth, caves, and grabs that one, as well.

"Oh my God," Jenni whispers reverently, clutching *Banana Split* and *Salted Carmel Almond* against her chest, not even caring a bit that it's freezing and beginning to melt against the incubator-like heat of her body.

It *is* ice cream.

Devin comes around the corner, sees her holding the two pints, and says, "Oh—hey, don't ya think it's early for dessert?" Her lips quirk.

"No," Jenni growls, protecting the ice cream like a football player ready for touchdown.

Devin's brows lift.

Ella is right behind her, brown eyes wide, taking in Jenni's attempt at breakfast.

"I like her, Mama. She eats ice cream before supper."

Devin throws up her hands, clearly exasperated. "You guys."

You guys.

Jenni smiles at Devin. "Thanks." A tight lump forms in her throat. She can't talk past it.

Devin stares at her for a beat. "Youbetchya." She walks to a small drawer by the sink. There's no dishwasher. She pulls out three spoons.

Jenni wants to cry but doesn't.

Instead, the three of them sit down at ten in the morning and mow through the best ice cream in the world.

CHAPTER 12

SLASH

*S*lash's first conscious thought is the burning in his wrists. They feel like they're on fire.

The sweat running from his brow eases the rust on his eyelids, and he slowly opens his eyes.

The environment is dim and dank. Slash doesn't turn his head, allowing his eyes to adjust. Onions hang in netted cages from a ceiling crisscrossed with hand-hewn floor joists. Shelves line the walls made of roughly tumbled local rock. The gruesome contents of glass jars stare back at him.

Eyeballs. Tongues.

A squat, wide jar topped with an ecru-colored lid holds what appears to be an entire brain suspended inside an undetermined fluid.

Non-human, Slash easily recognizes. *Fuck.*

Judging by his nose, he's still within proximity of the witch's dwelling. Her stench is everywhere, even in the depths of what is clearly a cellar.

Slash is not easily given to panic, but his mate's whereabouts are uncertain. His eyes search the murk, easily finding wide wood planks leading up to a door with a black porcelain knob.

He shuts his eyes, trying to disassociate the relentless agony of his wrists from his thought processes.

Della the witch is not omniscient. If she were, she would have known the buckshot, silver or not—is not enough to kill a Red.

But it hurts like a bitch.

And she's strung him up like a swine for slaughter. With silver bindings. *Fuck.*

Slash moves slowly, not sure how much care, if any, she took while getting him down here and hoisted. He finds his head doesn't swim with a concussion, nor does his neck feel as stiff as it should.

Yet his heartbeats pile up in a mountain of fear that's slowly building inside his body. He doesn't know where Adrianna is, and he doesn't trust that witch as far as he could throw her.

And I'd like to throw her. His palms dampen with want. Female or not, Della inserted something into his mate's food, sickening her.

Slash hears the growl before he's aware of it and silences himself as the door at the top of the flight of stairs opens with a dragging of the bottom and a creak of hinges.

Light pours forth, cascading down the dusty, flat treads descending to the dirt floor where his feet trail.

Quickly, Slash scans the items in the cellar, cataloging their usefulness. Maybe he can get free and get a weapon?

He could add Della to her own morbid jar collection. One piece at a time.

"You awake, Red?"

No reason to keep her in suspense. "Yes." Nothing comes out; his throat is parched. He clears it. "Yes."

"Good. Now don't get any plans. I have your mate right here."

"Adrianna," Slash calls out, and her name sounds more like a growl than a word.

"Slash," she answers, and he strains to hear and scent her state of being.

He can't smell dick. His body is trying too hard to heal, and the bindings of silver are continuous obstructions to that physical goal. Slash has never been great at using his senses when the agony of healing is upon him. "Do what she wants."

No answer.

Please, Adrianna, no stubbornness.

"Be a good bitch and tell him."

Tell me what? Slash's guts bottom out.

"Move!"

Adrianna appears, gripping the makeshift handrail that looks like it was assembled by an amateur a half-century ago.

Adrianna turns to stare at Della directly behind her. Her features are tight with anger. "Stop shoving me. I can walk on my own, cow."

The slap rings in Slash's ears, and his beast rises like a high diver surfacing to break free of the water.

Adrianna's face rocks back, and her palm touches where Della struck her.

"Move your butt, bitch."

Adrianna's shoulders slump, and she descends the steps slowly.

Their eyes meet, and tears that stood like water on glass begin to roll down her cheeks. "Slash," she whispers, her gaze skimming over him.

"Keep moving." Della shoves her with something he can't make out.

Adrianna stumbles on the last step, and Slash strains to reach her, barking out in agony as the bindings sink silver fire into his flesh.

Slash grits his teeth, unable to do anything but watch as Adrianna braces her fall with her palms on the dirt floor.

Plumes of dirt waft, and she coughs.

Della puts a foot on her rear and shoves her.

Adrianna flies forward, and Slash's eyes drill the witch. "I will kill you," he promises.

Della smiles, her earlier facade gone. A new woman sneers down at him in disdain.

Chestnut hair tumbles in loose waves around her shoulders. Modern pants and a fitted blouse cling to every bit of her tall, curvaceous frame.

But her eyes are like a ferret's: dark brown and resembling slits inside a face too angular to be considered anything but shrewish.

Della looks the part of witch. And her assuming a younger countenance doesn't make her less of a crone in Slash's eyes.

Slash hasn't lived almost three centuries to not understand another's intentions. Della's are plain. The process hasn't been revealed, but Slash knows she intends to do more harm.

"Obviously, you won't die."

Slash smiles, hating Della with every physical inch of him.

"Nope."

He forces himself not to look at Adrianna.

His beast wants to come. And that's fine.

Just not *now*.

Slash cannot hope to protect his mate if he plays that hand too soon.

And if he were a betting male, he would say Della's waiting for it. To spring some other torture at him.

Slash can bide his time. He's adept at that.

"I am a cursed witch." She hikes her chin as though deigning them with her news.

He says nothing, and Adrianna doesn't, either, which worries Slash. But he continues to give Della his full attention. Learning her motivations is all that matters right now.

Not his fatigue.

Not the agony of his burning wrists.

"My wards are a spiderweb of sorts." Her lips curl in a calculating smile. "Nothing gets through unless it is the *right* something."

"True love," Adrianna says from the ground, and Slash wastes a glance.

Her face is filthy. A smudge of dirt across the bridge of her nose hides the sprinkling of golden freckles he knows are there.

Slash feels his eyes go wolfen and quickly looks away

as his beast bulges beneath his skin, trying like hell to push out where it can.

His nailbeds begin to bleed as his talons burst loose from their prison of flesh.

He longs to rub his aching eyes.

"His beast does not like his mate in a position of vulnerability," Della says.

Drops of deep-red blood drip down his arms as his beast tries to force the change. The moon is near-full, close enough for a Red to form fully into his wolf.

Not now, he commands his beast. His body quakes. The change is a shining thing at the edge of his mind.

Adrianna's voice trembles, "No, Slash—she can kill you."

Della nods. "I can, and I will. I only need the whelp."

Slash's inhale is a sucking wound of stale air. "What, witch?"

She nods, obviously pleased with herself. "I need a newborn, begat from supernaturals who love each other. Once sacrificed, the babe will be my release." Her fingers clench into a triumphant fist. "He or she will be my freedom from the prison of my suffering."

Slash's face whips to Adrianna, heart crammed in his throat. "Are you with whelp?"

His beast roils so strongly that Slash feels gorge rise.

Adrianna nods numbly, rubbing her hands up and down her bare arms. "I'm sorry, Slash," she says in a small voice.

"Do not be." He turns his face to Della. "You should be ashamed."

The witch nods. "I should be, and so should you,

taking a barely out-of-whelp female and filling her with seed."

Guilt slays Slash. Those were his exact thoughts on mating with Adrianna. But he loves her, and she him. And now she bears his whelp.

The witch pokes Adrianna in the side with a crude wooden stick.

A howl bursts from his body, and the skin of his face splits. Slash gnashes his teeth, spitting and chomping at the one who would hurt Adrianna.

"Possibly," she strokes the side of Adrianna's head, and his mate jerks away from the touch. Della grips her hair, yanking her next to her side.

Adrianna screams.

Slash goes wolfen, and Della smiles.

Adrianna reaches behind her, trying to claw at the hands holding her. "She's forcing you, Slash. She tempting your beast!" Adrianna screams in warning.

The witch whips Adrianna around by the hair, and she bites her lip to keep from screaming again, drawing blood.

"After four centuries in this house, I no longer care how my salvation presents itself, or who pays the price for it. I. Will. Be. Free."

With a mighty shake, she throws Adrianna at Slash.

He strains against the bindings to get to his mate.

Adrianna rolls in a clumsy dive, landing in a pile at his feet.

Crawling to him, she sits up on her knees, wrapping her arms around his thighs, her face against his hip. "Slash," Adrianna cries.

Moon help me.

"Kill him."

Slash's face jerks to the witch.

Adrianna turns to look at Della. "I can't—he's my mate."

"I told you what I would do if you did not."

Slash gazes down at the female he loves more than his next breath. "What did she tell you?"

"That she'd rip our baby from my body."

Slash has never wanted to murder more than he does at this moment.

Della walks slowly to where Slash hangs. An unbidden growl splits his lips, which are misshapen in wolfen form because of the scarring that bisects his face.

From behind her back, Della produces a large knife.

Slash stiffens.

"Kill him, Adi."

Adrianna shakes her head. "No. I've loved him since I was a whelp. I'm not killing Slash!"

Her tears singe him.

Slash shuts his eyes, his decision made. If he acts now, there's a chance Adrianna will live.

"She's right," Slash says, opening his eyes. "Kill me so you can live."

"No!" Adrianna screams, clasping her hands together. "I'll never do it."

Slash looks at Adrianna. "Pick up the knife, mate."

"Don't make me, Slash."

He gives her a gentle smile. "Harsh choices, my mate." Slash feels the power of being an Alpha Red wash from him to her.

His will strikes her like a whip of fire.

"No," Adrianna says, but with less force, her body bowing under the power of his command.

"Yes!" Della hisses in triumph.

"Pick up the knife," Slash says.

Adrianna does.

The witch strolls forward, a smug expression affixed to her sharp features as she watches Adrianna climb his body with the fingertips of her left hand, kissing his flesh as she does, her right hand wrapped around the hilt of the blade.

Slash's body chooses that moment to get an erection as his mate licks the blood from his arms and torso. He's helpless to stop the involuntary reaction of his body when Adrianna is poised to slay him. Her nearness is still an aphrodisiac to his beast.

Even now.

She raises the blade. Her beautiful hazel eyes glimmer with fire like banked embers, flakes of green shimmering within.

Adrianna spins, flicking the long blade of the knife out and slashing it from left to right.

Della attempts to gasp, flailing backward.

Her throat opens like a second mouth. The white of the deep cut fills with blood.

She chokes, struggling to speak.

Adrianna raises the knife a second time, piercing the witch's eye socket with a blade now coated in blood.

The witch staggers back, and Adi leaps on Della's body, riding it to the ground. Yanking the blade free from the orb as they land together, Adi stabs her.

In the heart.

Slash closes his eyes.

His command was direct and comprehensive. Adrianna should not have been able to resist his compulsion.

Adrianna stands, Della's dying body beneath and between her legs, gore covering her arm to nearly the elbow.

She turns and smiles at Slash.

The expression is full and uninhibited. Adrianna quarter-changes, running to him and holding the blade high. For one, horrible moment, Slash thinks she means to end him.

She leaps, and with an ear-shattering howl, Adrianna sweeps the blade down, slicing through the silver tether that held his body in place.

He drops, gasping on the floor, and immediately sits upright.

But he's not too weary to catch Adrianna as she flings herself at him, weeping as though pieces of her are breaking.

Slash holds his mate, grateful to the moon for their lives.

And the life of his future whelp.

CHAPTER 13

LAZ

*T*essa's expression changes from open and soft to hard and surprised before Laz can blink.

"What?" she says in a loud voice, bouncing to her knees beside him.

"Offspring," Laz repeats with a slight frown. He tries to take her question seriously, but really, her nudity is a huge distraction. Her large breasts, perfectly formed and begging for a male's touch, sway as she rests her rear on top of her heels.

Tessa folds her arms, glaring at him.

Not the reaction he wanted after their first interlude.

When Laz is nervous, he steams. Now, if that were to occur in his natural environment of Hades, it would hardly be noticeable. And while he wore his human "suit," he could have hidden it then, as well.

As the humans say: there's no such luck. Laz has just filled his *need* with his Redemptive and has been stripped of falsehoods, physical or otherwise. He wears no suit—

no armor which to pierce. He is bare before Tessa, as it should be.

He rises also, lightly touching her shoulder. She tenses.

"Tessa," Laz says, running a hand from shoulder to wrist then prying her fingers apart. "What troubles you?"

She huffs, gently withdrawing her hand. "Nothing really. Except the assistance and cooperation Drek would give us hangs in the balance, Tahlia is gone. I just mated with the devil—"

"I'm not a devil." Laz frowns. "I'm a high demonic."

Tessa rolls her eyes. "You're *not* Lycan."

Laz's lips give an amused twitch. "No. I am not."

She nods and continues, "And now you lay it on me that I'm going to have a hotdog after all."

Laz's shoulders shake with laughter.

Tessa hits him. "Stop *that*," she hisses. "It's not funny."

"I will never be bored with you, Tessa." Laz smirks.

"That's assuming we stay together."

Lazarus stares so long and hard at Tessa that she eventually studies her folded hands instead of his face.

"I have found my Redemptive. The female that was made for me in this realm. It is so rare that there isn't anyone who has spoken to a demonic who actually had it happen. It's been purely legend. Until now."

"Until now," Tessa repeats softly, picking a single piece of black hair off her bare thigh and letting it fall to the floor.

He covers the hand that rests on her leg, greedily eating up her beauty. "Tessa..." Laz's other hands comes to rest at the back of her head, feeling the dampness of her hair from her recent shower. "Drek has retired some of the Lanarre's precepts. Tahlia is her own keeper."

Tessa opens her mouth as though she'll refute his words, and he presses a fingertip to her lips.

She smiles beneath his touch.

"That's better," Laz leans forward and stations his hands at the small of her bare back, rolling his lips against hers, and slowly, her hands creep around his neck. "You mated with a high demonic of mixed blood, and even now, you might carry my offspring. Is it not a wonderful potential to be pregnant?"

She sighs, nodding against his forehead.

"Then why are we talking about you birthing a hotdog?"

Tessa sits down on the bed, crossing her legs, and Laz gazes at her sex. Delicate, pink, and wet. His mouth waters at the sight.

"Perv," she says with a light voice, touching his chin.

"Pervert?" Laz asks, quirking a brow.

Tessa nods, but he's glad for the smile that graces her face, instead of the sadness and irritation of before.

Laz lifts a shoulder. "Let me stare at you." His fingers run down all the surfaces his eyes did moments before.

Her nipples pebble from his touch along the sides of her breasts, and Laz instantly dips his head, circling one of them with his tongue.

"Laz," she mumbles.

"Hmm," he says against her hot flesh.

"We should stop. You've sated my heat. The fire of my body is cool."

Laz releases her flesh softly and covers her flat

stomach with his hand. "And may your womb be filled with our child."

"Moon, Laz—" Tessa says, clearly frustrated.

Lazarus thinks that females are all fairly similar. Instead of wasting time with words, Laz shows.

Putting both hands on her face, he draws Tessa to him, kissing first her forehead then each eyelid before trailing his mouth down her face. He pauses to flick his tongue where his lips just were.

When he finally reaches her mouth, she's putty in his hands.

"Tessa?" Laz asks.

She nods. "I was really caring about all the hotdog stuff a second ago."

He presses another soft, wet kiss against her pliant mouth. "And now?"

Tessa opens her eyes, and her gray irises are so light, they appear nearly translucent.

"No shits given. If this is how a male will treat me, you could be a Martian, and I'd say yes."

Martian? Puzzling expression. "Yes to what?"

Tessa lifts her head from his hand, and he releases his hold, studying every micro-expression she has.

"To being your mate."

Laz grins. "You were always my mate, because you are my Redemptive, Tessa."

"So you weren't going to officially mate me?"

Laz is feeling the undercurrent of feminine anger and is very much out of his element.

"I can't ask what I already know. If you stay with me, we *are* 'mated,' as you put it. But in the realm of Hades, a partnership is typically different. Males claim female demonic."

"Oh. My. Moon." Tessa hops off the bed. "Claim?" she says loudly, crossing her arms again.

A foreign emotion fills Laz. Helplessness. His Redemptive is angry. He'll have to think quickly.

Slowly, Laz gets off the bed and approaches Tessa cautiously.

"No… you—" She wags her finger as he draws nearer.

Laz does not slow.

"Stay back. Whenever you get within a foot of me, my brains slip out my ears."

He smiles. It's involuntary, considering Tessa's staring at his cock. He grasps himself as he strolls toward her, and he thickens at the sight of her.

"Mother of Moon, look at you." Tessa's arms fall by her sides.

Laz wraps his arms around her. "I can't feign how gorgeous you are, how much I love you, how in Hades—it would not be as it is here, Tessa." He meets her angry eyes, where swirling clouds of gray like a gathering storm darken the irises.

"How can you love me? We don't even know each other."

Laz gazes down at her. "I know all that I need to. And you will be the mother of my offspring."

"Well"—Tessa shoves her hair behind her shoulder, crouching and ducking from Laz's hold—"we'll be outlaws then. A Lycan female choosing to be with something other than another Were? With as few female Were as there are? Pfft." She paces away.

Laz admires her fluid grace. Even angry, Tessa is beautiful.

She spins to face him, and Laz makes a monumental effort to look at her face instead of visually exploring her. Tessa consumes him.

She laughs. "You're obviously trying not to stare at my goods." Tessa puts her hands on her hips.

"Ah... they're *very* good."

Tessa smiles then shakes her head. "Oh hell, Laz—what are we going to do?"

Laz doesn't approach her this time. "We leave. Drek gave us a day of shelter, but I believe the longer we stay within sight of the Lanarre, the more they'll feel as though we're rubbing their noses in our union."

"No shit," Tessa comments. "Are you sure about this Redemptive stuff?"

He doesn't hesitate with his response. "Utterly."

Tessa shivers, cupping her elbows, and Lazarus can stand it no more. He walks to her side, grasping her upper arm. "Tell me."

She bites her lip and releases it just as quickly. "I can't help but think that even though you did Praile in, the threat's not gone."

Laz stares at the floor, inhaling deeply, then pulls her against his body. Hugging Tessa to him, he briefly rests his chin on top of her head.

"I'm not sure how adept I can be in hiding from the Master."

Tessa looks up at him. "Master?"

"The Dark Master—Lucifer," he qualifies in a low voice.

Her eyes round, she shakes her head gently. "I just can't get over that there's a *real* devil."

Laz chuckles. "I am living proof."

Her eyes sweep him. "Right. But you just got done telling me that you're a high demonic?"

He sees where it could be confusing. "I am. Though I'm of demonic blood, I am not of the devil."

She twists her lips. "A girl could get hang-ups with talk like that."

He rapidly digests her words, spitting out the rough translation of an answer. "It's a complicated way to say that I'm not the sum of my parts. I am from Hades, lived there. Tortured there."

Tessa flinches, but Laz won't sugarcoat his role there. He was second only to Praile. The great portion of their duties was to cause misery.

Now Tessa has made an alternate future possible.

"But now you're here."

He nods.

"What if more high demonics come looking for you?"

Laz won't lie. He doesn't want to. "It is a concern. Yet, that possibility isn't sufficient enough from seeking the existence I want."

He grabs her hands. "Tessa, I've been given a rare chance"—his eyes lock on to hers, holding her stare prisoner—"and it can't have been for nothing. There must be a reason why I am able to have a Redemptive and that I found you."

Cupping the side of her face, he continues, "Let us try. If you think there is something here that's real, then meet me halfway and let's exhaust what could be, instead of worrying about what might be."

Lazarus waits through a full tortuous minute before Tessa nods.

It's the best thing he's ever witnessed: her willingness.

CHAPTER 14

JENNI

*J*enni holds up the spoon, where a sliver of Banana Split Tom and Jerry's still clings, clearly mocking her ability to finish.

She studies it for a nanosecond then licks the cold metal clean.

Flavors too varied to begin to separate slather her tongue, and Jenni kicks her head back and sighs.

I could get used to this werewolf business. Especially in the taste bud department. "That's so decadent," she comments, nearly slurring her words.

Jenni lifts her head from the back of the couch, surveying the punishment she gave Devin's refrigerator.

There's not a crumb left.

"You can sure eat!" Ella says, giving a delighted clap. "I don't have any Tigger flakes left."

"Frosted Flakes, Ella," Devin corrects.

"Tigger!" she yells, then grins, revealing small baby teeth.

I wonder what my teeth look like now?

Jenni stands, carefully sets her spoon inside the sink, and makes her way to the bathroom.

She knows where it is because she can scent the used menstrual pads from the family room. Totally gross, but true.

"Hey!" Devin calls, chasing after her.

"Just going to get that shower going," Jenni says. But really, now that she's got a few hours of sleep under her belt and the bowels of the fridge has been emptied, Jenni's ready to see what she looks like.

"Oh! Right."

Jenni steps into a cramped, dated bathroom space that's as clean as a whip. Avoiding the mirror, she opens the cheap door to the shower stall. The glass shivers inside the cheap frame as she swings wide. Turning on the hot water full blast, she turns and inhales deeply.

Jenni gazes at the stranger in the mirror.

She doesn't look like the monster she was expecting, sprouting hair from every orifice.

Jenni doesn't know what she anticipated looking like. *Not this.*

Lifting her lip, Jenni inspects her teeth. She's brushed and flossed them three times a day since forever. It's a subtle difference, but her canines are a little longer.

Whiter.

And Sharper.

She extracts the finger holding her upper lip and lets her hand fall to her side.

The biggest change is her hair.

Before chemo, Jenni had rich, naturally dark-brown hair that matched her eyes. She always assumed her little bit of Italian heritage helped her along in that area. Once her hair returned after the chemo, she tried to dye it back to her natural color. But as everyone who uses hair dye knows, it's so much darker when first applied. The dye on Jenni's pale, baby-fine hair quickly faded to an unattractive sickly looking color.

Gone is the goth black hair that looked like a washed-out oil slick on hay.

Rich brown hair has taken its place, falling in loose curls around her shoulders. Glossy, thick, and fresh.

Jenni had become used to the sallow tone of her skin as she tried to apply cover-up each day to hide her lackluster skin tone. Then she would layer on blusher in an attempt to mimic the high-coloring she'd enjoyed before cancer.

She knows there's not a lick of makeup left on her face, but Jenni looks good. No—scratch *that*—fantastic. No makeup sold could lift her cheek color to the soft pink that glows from healthy, beautifully normal skin. Or the brightness of her eyes... the whites are like snow. The irises glitter like root beer hard candy. They're not the dull brown of yesterday's recollection, but a gorgeous, melted chocolate.

Jenni touches her face with shaky fingers, and the skin beneath her fingers is no longer dry and rough to the touch. The texture of this new skin feels like silk.

Holy shit, I've been remade.

Jenni can't tear her eyes away from the reflection of her throat.

The location where the Lanarre werewolf harmed her is smooth beneath her touch. She remembers the exact spot where the injury happened. But only healed flesh greets her stare.

And the wound from the branch as they marched through the forest?

Gone.

So healing is a *thing.*

And speed, strength, and totally taste and smell.

What's happening to me?

A knock at the door makes her jump a foot.

"Yeah?" Jenni asks, heart in her throat.

"You okay in there?"

Jenni nods, realizes Devin can't see her, and replies, "Yeah, just getting in the shower."

Only a tiny lie.

"Well, I left some clothes outside the door for you to borrow."

Jenni folds her hand against her chest, covering her mouth with the other hand.

Silent tears burn down her face, running over the dam of her fingers.

After a few seconds of regaining her composure, she says, "Thanks, Devin."

"Welcome."

* * *

HER FINGERTIPS ARE PLEASANTLY WRINKLED, and she's got a pair of yoga pants and a thick t-shirt on.

Devin's quite a bit taller, but skinny enough to be a human closet hanger.

The object of Jenni's thoughts breezes in, wet hair

wrapped in a towel turban. "You're *so* lucky," Devin points at her.

Jenni knows this, but it's probably not for the reasons Devin's thinking.

"It's my day off, girl." Devin grins, giving a quick thumbs-up.

Oh.

"So Ella is here because she's not old enough for kindergarten and only goes to Little People for part day, and I work night shift. It's great, she goes to sleep, and I go to work."

"Do you like your job?" Jenni asks.

Devin shrugs, filling a coffee carafe full of water from the kitchen tap. Without turning, she shifts two feet to the right and pours the cold water into the reservoir of a bright-red coffee maker. "I get food for free."

Jenni closes her eyes.

"They throw away almost as much food as they make. I mean, all those fast-food places have a limit on how long food can sit. And…" She presses the *on* button at the front of the coffee maker. Instantly, it begins to give throaty burps, nosily working toward Jenni's caffeine fix. "Sometimes the line manager doesn't get the count right. Y'know, making too many cheeseburgers for the rush —whatever."

She bends over, flipping her hair upside down, and begins squeezing the damp towel against her long hair. Devin stands, flinging the mostly dry hair behind her. "I mean, I'm not a real big fan of burgers and fries anymore, but it makes a turd, as my brother would say."

Jenni laughs, but it fades as Devin's face takes on a wistful expression.

She sits up straighter and swallows hard. "Where's your family?"

Devin lifts a narrow shoulder, her lips twisting. "They won't talk to me." She studies the remnants of her chipped black nail polish. "Tough love, I guess."

Jenni remains quiet for a moment. "Do they know you stopped using?"

Devin gives a swift shake of her head. "No, and I've tried to call and let them know I'm clean—and about Ella. But they won't take my calls." She looks down, toeing a plush toy on the ground. When she meets Jenni's eyes, a sheen of tears fill hers. "Can't blame them." She sucks in a breath then lets it out in a dragging exhale. "I was a lying, stealing, druggie."

"But you're not now," Jenni points out softly.

Devin nods. "No, I'm not. But I wrecked their trust. So there's *that*."

Jenni stands and walks to Devin.

"They'd want to know they had a grandchild. Trust me."

Devin just shakes her head and ducks her chin. "I fucked up."

"Listen, I know they would." Jenni's eyes fill with tears. "I know." Her voice is hoarse.

Devin cocks her head, studying Jenni's expression. "How?"

"Because my parents are dead. And I'd do anything for them not to be, and I know they wouldn't have cared what

I'd done. They'd still want a relationship with me, and definitely one with whatever child I produced."

She bites her lip, finally giving Jenni her eyes. "I-I don't know. I'm sorry about your parents."

Jenni gives a small shrug. She's used to the silence after she tells people about her parents, and she fills it with the answer everyone always wants. "Car accident."

"How?"

No one ever asks more. She meets Devin's direct stare, unaware her gaze has drifted, looking outside a window filled with fingerprints about the height a four-year old would make. "Drunk driver. Plowed into them when they were moving through a green light."

Devin runs her hand over her damp hair. "Damn, that's tough."

"Yup."

The silence stretches between them like a rubber band.

Finally, it snaps.

"Listen," Devin begins.

"Where's Ella?" Jenni asks quickly.

"I parked her in front of the TV for a half hour of cartoons."

Jenni takes a deep breath. Then another. "You've got questions."

Devin nods but gives a minute shrug. "You don't owe me."

"Actually, I do." Jenni's laugh is shaky. "I swooped in and totally threw your life on its ear."

Devin laughs. "Yeah, true. But I'll let you in on a little secret. My life's sorta chaotic anyway."

Jenni looks around at the general disarray of the place.

Things are cluttered and dated, but the surfaces are clean. "You have a little girl, and you're a single mom."

"Not by choice. But Bray…"

Jenni nods. No need for explanation there. "I'm a nurse."

Devin's smile is crooked. "Nice scrubs by the way."

That reminds Jenni.

Devin holds up a hand at her expression. "Got them in the wash. I don't know about all that blood, though." Her eyes narrow suddenly. "Are those stains really from an emergency gunshot wound victim?"

Jenni shakes her head.

"Knew it!" Devin whisper-hisses.

Jenni sighs. "So this Jane Doe's brought in."

"Huh?"

"A patient without an ID." Jenni thought everyone knew that. It's not a moniker exclusive to corpses.

"She was remarkable," Jenni says, remembering Adi's vitals—hell, the healing ability alone had sugar plums dancing in the head of anyone who got a load of her chart. "She'd been hit by a car. Shattered pelvis, multiple contusions, internal bleeding." Jenni swipes a hand through her hair, pushing the whole load behind her shoulder. "In fact, what didn't she have that was broken or bleeding?"

"What does this chick have to do with your… issue."

Jenni isn't sure how to begin. "She begins to heal. Heal in a way that no one's ever seen. We actually had a call in to the University of Washington. They were going to have one of their special sauce scientists make a trip all the way out here to PT and investigate it. Her."

"I guess it didn't happen." One of Devin's eyebrows lifts.

Jenni snorts back a laugh. "No. In fact, only five hours later, my mystery patient got out of the bed and with hardly more than a tense expression, tossed her clothes on, and went to leave."

Devin blinks.

Jenni points at her. "Exactly. *That.* I tried to stop her, and it wasn't going to work. Then she found out some guys were after her. She changed her plan. Improvised."

"Let me guess, *you* were part of the new plan."

Jenni nods slowly, threading her fingers through newly thick hair. "Thing is, I'm sick."

Devin's jaw works back and forth, and she cups her chin. "No offense"—her eyes give Jenni a quick scan—"but you look great."

"Now."

Devin frowns. "I don't get it. What do ya mean 'now'?"

"Because as near as I can figure, I'm a werewolf."

CHAPTER 15

ADI

"Evil bitch," Adi mutters, busy dressing the horrible wounds at Slash's wrists.

"Witch, you mean."

Adi cleans the deep lacerations a second time, and they're healing, but slowly. "Whatever," she says under her breath then looks up, meeting Slash's eyes. "How come these aren't healing up very well?"

"Silver," Slash remarks casually.

Things were anything but casual a few hours ago. "Right. They're super bad." Adi sits back on her heels, blowing a damp strand of hair out of her face.

"Super," he says and winks at her.

Adi sits up straighter, blinks at Slash, and promptly bursts into tears.

"My mate," Slash says, sudden worry saturating his voice as he draws her gently into his lap.

"I haven't finished!" she wails, hating the sniveling bullshittery she seems determined to be stuck in.

"I'll be fine." Slash tucks his finger under her chin and

lifts it. Kissing each salty tear away. "Why are you crying? The witch is dead. The wicked witch is dead…"

"This is *not* that old movie, *The Wizard of Oz,* Slash. It's so not a movie! It's our fucked-up *lives.*" Her lips tremble, and he lays a soft kiss on them then presses his forehead to hers.

"I am not making fun of you, heart of my heart."

Adi stills at the ancient words. "What are you doing then?" Her voice is barely above a whisper.

He leans away, and she gets lost in his dark eyes. They hold nothing but his feelings for her. "I am offering levity."

Adi cries harder.

Slash sighs and scrubs a hand over the sharp short hairs at his scalp. "I might be unsure about what's needed here."

"Really?" she says, hand pressed to her chest. "No shit?"

Adi awkwardly climbs off his lap and stands. She looks down at Slash, her heart constricting at the sight of his wounds. "I don't even know what that word means!"

Slash stands, as well, towering over her. "I am too old for you."

"Is this where we break up?" Adi asks, folding her arms. "Because I'm *not* good with that."

Slash chuckles.

She rolls her eyes at him, dropping her arms. "*Not* funny."

"There is no breaking up, Adrianna. I am your mate for life. But our age difference will rear its head on occasion."

"We were just starting to make sense of *us*. We got back together, and I'd forgiven you for your bullshit—"

"Bullshit?" Slash's eyebrows rise.

Adrianna glares.

"Ya know. That whole 'I gotta be the he-man and sacrifice my ass for my woman' thing."

Slash frowns. "I didn't think about us exactly in those terms."

"Yeah—*so* get that. But I did. I do. And if we're keeping count, I killed the witch. I didn't need a man to do it, if ya noticed?" Adi arches her eyebrows.

Slash gathers her against him. "I noticed, and it killed me to watch you put yourself in harm's way. My pregnant mate."

Adi stays silent, thinking about everything. "Probably because we have sex too much."

Slash barks out a laugh, hugging her tighter. "I can't think of that being a problem. But you *were* in heat. And that's what can happen when mates breed."

"I know," she says in a small voice. "I just—I'm going to suck at motherhood. I'm young, and I don't know anything and... *shit.*"

"You'll be fine, beautiful creature. You're a witch slayer —what more could our future whelp hope to have in a mother?"

Adi bursts out laughing. "You're just saying that to make me feel better."

Slash's mouth brushes her lips. "Is it working?"

Adi nods.

His expression turns serious. "We need to dispose of the witch's body and take everything from here that we can. We want to begin our short journey to the North-western. I want to leave this place. Badly."

The corners of Adi's mouth turn down. "Okay. You're assuming there's not another Red already part of the Northwestern Pack."

Slash cups her shoulders, not looking away. "Was there a Red when you left?"

Adi thinks back. Besides Jason, who was the feral, Reds were like UFO sightings: had to see them to believe them.

"I doubt it. Jason Caldwell was the first Red we'd ever had, and Lawrence and Tony made sure he was locked up."

"You took care of him?" he confirms.

"I did. I mean, back then."

They share a moment of silence, both thinking their own thoughts about Jason's life—and death.

"It's the best option." Slash says what she's already thinking.

Adi nods. "I know. But things haven't been settled since we got together."

His mouth twists, pulling the rope of scar tissue taut. "We *did* establish our relationship in the middle of a Singer war."

"True."

"Then you ran off, and we stumbled into a witch's lair." Slash's eyebrows pop.

She laughs. "Okay, I guess our start was kinda bumpy."

"Very." Slash's voice is droll.

Adi smacks him in his tight abs.

He covers his stomach like it hurt, and Adi catch's sight of his wounds again. "Oh *moon*, Slash—I'm sorry."

His smile tells her it's okay.

That everything will be.

* * *

"MAN! SHE WEIGHS A TON!" Adi says.

Slash smirks. "On the count of three!" he says loudly. "One, two—three!"

They swing Della hard, releasing her arms at the exact same moment, and she flies off the old porch.

She lands with a plop, forest debris exploding in a violent cloud.

Adi dusts off her hands. "That felt awesome. What a nasty bitch she was."

"Witch," Slash says conversationally.

"Pfft!" Adi stomps back inside the cottage.

Slash follows at her heels. "Are you hungry?"

"Yup!" She storms ahead directly into the kitchen and tears open the fridge.

A bunch of glass jars line the inside of the fridge.

Eyeballs. Tongues.

Brains.

"Ewww! What the hell is *this*?" Adi turns her face to Slash, mouth agape. "Is there anything in here to eat?"

Slash laughs. "She's all stocked up on body parts."

"Gross *and* nasty," Adi mutters, slamming the door. "Okay!" She brightens. "If she was really related to the Hansel and Gretel witch, shouldn't she have proper food —y'know—to lure people?"

"Depends on who you ask."

Adi smacks him again. "Eyes and brains aren't food."

Slash grasps his chin, rolling his eyes toward the ceiling, but she can tell he's having fun at her expense.

"Men!" she yells, starting to walk out of the kitchen.

Slash grabs her around the waist, easily hoisting her off the floor, and hold her against his hard body.

"I've done a thorough inventory while you were using the shower. She has some food."

Adi wants to cry in relief. "Slash, I'm so hungry, this isn't even funny." She searches his eyes, trying to appeal with a look.

He slowly lowers Adi to her feet. "Nothing is more important than my mate's needs. Especially my mate who carries my whelp." He lightly places a hand on her flat stomach, and Adi covers it with her own.

Slash flicks his eyes, which have gone green at the edges from his wolf, to a bag on top of a small table within the tiny kitchen nook.

Adi follows his gaze and runs over to the bag and pulls out cheese, beef jerky, and dried fruit.

"Did you eat?" she asks quickly.

"I'll eat when you have your fill."

"Slash—"

"Eat," he growls.

Adi doesn't have to be asked twice.

The first taste of the cheese is succulent, springing on her taste buds and making her think of butter and cream. Yanking off a hunk from the stick of beef jerky, she sinks her teeth into the first bite. Notes of smoky flavor and mild spice make her mouth water.

Adi saves the dried dates and apricots for last. She tips

her head back. The taste of the sugary-sweet fruit bursts in her mouth, filling it in a wonderfully satisfying way.

Adi sucks the juices from her fingers and looks at an amused Slash. "This better not be poisoned food. Moon, that *sucked*."

"No," Slash assures her. His strong body leans against the door threshold, and regarding her, he smirks. "I sniffed that until my nose fell off."

Adi nods between mouthfuls. She rises on her tiptoes and kisses the underside of his jaw, and his rough two-day beard tickles her lips.

He lowers his head, and Adi kisses his nose.

"Nose is still there, stud."

Slash has a small smile just for her. "Yes." He runs a finger down her face and plucks a small bit of food from the corner of her mouth before putting it into his own.

She watches his finger work, and a sudden surge of lust seizes her.

Slash's nostrils flare.

"Don't think I didn't notice your hard-on when I was about to stab you." She twirls a piece of fruit from her fingers, and he wraps his lips around her fingertips.

Adi sucks in a breath, leaning forward. "Are you a sadist?" she whispers.

He shakes his head slowly. Grabbing her wrist, he moves his lips to the base of her fingers, sucking the juicy piece of fruit from the tip.

"No, but a mate has that effect on a male Were. And you were licking my wounds and body. I could hardly stand up to that." He shrugs. "I'm only a Lycan."

She smirks, and his hands go to her waist. "You were standing up, all right."

"Yes. I was—as I am now."

Adi's smile broadens to a grin. "I feel that."

His face grows serious once more. "I can hardly help it, Adrianna."

"I can," she says.

Slash looks at her for a heartbeat then closes his arms around her petite body.

He speaks against her temple, stirring her hair with his warm breath.

"I know."

* * *

ADI LIES ON HER SIDE. Her hands are folded beneath her head as though in prayer. She gazes at Slash within the deep shadow of the guest bedroom of the witch's cottage. "Doesn't it feel weird to be inside Della's house when she's out there cooling her heels—rotting."

Slash chuckles, cupping her side at the valley where her waist dips.

He shrugs, cocking his head to the left. "She's dead, Adrianna, and thank Moon for that." His fingers work small circles on her skin, and she shivers at his touch. "We need whatever resources we can procure before we leave. Rest, showers, and especially, food."

Adi rolls over onto her back, and Slash props his naked body above her with an elbow, staring down at her.

"If I eat another bite, I'll barf."

Slash roars out a laugh. "Oh, my mate, you don't lack for interesting expressions."

Adi arches an eyebrow. "Is that a problem?"

His smile gradually fades, but the laughter edges his lips. "Never. You are a breath of fresh air. Vital. Engaging. I hope you never change. But I will say, I'm in for interesting times."

"What you really mean is, I'm not boring."

He nods. "Never."

Slash lays the side of his face gently against her stomach. "I can't believe a tiny whelp grows within you."

Adi puts her hand against the short hairs of his scalp, rasping over the top, the bristles tickling her flesh. "Me, either."

"Are you happy?" His words are soft, his meaning deep.

She thinks about it. "I'm happy with you. I'm worried about our future. We just seem to escape from one mess to the other. I want the chaos to stop. I want peace for our baby."

Slash lifts his head to stare at her, and Adi's hand slides from his head. He captures her fingers, threading his through them. "That is why the Northwestern is the most important next step. We can belong to a pack, have protection, be a part of the whole. You know how unhealthy it is for Were to not be part of a pack."

Adi knows. That's probably the reason she feels so horribly unsettled. She needs other Lycan. It's their nature to be together.

"What about Jenni?" It feels like each one of her heartbeats are a sick thud when Adi thinks about the nurse she left behind.

"The nurse?" Slash asks.

Adi nods. "I really want to go find her. Y'know—bring her into the fold."

Slash shakes his head, eyes blazing momentarily. "No. It's suicide. All that happened too close to the Lanarre of the Hoh. We'll be instant targets if we go back." His eyes tighten. "And I'm not sure what happened to the bodies."

His eyes move to wolfen as his body hangs balanced between partial and full change.

Adi goes quarter-change just by proximity. "We left behind proof."

He nods. "You turned a human."

"She was diseased—dying." Even Adi can hear the defensiveness in her voice.

Slash's eyes skate away. "You're very young, Adrianna."

"Listen, *you*!" She sits up, and his head falls away from her belly. "Don't get on your high horse. That *human* girl tried to shelter me, even after Jenni knew all the supernatural goodies. And she didn't have much life left. I wanted to help." Adi hits her chest with a thunk.

Slash captures her hand, dragging Adi against him.

She doesn't struggle in his hold even though she's pissed.

"I'm not saying you're not an honorable female. Saving Jenni was a noble gesture, to be sure."

Adi holds her breath. Releases it. "But?"

"The truth is, now there's a female rogue out there who doesn't know anything about being a Were. And she's in Lanarre territory." Slash's eyebrow hikes, and Adi nods.

"Jenni needs to extract herself. I will not sacrifice my mate because she feels responsible for this human."

"She's a Were now, Slash."

He nods. "She is."

"Then why can't we get her?"

Slash palms the side of her face, pressing his forehead to hers. "Because I will not put you in a position of vulnerability."

Adi feels a full pout come on.

He studies her expression. "That will not work, either." Slash tucks a hair behind her ear. "No matter how much your happiness means to me."

"Really?" Adi asks, flummoxed.

Slash nods. "Nothing is more important than your safety."

Adi is beginning to see that Slash is really serious about that.

She's a slow learner.

CHAPTER 16

DARK MASTER

The Singer's lifeless corpse lies motionless on the central tableau, one hand dangling over the side. The skin is covered in so much blood that the mangled fingers look like cerulean worms.

Dark Master is disgusted. His foolish high demonic servants botched the handling of the male, necessitating a more rapid execution of his death. He had no time to *play* with the angelic. Dark Master is not usually inclined to pout. There simply are too many dealings in Hades for which he is responsible.

Yet sometimes, he longs for a bit of *fun*. And the buffoonery of theirs has robbed him of his sport.

He sighs, surveying the gore. Little remains, and what does, sinks into the fissures on the stone's surface. He learned nothing of Praile, except the confirmation that a "Peter" had made an appearance at Region One of the Blood Singers' compound, posing as a male Singer who hailed from Region Two.

Of course, Lazarus had been with Praile. Both claimed

to be survivors of the massacre perpetuated by Laurent, and the whole of Region One welcomed them with open arms.

Dark Master has no doubt that the Singer told the unvarnished truth. He is too skilled with torture to believe any being could maintain silence through the execution of his tender mercies.

He walks to his high demonic servants.

They cower.

Sometimes that happens when he's been a might enthusiastic with his tasks.

They worry the Dark Master's attention may turn to them in the same manner. They do not realize his artistic passions would never drift to them, and he is too happy to remain silent on the matter. It is not entertaining to torture one's own kind.

Dark Master prefers a challenge—to employ finesse.

That is why he might be forced to surface to Between. Praile is unreachable, and he has never been able to confer with Lazarus.

He must ascertain what has occurred with the Rare One. *I need Praile.*

The undertaking of going Between is a horrible process. Dark Master is the ruler of Hades. He is not *meant* to surface to other realms.

And just that thought alone is enough to manifest stinging sweat at his temples, pits, and crotch. He rubs his hands together, and they're tacky with dampness.

"Stand!" Dark Master commands.

The high demonic who have been in bowing positions on the hot ground for a half hour rise to their feet.

Their kneecaps, worn to the bone while they kneeled, gleam dully. Only the soles of the high demonic are immune to the extreme heat generated by the ground within this realm.

The remaining bits and pieces of their bodies are vulnerable.

"Master..." Rernard bows his head, not daring to meet Dark Master's eyes. Dark-red hair curls softly around his ears. "All communion with Praile has failed."

He waves his hand around, clearly indicating silence is the order of the moment. "Yes, *thank you*, Rernard. That is why I must vacate Below for Between."

The howls and tribulations the lowly demonic beat and torture from those deserving souls who end up in Hades begin to fade with this new proclamation.

"I will make you in charge of Hades in my stead."

Rernard's deep eye color, very like obsidian metal, shines back at Dark Master in the gloom, Thin, opaque skin like paper covers Rernard's healing kneecaps. He drops to his knees, cringing as the hot floor burns the brand-new flesh off a second time. "Master, I have already failed you once. I cannot do so again."

"Stand."

Rernard presses his palms to the floor and heaves himself upright. Fresh blood dampens his palms, the flesh of his knees bleeds—the bone like broken eggshells.

"You know what will occur if you fail me in this, Rernard."

As he gives a quick series of jerky nods, the horns atop his head, which match his unusual eye color, catch the light.

Rernard is a handsome high demonic specimen. Not like the ugly duckling of Dark Master's servants, Lazarus.

"And what of Lazarus?" he inquires.

Rernard gives him sharp eyes then flicks his gaze away. "No one can ever reach Lazarus, Master. You know his mixed blood blocks many things."

Dark Master cups his chin, lightly tapping a talon against the hot flesh of his jaw. "Yes," he agrees in curt reply. Lazarus is already so disadvantaged in looks, Dark Master does not wish to think of more prejudice to heap upon him. After all, Lazarus has done much to advance within the hierarchy of Hades. Most of it horribly fitting.

"Master, what if you do not return?"

Rernard's Adam's apple bobs.

"If I cannot commune with Praile, I must do the job myself. You understand the importance of my work, Rernard."

He nods again, but Dark Master can see from his expression that he does not fully appreciate the position Praile's put them in—all of Hades.

"You cannot ascend, Master. Our Dark Master cannot go Between."

"I can if I take certain measures."

Horror flows over Rernard's expression. "Are you thinking of—"

He meets Rernard's eyes. "Yes."

"But you will be maimed forever."

"Yes."

They turn their attention to the fallen angelic on the tableau. "Ready his blood," he instructs in a bald voice.

Rernard thinks to touch him.

Dark Master stares at the other demonic's fingers upon the flesh of his arm until he removes his hand. Dark Master can still feel the ghost of his servant's talons on his body. "Do it."

Seconds pound between them.

Then Rernard says, "As you command, Master."

* * *

DARK MASTER HAS no voice left with which to scream. His vocal chords have grown hoarse from the many times he shrieked during the process to ascend.

He can merely whisper. "Come," he croaks to Rernard. And though the call is whisper-thin, little more than breath and heat, like all high demonic, Rernard possesses excellent hearing. He moves with great reluctance to the soft bed of feathers that Dark Master rests upon. The feathers are from angel's wings.

The procurement of such from Above is truly dangerous. Yet nothing is softer. Nothing promotes greater healing.

Dark Master sleeps on a bed of angel's feathers each night. Though he does not require food, he must be at rest for a few hours each Hades day. Rejuvenation is critical.

Dark Master dreams while he slumbers. He dreams of beautifully violent scenarios.

Many of which involve the Rare One.

But he must bide his time. The transfusion of angelic blood into his body was a most *unpleasant* experience.

He burst all the minute blood vessels of his face screaming—no begging—for a hiatus from the misery.

None came, for he'd thoroughly explained what would occur if Rernard did not complete the metamorphosis.

True Death. Eternal death. The type of demise reserved for the heinous who dwelt in Between during their time alive.

Dark Master offered his high demonic the eternal licking by fire while falling, yet never landing. For eternity.

Rernard was uninterested in that option.

He can feel his lips curl, remembering Rernard's expression. It had been a mix of terror and trying not to show it.

Dark Master attempts to sit up.

Rernard rushes forward as though he might assist.

"Touch me and die."

Rernard halts.

Dark Master gives him a searing look.

Rernard's beautiful red skin splits wherever his eyes touch him.

"Please, Master," Rernard pleads, his newly torn skin oozing and weeping black blood, "I have done all that you asked."

True.

"Bring me a hand mirror."

Rernard cringes, quickly looking away at what must be the horrible sight of what he has become.

"Are you sure?"

Dark Master's eyes narrow. "Do I look unsure?"

"No." Rernard vigorously shakes his head.

"Fetch it to me then."

Rernard races off, and Dark Master scans the parts of his body he can see.

Smooth flesh like alabaster greets him. Pure, white. Disgusting.

Dark Master shuts his eyes tightly. *I shall not be vain.*

Rernard's hurried footsteps return.

Keeping a good distance, he extends his arm away from his body, the hand mirror barely gripped between his fingers so as that his body is not too close to Dark Master and his metamorphosis.

The image in the mirror will be irrefutable proof.

Ones from Above cannot sully themselves with blood from the demonic and hope to survive. He who shall never be mentioned has given that assurance to those who are in league with Him.

However, the demonic, though completely altered physically, can withstand the process.

Though it is a permanent one. There are no "take backs," as the humans from Between would have them believe. There is only forever.

Whatever the image in the mirror, Dark Master must live with it for eternity.

He yanks the mirror from Rernard's lifeless grip and flips it over.

With supreme restraint, he begins to raise the heavy glass.

Dark Master tells Rernard that looks are not important, that succeeding in one's duties is more important than the beauty of black irises, ruby hair, and horns. More important than having a magnificent battle tail.

Then he sees what he looks like.

Dark Master rears his head back and roars his grief into the tombs of Below.

The sound reverberates back to him like a boomerang, his grief sent home like a well-aimed sucker punch.

Being ugly forever will give him even more motivation to kill the Rare One.

And if there is one thing that isn't lacking in Hades, it is motivation for wrongdoing.

He opens his fingers, and the mirror falls, shattering into a million tiny shards of reflective crystal on the smoldering floor.

Dark Master orders all mirrors share the same fate as the one reflecting his ugliness.

Before the hour is through, glass is melting everywhere it once hung.

CHAPTER 17

TESSA

*T*essa's heat flares, momentarily stealing her breath.

It's been an entire day, and already, her cycle is building again. She squeezes Laz's hand, and he squeezes back. His unhurried study of the great house's interior of the Lanarre prince does not affect him in the least.

Tessa is in awe.

Her eyes run over all the lavish details that are like icing on a cake. Huge, old-growth Douglas fir timbers anchor all the load-bearing points throughout the ceilings, which are higher than fifteen feet.

She cranes her neck, fingers nervously trailing over the back of Laz's hand.

He remains stoic and seemingly unafraid. While Tessa is sure that they've been given a respite—only to have to fight their way out of the Lanarre Hoh pack.

Tessa's afraid. Not in the way she was for the two decades that Tramack pursued her. *No.* It's not the adrenaline-fueled fight-or-flight instinct that clung to her body as she hopped from one location to the other, but a deep-seated fear arising from her time as whelp. Every whelpling is taught about the Lanarre from the moment they can change. They are Lycan Royalty.

Supreme Were. The ones who set the boundaries, limits and laws for all Lycankind.

Now here her and Laz sit, as though judgement's already been passed. The only thing that serves as a distraction is Tanya, the imposter.

She sashays around the room as though she owns it.

What a bitch.

Tessa bites her lip. She and Laz don't need to make any waves. As it stands, every pair of Lycan eyes that fall on them is filled with disdain.

Some hold envy. Tessa doesn't like that combo. It doesn't bode well.

"You're going to let Tessa leave with that demon, Drek?" Tanya purrs, her ripe body pressing up against Drek.

Oh, what Tessa wouldn't do to for an ability to barf on demand.

Right on Tanya's tootsies.

Laz sits up straighter, as though aware of her train of thought.

A low growl seeps from between the lips of a Were she can't identify. Tessa breathes deeply, trying to calm down. Normally, her emotions wouldn't be so close to the surface, but with heat riding her... all bets are off.

Drek frowns at Tanya, his eyes raking over her curvaceous form. He physically removes her from him.

Tessa gazes at the rough slate floor that borders the sunken living room, so no one sees her smile.

Warmth from a roaring fire in the massive, all river-rock fireplace chases away the chill.

Lazarus doesn't seem to mind the heat.

Tessa cups a hand over her mouth to stop a hysterical giggle from interrupting Tanya's pathetic attempts at ass-kissing.

"You have shown that you're willing to take away a royal Lanarre's bid for the throne."

Tanya's eyes narrow. "We share the same blood."

"But not a shred of the same integrity," Tessa notes in a dry voice.

Laz gives her a look that silently begs for her not to speak.

Like that will ever work. Tahlia is a fine Were—brave, strong and foolhardy, like all Were just out of whelphood —but she is not the conniving slut Tanya is.

Tanya shoots a look her way that smacks too closely as a warning for Tessa's liking.

Tessa stands, and Laz does, too. "What are you doing?"

Her eyes narrow to slits. "She's challenging me." The alpha inside Tessa rises, growling. She wants to charge Tanya so much, she can taste the other Were's blood on her tongue.

Tanya's lips curl into a knowing smile.

"Who cares if she challenges you?" Laz asks logically. "Our bid is to go. Let the Lanarre sort this mess."

Tessa gazes up at him. Though she is quite tall herself, he is nearly a foot taller.

His normally pale-blue eyes are deep charcoal.

Lazarus senses battle, her beast, or something. Whatever she does next will matter to them both. Her behaving in a volatile way isn't helping.

However, sometimes, her beast rules.

Tessa fights her nature.

Drek says, "What I do or do not decide in regard to this rogue Alpha female is mine to decide. I will not take the advice of a female seductress who was intent on usurping the rightful female."

Tanya fists her delicate hands. "Tahlia didn't even want you!"

Oh shit. Tanya cringes inwardly.

Conflicting emotions wash over Drek's face. None of them good, especially the last one.

Anger.

"You drove her from the protection of the Hoh pack!" Drek finally loses his patience. "She would be here if it weren't for your interference."

Tanya leans back, juts out a hip, and points at Drek. "It was *your* wolves who beat her down. Didn't use their noses, and for some reason, you tied us both up. Now, is that any way to treat your betrothed?"

Drek pivots, giving Tanya his back, and paces away from her.

Another Lanarre approaches him, whispering something close to his ear.

Drek gives a vehement shake of his head.

"I don't have time for this, Bowen."

"Your highness." Bowen's eyebrows lift, and Tessa intuits instantly that they are closer than the formal words would indicate.

She can scent kinship anywhere—it's one of her gifts. This Bowen has the blood of the Lanarre. *Maybe he's distantly related to Drek?*

"You must make time. Figure out what to do with this female so you can take care of important matters."

They discuss something beyond what Tessa and Laz can hear. After about five minutes of heated back-and-forth discussion, Drek turns.

He looks directly at Tessa. "I'm sorry. I know that we'd discussed your leaving." Drek's gaze shifts to Laz.

Blood oath. Tessa can feel his heartbeat wildly thumping inside her damp grip. *Probably keeping time with mine.*

"I-I don't understand." Tessa looks first at Drek, then his right-hand Were, Bowen. "Laz and I want to leave. I helped get Tahlia to you, and even though Tanya is a snake"—Tessa ignores her insulted huff in the background—"she has a point. There was a breakdown in command, hierarchy… whatever. Tahlia and I were treated like shit. By *your* males."

Bowen's face becomes ruddy under her scrutiny. "We're aware, female—"

"Tessa." She frowns. This is going backward. Fast.

He nods. "Tessa. We're aware that things could have been handled better."

Tessa lets go of Laz's hand and folds her arms. Her glare sweeps over Drek, Bowen, and Tanya—*hell*, the entire room of Lanarre aren't immune to her disdain. *Asshats.*

"I have fought to stay out of the talons of Tramack, an insane Alpha from the Western."

Drek nods. "We ran into him."

Tessa sweeps a palm up. "So you know. He's a nut bunny."

His lips quirk. "I wouldn't go that far, but he'd healed significant damage wrought by a demonic."

All eyes go to Lazarus.

Oh shit. *Not* what she wanted—their attention on Laz.

She unfolds her arms and takes a quarter-step in front of her male, ready to fight off anyone who would dare come between them.

"Relax, female." Drek holds up a palm, but his eyes have gone wolfen. "We have no intention of harming the demonic."

An uproar ensues, voices growling and leaping around the room within the open acoustics of wood, stone, and tall ceilings. A wave of their anger strikes Tessa, and she clings to Laz's hand, pressing her body against his.

Laz doesn't return the hard hold, and she realizes he's readying himself to step away from her—to fight if the need arises.

A sharp and commanding bark splits the air, causing her eardrums to thrum, and she cringes.

"Enough!" Drek roars, slowly revolving, catching the eyes of every Were who would meet his dominant stare.

None do.

"I am your prince. And Tahlia, no matter what the circumstances of her coming here, was your future princess. Through a series of bungled communication and rash thought processes, she has fled. In *bird* form." His tone is disgusted.

Everyone in that huge room understands how difficult

tracking a Were who can shapeshift into another form will be. Especially one who is a bird.

A needle in a haystack.

"To be fair, Prince Drek," says a Were who leans casually against one of the huge round timbers in the center of the room, "it was confusing to have who we now know was Tanya claiming to be your intended. When we understood you and Bowen to be searching for her."

"Her party was late," another Were states as fact.

The two Weres exchange a loaded glance.

"That was partly my fault," Lazarus speaks for the first time, and now it's Tessa's turn to grab his forearm in warning. Her heart climbs her throat.

He doesn't listen, of course.

Aren't we a pair.

"Speak," Drek commands.

Laz touches her hand lightly. "I was sent on a mission from Below. Praile and I were to dismantle the Region One Singer compound and slay or infect their Rare One."

Murmuring begins, and Tessa wants to cover her face with her hands. Now they'll never let them go. Laz has admitted his willingness to commit an atrocity against another supernatural group. What's to stop him from doing the same here?

Why *would* they let him live?

"And?" Drek asks.

For the first time, Tessa has a sense of grudging respect for the Lanarre prince. Maybe he's not just a figurehead. Laz has confessed to something awful, and Drek hasn't had him executed on the spot.

"When I arrived, Tony Laurent, a Were from the

Northwestern had committed murder of the entire Region Two in collusion with the low demonic. There were few survivors, and the Rare One was successfully infected with a piece of our essence."

Drek scowls. "What does this have to do with your role in Tahlia's murdered guardians?"

"Tony Laurent was insane. He would have taken after, dismembered, and slaughtered anyone he ran into. That some human guardians, long serving humans from Tahlia's pack, happened to be in his proximity is most unfortunate."

Most unfortunate. A hot tear of frustration runs down Tessa's face before she can stop it.

She remembers Talia's fragile and haunting recounting of how she barely escaped the crazed Were before coming to Tessa's aid at a gas station.

The Lanarre who'd been lounging against the thick post moves away from the solid wood to face Laz, eyes going wolfen. "So you're responsible for the prince's female having barely escaped with her life?" His hands bunch into fists.

Oh shit, shit—shit!

With apparently no sense of self-preservation, Laz answers, "Essentially, yes. Praile should have terminated Laurent. Instead, he released him to rampage around, finding whoever he tripped over to slaughter."

A vein in the Were's temple begins to throb in time with his heartbeat.

Tessa steps in front of Laz.

"Move out of the way, bitch—we have a demonic to kill."

Tessa goes quarter before her next breath. "Fuck off, fang face."

"Neil, step down. Control your beast."

Neil, the Were with long fangs and not much else, turns to his prince.

No words are exchanged, but Tessa gets the backwash of the Alpha's power as he lashes it against Neil like a whip spiked in fire.

The large Were drops to his knees.

"I don't reward deceit, no matter how ugly the truth." Drek pushes more power over the assembled Lycan, and Tessa goes limp. Laz has no option but to tuck her against him to prevent her from sliding to her knees like the others.

"And Lazarus of Hades has confessed an awful truth." Drek turns to Laz. "Tell me why we should spare you?"

"I didn't realize I was on trial." Laz slowly surveys the room, and Tessa doesn't see one pair of neutral eyes staring back.

"You are a demonic. You've killed my Were. You have mated with an Alpha female. Regardless of rogue status or not, Lycan females are rare enough we aren't inclined to let them go."

Drek gives Tanya a speculative look, and she arranges her body in a pleasing posture.

She makes Tessa ill.

"Though they might lack certain qualities."

Tessa snorts.

Tanya spares a glare for Drek but, thankfully, says nothing.

Drek returns his attention to Laz. "Why do you admit your duplicity?"

"I want everyone to know that Tessa is my Redemptive. Her existence has freed me from the command of the Master. My compulsion to return to Hades has been lifted. I now have a chance, however slim, to live a life I never imagined possible."

"And before?" Drek asks slowly.

Laz answers just as slowly, as though the question posed is a stupid one. "Before I had to perform the tasks given to me."

Neil sneers. "What was that?"

Laz replies, but addresses Drek. "Whatever the Master —or in his absence, Praile—would have of me."

"The demonic who's skull you crushed?" Drek asks. "The one who nearly killed me?" His eyebrows cock high at his forehead. "Without your healing abilities, even now, I would be dead."

"Yes." Lazarus's exhale is labored.

The two males stare at each other.

"There is the other matter, my prince," Bowen interrupts.

Drek's eyes go hard.

"Three of my Lanarre soldiers were found dead, beheaded in the underground parking area of the local hospital in Port Townsend."

Tessa's eyes rapidly shift between Drek and Bowen. She flares her nostrils.

She doesn't like what she smells. *Certainty.*

Laz shrugs. "Their loss of life is not by my hand, if that's your inference."

Drek threads his fingers together. "Their death took place before your arrival here."

Tessa blinks.

"When Tessa would have been throwing off pheromones with her heat that would have brought every Were within a hundred miles to her side."

Laz laughs loudly, startling many of the others within the large space. "I don't have a sense of smell like a Lycan. Can't *you* detect who was responsible for this crime?"

Bowen shakes his head. "The local human police contaminated everything. But there was the residual scent of a female in heat. There is no male alive who wouldn't recognize that smell. It's instinct. And the demonic are scentless."

"This is ridiculous!" Tessa shouts. "We are going. You gave blood oath. I'm not hanging around for some witch hunt and burnt offering at the stake because you guys think that Laz offed three Lanarres because he's here and available to be condemned."

"Tessa," Laz says, but she ignores him, having worked herself up into a head of steam.

"You will stay, or we will kill your demonic... mate," Bowen says.

Tessa feels the force of his command, and tears of pure frustration claw their way down her face.

Laz looks down at her, quietly telling her to bide her time, while Tanya's soft laughter is acid that's burning the inside of her ears.

CHAPTER 18

*D*evin points at the door. "Get out." She moves so that the couch is between them.

Jenni stands. She knew it was a possibility Devin might freak. Who wouldn't? The story is like a bad fiction novel.

"I'll go," Jenni says quietly.

Devin scrunches her nose. "Keep the clothes."

Jenni picks up her purse, arranging the strap across her body. "I'm really sorry," she whispers.

"It's okay, just go. I got Ella to think about. I can't have a crazy in the house. No offense."

She just nods. What can Jenni do to defend herself after the stuff she told Devin? Nothing. What would *she* think if some girl she'd just met told her that stuff?

Jenni would think she needed a straitjacket.

She picks up her hoodie and slips it on. Zipping it up, she takes an experimental whiff. It smells like forest and dirt. Great.

She places her hand on the cheap doorknob, hoping

she hasn't endangered Devin or Ella. *What if this Lanarre group comes sniffing around and hurts them?*

Adi seemed to think the males were protective of females. Not from what she saw. Not a bit. Maybe Adi's man, Slash, is.

"Wait!" a little voice yells from behind her.

"Stay by Mama, Ella."

A small foot stomps, and Jenni presses her head to the door, indecision making her pause.

"She eats ice cream for breakfast! I like Jen-Jen. I want Jen-Jen. She's more better than Dar-Dar!"

Jen-Jen. She smiles despite herself.

"No, Ella. Jenni thinks she's a wolf."

"Cool," Ella says reverently.

Jenni turns.

Devin glares at her.

"I don't know if others will come looking for me. I might be held responsible for what went down in that parking garage."

Devin pales before her eyes. "What do ya mean?" She winds her arm around Ella, tucking her tightly against her slim frame.

"I mean that I really am what I said I was. And that I was just… at the wrong place at the wrong time. It wasn't a plan of mine, you know."

"You becoming a werewolf?"

"Cool!" Ella repeats, wiggling out of her mother's grip and running to Jenni.

"No!" Devin cries, jumping like a gazelle after Ella. But Ella reaches Jenni first, leaping into her arms.

Jenni catches her.

Big brown eyes peer into her own. "Are you really a woof?"

"A woof?" Jenni asks, a smile stealing over her face.

"Yeah," she nods vigorously, "a woof."

Devin meets Jenni's eyes over Ella's shoulder. "She means wolf."

Jenni nods. "Kinda like a wolf, but not *all* the time." *At least that's what I assume.*

"Can I see your teethies?"

Jenni nods and opens her mouth.

Ella touches each tooth, appearing disappointed as she gingerly explores the interior of Jenni's mouth. "I don't see nothin' sharp."

Jenni's laugh is muffled with the small fingers in her mouth.

"Don't be telling her stuff like that." Devin crosses her arms over her skinny chest.

Gently, Jenni lowers Ella to the floor, but the little girl clings to her legs.

"I don't know what's gotten into her. She never takes to people like this."

"I feel honored."

Devin's tense, eyes full of defiance. "Well, I don't."

Jenni tries to reason with her. "Listen, what happened with Bray? How do you explain that?"

Devin stares at her then eventually drops her eyes. "You got me there. I can't. It was weird, how you handled them." Her chin hikes. "How you dodged bullets…"

"And carried you most of the way here."

"You carried my mama?" Ella grins.

Jenni looks down and sees round brown eyes searching her face for an untruth. *Keep it simple.* "Yes."

"She's heavy!"

Devin and Jenni laugh. "Thanks, Boo—every woman's dream phrase."

"Boo?"

"Mama calls me Boo because it keeps the ghosts away."

Jenni puts her hands on her hips. "And I shouldn't be telling Ella about being a werewolf?"

Devin blushes. "Okay, so don't judge, but she used to have nightmares about ghosts. I told her that if I called her Boo once a day, the ghosts would get scared and not come around."

"Not too bad." Jenni grins.

Devin's smile is slow, but Jenni's glad to see it. She ducks her head. "Yeah."

A few seconds pass in silence. "You still want me to beat feet?"

"No," Devin admits sheepishly. "You just threw me. That story." She gives a little shrug with one shoulder.

"So you believe me?"

Devin regards her for a moment. "I don't know. But I like you. Ya helped me, and I can tell you've had a hard life."

Jenni can't refute that observation.

Ella makes the most of the awkward situation and tows Jenni away from the door then pushes her back down on the couch. "There," she says, carefully arranging Jenni's legs in front of her.

"Bossy little thing," Jenni comments, amusement curling her lips.

Devin laughs. "You've got *no* idea."

"Let me see whatchya got in your purse?" Ella tugs at it.

Jenni takes the strap over her head and unzips the top.

"Look at this!" Ella squeals in glee, eyeballing all the zippers for different compartments within the main body of the handbag.

"There's no killer meds or something in there, is there?"

Jenni looks at Devin. "Nope."

Devin's shoulders slump in clear relief. "Good."

They look at each other.

"Okay, so give me the rest of the story."

Jenni does. When she gets to the part about her terminal diagnosis, Devin sighs, her face going sad. "My nana died from cancer. She practically raised me 'cause my parents didn't have no money."

"I'm sorry," Jenni says.

"Were you really going to die? I mean, it's hard to believe with you being so young…"

Jenni glances at Ella, who's deep into inspecting her coin purse that twists to open and close. Carefully, she removes a penny then, with a frown, returns it into the leather pouch. She swivels her tiny hand over the top, and it closes. She repeats the process, and it opens. Ella smiles, fascinated, forgetting the money inside.

"Yeah. I have that gene. The one that means not *if,* but *when,* I'll get breast or uterine cancer."

Devin nods. "So you think?"

"I do. You should have seen me yesterday. I think Adi gave me a gift."

Her eyes run over Jenni again, and a tiny frown plants itself between her brows. "Seen what?"

"I looked like I was on death's door."

"Because you were," Devin replies.

"I need to go," Jenni admits.

Ella doesn't look at Jenni. "Don't wanna have Jen-Jen go."

"Why would you go?" Devin asks, obvious discomfort in her voice. "I mean, now that I'm not throwing you out."

Jenni tells the truth. She's not much for lying anyway. "I should try to find Adi. She can help me. In fact, I'm pretty sure she was trying to save me by injecting me with whatever werewolf magic that was when she bit me." She meets Devin's stare. "Because Adi knew that if I'd never met her, I wouldn't have been caught in the crossfire of some weird werewolf thing."

"Yeah, what's going on there?" Devin asks, glancing at Ella.

She has all of Jenni's stuff out and is applying scarlet lipstick, making her small lips into big clownish ones. "Pretty!" she says, twisting the lipstick until the entire red-colored stick is extended, clearing the tip of the enamel tube.

"Boo, put that back," Devin chastises. "With the lid on."

"No biggie," Jenni says, smiling at Ella. Lipstick Death by Preschooler is the least of her concerns.

"I'm not sure. Adi said something about being in heat, and they could smell her."

Devin's nose wrinkles. "Eww."

"Yeah," Jenni agrees. "So her husband, or whatever they call spouses in the werewolf world, showed up—

and like I told you, he messed up their day. Permanently."

Devin shivers. "Sounds pretty gross."

Jenni nods, though she's seen some pretty sick-looking stuff in her time. "Anyway, if I can find Adi, maybe she can help train me or something. I get it. She couldn't hang around for the humans showing up. There were things she needed to figure out with Slash. But she left me high and dry. I know less than nothing."

"And," Devin leans forward, elbows pressed to her knees, "it's almost a full moon."

Jesus.

"Do you think the myth stuff is true?" Devin asks excitedly.

She can be excited for both of them. Right now, Jenni is just plain scared of the unknown.

"Here, *ah*—Ella, can I have my cell?"

"Ah-huh," Ella says absently, handing Jenni the phone. Every bit of the crystal display is smudged with itty-bitty fingerprints. And the *low battery* light is on.

Damn. Of course the charger is at the condo.

"What are you doing?"

Her finger rapidly scrolls to the Google symbol then she taps in the query words. "Checking the moon's cycle."

"This is too weird."

Welcome to my world.

"Yeah."

Four days.

Her display blackens. Damn thing's already dead. "Figures," Jenni mutters.

"What? How much time?"

With shaking fingers, Jenni pushes her damp hair behind a shoulder. "Four days."

"That's not very long."

Jenni refrains from the eye heave she was going for and sighs instead. "Maybe it's all bullshit." Even to her, she sounds wistful.

"That's a bad word," Ella says, busy emptying Jenni's purse of every piece of lint, scrap of paper, gum wrapper, and purse dredge she can find.

"Sorry," Jenni mumbles. A sudden urge to cry washes over her, and she puts her face in her hands.

Little hands cover hers, pulling them apart. "Why you crying?"

Devin silently hands Jenni a tissue, and she loudly blows her nose.

They look at Jenni.

She returns their stare, not really sure how to answer when *she* doesn't even know what her problem is.

I'm alive. What the fuck is this ungratefulness? Why can't she just accept the unbelievable and hold off on the pity party for later?

Like next year. The year she wouldn't be living if she hadn't been on shift when Adi was wheeled in.

But it's the four-year-old who's smarter than everybody. "You don't wanna be a wolf?"

Jenni nods. "Yeah. I don't think I'm on board with the whole howling-at-the-moon thing."

"But ya get to chase stuff. And be warm and run fast and eat everything," Ella says in a dreamy voice. "And be fuzzy."

"Furry," Devin says and meets Jenni's eyes.

Jenni sets Ella on her lap. "You know, has anyone ever told you you're a smart little girl?"

She tweaks the tip of Jenni's nose. "Ah-huh."

A laugh bursts out of her. "I'm glad you're my friend, Ella."

Jenni thinks she might be falling in love with her.

"I've never had a wolf friend before. Even at yittle people."

"Little." Devin corrects her, but she strokes Ella's long golden hair.

After a minute of Jenni getting her emotional act together, Devin says quietly, "You can't really go to your place, Jenni. Cops are gonna be there. You know, that disappearing act you pulled was kinda..." She waves her palm around.

"Spectacular."

They're quiet for a minute, each in their own thoughts.

"I have to go. I'll need my things."

"Listen, what kind of money do you have?"

Jenni feels her brow knot. "A lot. As a matter of fact, I have a big insurance payout from my parents' death." She breathes through the sucking chest wound of grief then continues, "And I don't have a mortgage."

"Oh, yeah, mortgage."

Jenni looks around the apartment of a twenty-two-year-old who works at McDonald's. She's probably never thought about owning a place. Probably just rents the apartment month to month.

"I can quit, pack my crap, and come with you."

They look at Ella.

"It's not safe."

"Not gonna lie. I can feel the heat from Bray. Don't want to be around right now."

Oh, yeah. Bray the Magnificent.

"I'd want to die if anything happened to Ella."

Devin laughs. "Like I wouldn't?"

"I'm not a gonna die." Ella is carefully putting all Jenni's stuff back in her purse. "I clean your purse."

An assortment of wrappers, papers, and general junk is piled on the coffee table.

Devin bursts out laughing. "I swear that kids going to be organizing my life before she's five."

Jenni scrutinizes Ella.

Ella smiles back.

Maybe.

CHAPTER 19

SLASH

*N*o matter how much he wants to make Adrianna happy, her concern over the human pet she changed to Were cannot take precedence.

The Hoh pack *will* hold them responsible for the deaths of the Lanarre scouts.

Even if he was within rights to defend his mate, he was not in attendance of said mate when they picked up her scent. They assumed she was rogue, in heat, and in need of breeding.

Simple, right?

No. Slash feels his eyes go wolfen and he clenches his hands into ready fists. Just the inkling—the whisper of an idea that another male would touch Adrianna nearly brings his beast.

He's continually surprised by how completely he's taken to the role of mate—a position he never thought to hold.

Now he can't imagine *not* having it.

He watches Adrianna as she whistles tunelessly, assembling supplies to put inside a battered backpack.

His eyes linger over remnants of the print that obviously covered the backpack. He frowns. "Are those unicorns?"

Adrianna tosses an irritated look his way. "I'm not giving this baby up, even if it took a beating on the highway."

Adrenaline spikes. "Are you referring to throwing yourself out in front of human traffic?"

She sighs, absently rubbing her nape. "Yup. And I'd do it again. Those douche nozzles were gonna try and breed me. I'd rather *not*."

Rather not. "Douche nozzles?" Slash says, tramping his wolf into submission.

Adrianna glances his way then stops rummaging and packing the tattered backpack. "Slash, your eyes."

He looks away, concentrating on the unending forest seen through a large glass window facing the porch, instead of his fragile mate in front of him—and the proof of hurting herself to escape Lanarre males.

Because I wasn't there to defend her.

"Hey."

He senses her nearness and regulates his breathing. Measuring each one. Spacing each inhale and exhale until he can feel his wolf settle.

Finally, he raises his eyes from his worn boots.

Adrianna is before him. "It's not your fault. You had that messed-up paralysis thing…"

He grins despite his guilt. "Ah, yes—that."

"Yeah." Adrianna returns his smile and takes hold of the lapels of his jacket.

Slash's heart fills with a terrifying emotion.

Joy.

Simple happiness that this female changed his *existence* to a *life.*

"Now you're all better," she says, her fingers sliding down his lightweight coat as she turns away, and he grabs her hand, gently pulling her back and folding her against his body.

"You won't have to worry about that happening again." He frowns. "But… is there anything the witch has that we can pilfer so I don't have to look at the unicorns?" The pack serves as a constant reminder of what Adrianna went through without him by her side.

Adrianna studies the pack. "I guess the road rash *is* pretty bad." Her attention shifts to Slash again. "To be honest, I don't want anything of hers." She shudders. "I'd rather use my backpack with all the glitter scraped off and beheaded unicorns than touch or use something of Della's."

Slash waits a heartbeat. "Okay. Just food and drinks then."

Adrianna leans her head back. "Or whatever small crap might be worth something. I'm all about thieving off an evil witch who was going to take our baby."

Slash crushes her against him, and Adrianna gasps. "No one will ever touch you—or our whelp."

He tips her head back with a finger, searching her riveting hazel eyes. "Do you understand me, mate?"

"I love it when you get all dominating."

Slash rolls his eyes. "I'm serious, Adrianna."

She kisses him, wet and deep, then whispers, "Me, too."

* * *

"I'm surprised I can walk," Adrianna says with a wink.

Dull heat spreads over Slash's neck as he thinks about yet another session of their lovemaking.

He cannot get enough of her. Adrianna has begun something deep inside Slash that he is helpless before—and hungry for.

Her eyes widen. "Are you blushing?" Adrianna's voice is teasing.

The heat grows more acute. "No," he growls.

"Liar."

Slash dares to look at her, expecting to see Adrianna laughing at him.

Instead, her face glows with love, pleasure, and happiness.

Moon, do I adore her.

Slowly, Slash walks over to Adrianna, and cupping the back of her head, he draws her to him, kissing her face and finally, her lips.

"You sure have a lot of stamina," she says a little breathlessly.

"I am a Red. We are known for that."

"Ah-huh."

Slash forces himself to let go of her hand and begins to thoroughly scan the woods from the witch's porch. They must go.

"I won't miss this dump," Adrianna comments.

But Slash is riveted by something that's caught his eye. It is absent of smell.

Della.

"Adrianna," he calls out softly.

Clearly recognizing the caution in his voice, Adrianna turns slowly to him, rolling her right shoulder and settling the backpack more firmly between her shoulder blades.

He watches her draw nearer, and there's a glow to her skin that wasn't there before. Unlike some with her hair color—blond begging to be light-brown—Adrianna isn't fair-skinned exactly. But the remnants of fairness take up the bridge of her nose, where freckles are sprinkled liberally like flakes of brown sugar on her skin. Soft pink color spins across her cheekbones as though brushed on with the lightest stroke.

Her long hair plaited tightly to her head, she appears like a flower in full bloom. Slash looks down again so Adrianna won't see so obviously what he feels.

Della had an archaic washer and dryer, and Adrianna laundered their clothes, grumbling all the while that he would be the one to clean them next time.

Slash quipped that if he could handle her panties, he wouldn't mind.

Adrianna was quiet after that, but a smile had ghosted her lips.

He looks up, noting how the fresh clothes cling to her body, and Slash can't help his body's response to hers, hardening at the sight of his mate moving nearer.

"Good Moon, look at you," she says softly.

Slash shakes his head, dismissing his body's traitorous response to her nearness. "It's not me."

Her eyes run invisible fingers over his body. "It *so* is." Her open smile warms him. But the heat fades as he indicates Della, about fifteen feet from where they stand.

Adrianna flares her nostrils. "What?"

"Can you scent her?"

Her nose scrunches. "No, thank Moon."

Slash stares at her for a long moment.

Her eyes round with understanding. "I *should*."

"Yes."

"Slash." Her voice is worried, and he hates it.

"We need to investigate."

Adrianna puts her hands on her hips. "Is this like one of these *B* horror movies where the dumb-ass main character has to go down the dark hall, basement, or creepy house and *check* shit out?"

Slash frowns.

"I don't care about Della. I just want to go." She cups her elbows, looking around.

He scents her anxiety.

"We're going. But I want to know why the witch you stabbed in the heart—"

"Three times."

Slash nods. "Is not scenting of death."

"Okay." Adrianna's voice is small.

They knit hands and advance on the lifeless body.

When they're within a couple of feet, Adrianna will go no farther. "Look at her."

"Yes."

Della looks as though she's sleeping—not dead.

Luscious, full dark-brown hair fans around her body as though the locks were just artfully washed and styled, arranged as if waiting for a prince charming to wake her with a kiss.

Her skin is not the grayish-yellow of the deceased, but appears like burnished alabaster with a lick of soft rosy color.

"Stay back, Adrianna."

"You don't have to tell me twice." A few seconds pound by. "Slash, she doesn't look dead."

Dried blood coats the shredded clothes at her breastbone, and her body has already shed rusty flakes into the decayed leaves and forest debris nearby.

"I didn't remember her being on her back," Adrianna says, a slight tremor in her voice.

"There's no life around her." Slash can feel Adrianna's gaze prowl the area then meet his own, though he's uncomfortable looking away from Della for even a second.

"The blades of grass are bent away."

"As if avoiding her."

Their attention returns to the "corpse."

Slash slowly circles Della's body. "If I didn't know better, I'd say she was a vampire who'd been turned and was waiting for night."

Soundlessly, they both look at the canopy of trees which soars above their heads. Puzzle pieces of light scatter above them, sprinkling chunks of illumination at their feet.

The forest holds its very breath... then one crescent of light falls directly on Della's closed eye.

Slash isn't surprised when the eyelid suddenly opens, revealing a malevolent stare directed at them.

* * *

ADRIANNA'S PIERCING scream splits the air with the precision of a sword swung hard, ringing in the silence like a discordant musical note.

Slash leaps backward and toward Adrianna, jerking her against him.

"Slash," she moans, skin clammy to the touch. "I killed her."

"No."

The trees appear to shiver as huge beasts emerge from the deep green folds.

Trolls.

Exaggerated brow ridges, huge hooked noses, and small beady eyes in a variety of jewel tones fall on the witch.

Della struggles to sit up.

Slash backs away, securing his mate more tightly against his body. "Wrap my waist, Adrianna."

She does better than that, circling her arms around his neck and doing the same with her legs around his waist. She burrows her head against his neck, and he secures her with hands palming her rear.

"Are those the trolls?"

The beasts are huge, like small mountains, bigger than Slash in his wolfen from.

"Lycan," the one who is the smallest but clearly in charge strides toward them.

"Step no further. I hold my mate in my hands."

The troll stops, moving his shoulders back like independent boulders of muscle, then stills. "The witch is ours."

Slash nearly laughs.

"Have at her," Adrianna murmurs against his neck.

"Adi—shh."

"We have no quarrel with you." What must pass for a smile flickers across his face. Bestowing a grin on them, he peels back his fleshy lips, revealing square slightly yellow teeth.

Slash is very glad Adrianna is turned away.

"No!" Della begins to scream, and the troop of seven-foot tall trolls turn to her as one. Each has a club in his burly hand. Forearm muscles bulge as they lift the thickest ends of the tapered and gnarled wood high.

"Your curse has lifted, and with your death, so will ours," the leader says.

They move forward, and the ground shakes with their footfalls.

"Slash."

"We're leaving."

The lead troll turns. "You must bear witness."

Shit.

"They could have killed us when we passed through the first time," Adrianna softly points out.

Slash still doesn't like a bunch of males standing around with weapons while his mate clings to his body. *Feels wrong.*

His lips twist. *What a fucking understatement.*

199

"Yes," Slash replies. He can't hope to escape with so many, so close.

They return their attention to Della, who's on her feet now.

"With violence, you were beget. With violence, we return you to the earth."

Della holds up her hands. A wand appears in one.

The very thing she claimed not to use or need anymore.

The tip sparkles in the scattered light, and Slash can make out a crystal sphere catching whatever illumination floats in the gloom between tree trunks.

Adrianna turns just as Della raises the wand and points the shining tip at her.

With a downward arc, the wand slices the air, and a brilliant, iridescent ribbon untwines like a cracking whip toward Adrianna.

A troll leaps, inserting his body midair between the witch and Adrianna.

A wound the size of his torso opens him neck to crotch like a yawning mouth. Entrails pour onto the forest floor in a steaming, glossy pile.

The troll wails in agony.

Slash's beast bursts from his body in a painful explosion, throwing Adrianna to the ground in a pile of his discarded flesh, skin, and gore.

Slash roars as he leaps, and the sound echoing in the woods like a broken, hoarse siren.

He attacks the witch, tearing at her leg until he removes it from her body.

Della's wand falls, already fractured and sheared off at the tip.

Slash backs away, head down, jowls full with the spoils of ripping her apart.

The trolls advance on the defeated witch, their killing intent sings within the tense posture of their clubs, free of blood.

For now.

CHAPTER 20

LAZ

"Neil should not be chosen as our guard."

Tessa kicks the door and is rewarded with a dent in the wood for her trouble. "He's just the first dickhead who volunteered."

The corners of Laz's lips lift. "Yes."

"Tahlia's gone. Drek should be looking for *her*—not keeping us until the proper murderer is discovered."

"Agreed."

Tessa looks at him. "Then why don't we sneak out of here. I mean—isn't the guy from the Hot Place going to send more minions after you?"

He would laugh, but not while his Redemptive has worry tightening the edges of her eyes.

Laz doesn't hesitate. "With certainty." Every moment they remain is an additional one they don't have to spare.

Tessa comes close to him, and he reels her the rest of the way by her hands. "Redemptive, you are most impatient."

She laughs. "And you're more patient than me?"

"Infinitely." Laz gives a tight smile.

Her brows pull together. "What's with all this cloak-and-dagger shit, Laz?" Tessa pulls away, and he allows it, though he feels better in every way if a piece of his body is always touching hers.

Laz supposes that's not a reasonable thing to ask for, and badly suppresses another amused smile.

"What are you grinning about?"

Laz runs his eyes over her form. "I was only thinking that I'd like to touch you always, rather than be parted."

"Moon, you are an addicting male." She shakes her head as though wishing it weren't true.

"Is that a good thing?"

She nods.

A pocket of silence fills between them.

"Why do you say we need to have patience?"

"I believe Drek was only keeping us for the moment, to let us go later. The Lanarre prince took a blood oath; he would be a fool to go back on that. He is..." Laz searches furiously for the correct phrase. "Saving face." Laz sweeps a palm where a disgruntled Were waits on the opposite side of the dented door. "After all, how would it look if he released us, after I killed his Lycan, and three others have been murdered where the killer has not been identified? Even though I healed the prince from damage wrought by Praile, I am not fully exonerated."

"I love the way you talk," Tessa says, and Laz is suddenly self-conscious.

"I am old," he says in his own defense.

"Not *that* old," Tessa says lightly, though her eyes hold heat when they run up and down his body.

He raises his chin. "I am nearly a thousand in Between years."

As they stare at each other, Laz can literally see Tessa searching for how to respond.

Then she's smiling, and it reminds Laz what she looked like when the moon appeared from behind the clouds.

Radiant.

"You're just robbing the cradle then."

Laz smirks. Tessa has a wonderful sense of humor. A trait utterly missing from Hades. Missing by necessity.

Thinking about his dark home dims Laz's humor.

"What?" Worry creases her face, and Laz desperately wants to erase the cause.

He shakes his head, dispelling what she saw in his expression.

Tessa takes both his hands, threading her fingers with his, and holds them up so the knuckles point toward the ceiling. "You expect me to just be mated to you and buy all this Redemptive stuff, and *then* you don't share what's on your mind."

"Essentially"—he pulls her closer, rotating their hands down and between their bodies—"I killed my boss, second only to the Master himself."

Tessa sighs. "He had to go. Chopping off his dick a couple of times didn't seem to slow him down, either. It had to be a full head-mashing."

Laz doesn't laugh.

"Hey…" Tessa drops his hand and traces his full lips with a finger. "You have to lighten up."

"As soon as we're free from here and making our way, I will rest easier."

"Making our way where? And won't they find you?"

"I plan on taking measures to erase my demonic signature in this realm."

Tessa's eyebrows slowly rise.

Laz answers her unspoken question, "We leave for the fey mound, gain safe passage, stay for a time until their search yields nothing. Then, when the threat of demonic presence has lifted, we leave."

"Oh, right." Tessa steps away, folding her arms. "The fey will just welcome us with open arms. That whole plan seems so easy. I remember those guys as being a mixed bag, at best."

Laz senses his irises darken. "I admit going there holds a dual purpose. I can finally find what blood I have running in these veins. I am mixed. There must be some reason why my Redemptive is a Lycan—that I have one at all."

"Should I be offended?" Tessa chides.

"No." He runs a hand down her bare arm, and she shivers. "Complimented. There are few of Hades who could claim any female outside Below."

"I know, I know. I'm your Redemptive."

Laz nods. "Your status is more important than you know."

"And the faeries can determine what you are?"

"They are a neutral species in many ways. Their very nature is mixed, their ground is magic—the sithen is a living thing. They can see and ascertain many things. And they might keep us safe from those who would pull us asunder."

"That doesn't sound great. Not getting a wonderful visual, Laz. More like we're a couple of voodoo dolls getting stuck with pins."

"As a metaphor, it works."

Tessa tucks a loose hair behind her ear. "That option terrifies me."

"I would rather go with the evil we don't know than the one we do."

"So we get the hell away from the Hoh pack, find faerie, and bust a move."

Laz draws her in again, their bodies molding to each other. Tessa lays her head against the muscular planes of his chest, directly over his heart.

He runs his hands up and down her back, taking comfort in her closeness. "I don't speak as you do—"

"But you could." Tessa grins.

His lips curl. "Yes, though it doesn't come naturally."

"Anyways, we do our thing in faerie, then we leave. You'll know what you are, and the demonic will have given up searching for you." Tessa looks up at him. "Is that how it will work?"

Laz badly wants to respond with a yes and allay her fears. Instead, he replies with the compulsion for truth, "The demonic don't give up easily."

Tessa's exhale is frustrated. "Then why are we bothering with going all the way to the faerie mound?"

"Because," Laz looks deeply into her pale-gray eyes, "it is our best hope among bad ones."

He doesn't tell her that, as he views it, this choice is the only one.

* * *

Tahlia

SHE DOESN'T REMAIN to see Drek mate with Tanya—or to continue to be tied up and dismissed. Tahlia is Lanarre and should at least have deference for that. Yet, she doesn't.

So she leaves.

Guilt over leaving Tessa to her own devices doesn't stop her, either. *Can't stop.* Tessa has Laz, though how she could trust a demonic makes no sense to Tahlia. Even if he was able to sufficiently prove his worth, he is of the devil.

And Tahlia doesn't trust the Lanarre of the Hoh enough to stay and take her chances that Drek would come to his senses and claim her as his chosen as he was supposed to—if she's even willing to accept.

Tahlia doesn't fly in the direction of the Redwood pack of the west. They won't help her. They'll assign blame.

A Lanarre female who was apparently rejected by a Lanarre prince, she would be shunned. And Tanya somehow easily usurped her position by just streaking through and jiggling her considerable assets.

Tahlia can't cry because of the bird form she holds.

She has no pack. Effectively, Tahlia is a rogue female. Not an ideal position for a female Lycan.

She finally sets down on a low branch and wraps her

delicately sharp talons around the wood. She tucks her body tightly against the trunk, and her eyes immediately begin to droop, lulled by the soothing smells of cedar, fir, and forest. She's exhausted from the events and the emotional injustices she's suffered.

At the exact moment Tahlia drifts off into sleep, she remembers Drek. And in that paper-thin veil of gray between wakefulness and sleep, she recalls a single shining moment where Tahlia thought the prince might have been something far more than an arranged match between Lanarre packs.

For a breathtaking few seconds, Tahlia had thought Drek might be a male she could love.

* * *

Drek

"I DO NOT CARE!" Drek seethes, gritting his teeth.

"You can stop shouting—I hear fine," Bowen remarks.

Drek shoots a killer scowl at his second.

"You can't release the demonic *and* Tessa, Drek. Not without causing a huge uprising. You must punish the demonic in a showy way, so everyone gets the idea you're not soft." Bowen flips his palms over, facing the ceiling, giving an exaggerated shrug.

"I hate how rational you are. And I hate fucking politics. And I took a blood oath."

Bowen sighs, rolling his eyes at the ceiling. "Fuck— Drek." He hangs his head. "Somebody's gotta be. You're out of your gourde because Tahlia is unprotected. Admit that and we can move on. And as far as the blood oath goes, just don't see him dead." Bowen meets Drek's eyes. "Because the moon will see your blood spill if you do. What possessed you to give a blood oath—ah yes, demon boy saved you." Bowen rolls his dark eyes. "And I know you had blood connection with Tahlia."

Moon. "It's that obvious?"

"Yes."

"Lazarus is demonic, yet he healed me. I owe him his life for my own." Drek closes a fist, placing it above his heart. "I wouldn't be standing here to worry about Tahlia if he hadn't."

"And it was Praile, the other demonic, who injured you."

Drek gives a miserable exhale. "That's all they'll see. But yes, if not for Laz's interference, I'd be dead."

"We're Lycan. Were are not exactly known for being rational. We're ruled by the moon, for fuck's sake."

Drek smirks.

Bowen snorts. "I know—you adore me."

He nods. "I do. You're rash, and aggressive—"

"And I make an assload of sense." Bowen nods, spreading his muscular arms. "Admit it, prince."

"Don't call me that in private, Bo," he says to the male he was whelped beside.

Bowen shrugs. "Hurt the demonic—slap on the wrist—shit, then release him. The pack will honor that as a wash. Lazarus murdered two Lanarre in defense of his mate, and then he healed you against wounds caused by one of his own."

"I cannot believe a female would be with a demonic."

Bowen shrugs again. "We have honorable males that would do quite a bit to be with a quality female such as Tessa."

Their eyes meet.

"Even though she doesn't have royal blood."

"That is important to this pack," Drek begins, "though it is not important to me. Moon knows, we Lycans do not have sufficient females for the luxury of pickiness on royal blood."

"I get it—I'm unmated." Bowen's eyes meet Drek's, and they've gone silver at the edges with his wolf. "But this is what you must maintain for power, Drek. If one of the alpha's suspected that royal blood no longer mattered, you'd be fighting all of them for the throne. Beginning with Neil."

Now it is Drek's turn to roll his eyes. "The hierarchy is antiquated. I want out. I want to be a male. A Lycan."

"You were born royal—automatically Alpha. It is your birthright and can't be changed, Drek."

He slams his fist on the giant wood table that has sat in the exact spot for a thousand years. "And look what it has cost me," he finishes in a low voice.

They say nothing for a strained moment.

Finally, Bowen articulates Drek's worst fear, "You have to wait to search for Tahlia until this Laz thing gets handled. The sooner the better. Or Neil will find others, and bring something formal to do to him. You want to be the one, as our leader, to decide his punishment. Not that fucker wannabe, Neil."

Drek chuckles. "I still don't care how much our pack might feel the need for justice against Lazarus. Every moment we delay searching for Tahlia, she is in more danger. Let's handle the Lazarus issue swiftly."

"Agreed, but you can't take off on a wild-wolf chase with the pack this unsettled."

Drek hates his choices, for he has none.

He stands, and with a nod at Bowen and a heavy heart, he makes the trek to the cabin where Tessa and Laz are being held.

CHAPTER 21

DARK MASTER

*I*n many areas of Between, there are places where the veil that separates each realm is opaque. Fragile.

Dark Master has always avoided such pulsating tumors of separation because of the poisonous chasms they represent—a sucking void into a dimension that means sickness to him.

Until now.

His talons are gone, replaced with fresh pale-pink nails. His skin is fair like snow brushed by the first blush of sunset.

Dark Master couldn't bear to look at his image a second time. The faces of his servants tell him much—more than any mirror. Their repulsion is reflection enough forever.

He has never felt shame before. Now, as his kind look at him then quickly away, Dark Master knows he'll be forever marked.

However, if he can get at the Rare One and expunge

her from the face of this realm, the demonic will gain a foothold Between. A measure of power that even the angelic do not possess. Like a stain, the demonic will spread their blackness Between.

That is, if he can ever regain his strength.

"Rernard!" Dark Master barks, his jealousy spiking as the high demonic draws nearer. *Perfectly* handsome.

Deep-red skin like freshly spilt blood wraps an impressively muscular body. Black horns and irises shine with malevolent beauty. Rernard even possesses an impressive battle tail, a coveted feature of the high demonic.

Hate seethes within Dark Master for the permanent loss of his handsomeness.

The Rare One will pay a steep price for continuing to exist and forcing him to cross the shroud from Below to Between.

"How long will I be..." He cannot finish the question, taking a look at where he lies on ground so cold it should not be a part of nature in any realm.

"I am not sure, Master. One of your stature has never attempted the transference before."

With great effort, Dark Master rolls onto his back, staring for a moment at the ugliness of the sky of Between. Gone is the slick heat of blackness present Below. Instead, crisp pure white clouds happily trot across a blue sky that reminds him of the insipid eye color he now owns.

Fighting the urge to dig his new eyeballs out of his skull, he heaves himself upright, measuring Rernard's cautious approach as he places a stack of ugly garments, most typically worn by those who dwell Between, beside him.

He clenches his eyes shut, immersed in his misery. Finally, after a full minute of self-pity has passed, Dark Master opens his eyes.

"Master, let me assist you—"

"Go to hell."

Rernard gives a curt bow. "Thank you, Master. However, I feel that I must insist."

Of course he must. Though he loathes being weak, Dark Master holds up his hands. Rernard and a low demonic each grip his outstretched arms, yanking him upright.

Colors swim before his vision. Everything that surrounds him is bright and jarring, not the deep familiar warmth and low molten light of Below.

Not this realm. *This* place is a rainbow of nauseating colors. The rich greens of the spectrum Between trigger his gag reflex. *Trees,* his overstimulated mind attempts to rationalize. *That* is what the wretchedly fresh-smelling living tapestry is.

And it's cold and wet. He shivers. *Why is it bright?* Squinting, Dark Master looks through the spaces where the forest's massive canopy of needles and leaves allow patches of open sky to penetrate.

Pain explodes as cool, late-autumn sunlight crawls over his new, sensitive skin. He doubles over, and only Rernard keeps him on his feet. Another fact Dark Master hates. The second insult is heaving the last bit of food he consumed while Below.

After Dark Master finishes releasing the contents of

his stomach, the steaming pile of his last meal sits before them.

He spits to the side, his saliva sizzling where it lands against cool ground. Dark Master gives a weak smile at that small comfort. "Take me away from my own leavings, Rernard."

Rernard had attempted to convince Dark Master that more of the low demonic should accompany them to Between. In that way, Dark Master could have all the assistance he might require.

But his vanity kept that suggestion as only that. He did not want more of the demonic to see how he would need to persevere to get the job done—or what he would become.

A piece of Hades hides deep in the gut of the Rare One. If she is mated to another of the angelic, his very proximity would offer protection from the ill effects of the spore.

What she must never do—*ever*—is find her way to Hades. Because she possesses a piece of them within her, she would be allowed entry to Dark Master's realm.

Without her mate, Julia Caldwell would eventually wither and die. With him, she has opportunity for entry into Hades. The special evil piece of the demonic will behave like a Trojan horse that would destroy them and all the majestic darkness Dark Master has built.

His solitary consolation is that she remains ignorant of that power. Or possibly, she is not brave enough to traverse from Between to Below.

He scowls. The angelic are many vile things, yet they have an unfortunate propensity for bravery and self-sacrifice. As a Rare One, Caldwell would be disinclined to acts of cowardice.

They reach the edge of a vast forest. Dark Master encircles his servants with his arms, leaning on their superior physical strength.

"You are made vulnerable in this realm, Master," Rernard says quietly.

"Do you think to remind me that my immortality hangs in the balance while I breathe the foul, cool air of Between?" His breath steams, briefly obscuring his disciple's features.

Rernard bows his head. "I fear for you, Master. And Praile. Even Lazarus, as ugly as he is, is a fine high-demonic warrior."

"I will return with the blood of the Rare One coating my fingers, her heart warming my belly."

Rernard nods.

"How far to the fey sithen?"

The low demonic holding up Dark Master's left side cringes at the mention of the faeries.

"Days," Rernard says.

Dark Master scowls. "My abilities are greatly limited."

"There are humans who have the blood of the demonic in their veins. They will heed the call of your presence. You can assign them as your temporary servants. You will tire and need food as well as water. Possibly transportation."

"Yes-*yes*," Dark Master hisses, irritated by the reminder of his neediness Between.

"We will stay with you until you are well enough to travel."

Dark Master looks at Rernard until the demonic drops his eyes. "Return to Hades, Rernard." His quiet delivery rings with authority, and the low and high demonic instantly back away from the deadly timbre of his words.

Rernard blinks at the veiled command hiding within the compliment. After a moment, he replies with the only answer he can, "As you wish, Master."

They set him on the ground.

He does not watch their exit, but scans the landscape, where far in the distance, beyond rolling hills of emerald dotted with brightly colored trees, the twinkling lights of a city are visible.

That is where his servants will be.

Dark Master has many servants. Many more than those from Above.

* * *

Jenni

"WHAT ABOUT YOUR OTHER STUFF?" Jenni asks, surveying the lonely assortment of boxes and a couple of backpacks stuffed to the brim.

"Never planned on staying here forever. Not close to my parents because of… y'know."

Jenni cups a hand on the taller girl's shoulder and gives her a reassuring squeeze.

"Ow!"

She immediately releases her hold.

"You're strong," Devin says, rubbing the spot where Jenni's hand just was.

"Sorry."

Devin lifts a shoulder. "No big thing… but *damn.*"

"Bad word, Mama."

They look at Ella and smile.

"Thanks, little cop."

"Welcome," she says without missing a beat.

"Did you forget your dolly, Boo?"

A solemn nod is her answer.

Jenni smiles. "Can I see your dolly?"

The doll is not a practical choice, taking up half the backpack. When Ella finally extracts the whole thing, Jenni gasps. "Is that a Cabbage Patch?"

"Ah-huh! And look, she got brown eyes like me." She flips the ugly doll back and forth, so Jenni can't really tell the eye color.

"I haven't seen one of those in forever."

Devin gives a sad smile. "It was my mom's, believe it or not. She was in high school when they were popular and… well, I—it's not much, but it's what I got."

"I love 'er." Ella says, giving the doll a tight hug, effectively strangling its neck.

"Then she's coming with," Jenni says decisively.

Ella gives Jenni a horrified look. "Yeah! Duh!"

"Ella," Devin warns with a frown.

She shakes her head, hair flying with the vehement motion. "We don't leave Tiki."

Tiki.

Devin's exhale is soft and a few of her inky dyed hairs flutter around her jawline. "I can call my daycare tomorrow and let 'em know."

She shifts her weight, biting her bottom lip. "I feel bad, taking Ella and you out of your environment."

Devin shakes her head. "I'm not tied here. I can do whatever. I don't like giving crappy notice, though. Dale's been pretty cool."

She gave up her life here fast. But with Bray circling them like a shark scenting blood, choices are limited.

"Hey"—Jenni gives her a significant look—"tell Dale about Bray, give him an abbreviated version of events. He might think it's pretty cool that you saved McDonald's."

Jenni lifts a box off a threadbare harvest-gold shag rug, and they trudge up and down the flight of stairs a few times until all ten boxes are inside the car.

When Jenni's vehicle's packed, they grab Ella's booster seat from Devin's car and pile in.

"I'm paid up for rent for the rest of the month." Devin spares a pensive glance at her car. "My ride's too much of a beater for anyone to bother with."

Jenni nods. "Not sure how safe it is to go by my house."

"Aren't you, like, supernatural now?" Devin says in a whisper, as though they're co-conspirators.

Ella hears anyway, and chimes in from the backseat. "What?"

Laughing, Jenni starts the car. "I'm not a superhero."

She heads onto the main road and drives toward her condo at the edge of Port Townsend.

* * *

DEVIN SURVEYS the area as Jenni's condo complex comes into sight. "But you can run in your place, grab your crap, and get back to the car."

She thinks so. "I'll need a half hour, maybe less." Jenni doesn't say how her place doesn't really have much inside. Jenni was dying.

Jenni's way of coping was getting rid of all her things.

She steers the car down the winding lane that leads to some of the first condos built in PT in the late 60s. They were renovated in the early 90s and not touched since.

Clouds hover over the Olympic Mountains like shrouds of icy gray dust.

What Jenni likes about her condo is the space. The greenbelt. Her unit is fourth floor, and about twenty years ago, an elevator was installed. Over the years, seniors had moved in, wanting a no-maintenance, zero-climb place to call home.

Jenni is the only person under seventy years old living in the building.

The quiet of the surrounding woods that greets her as she climbs out of the VW is not unusual.

What *is* weird are the new senses that come alive once she's left the metal and glass of the vehicle behind. *How could I have lived twenty-eight years without sensing the presence of all this life?*

The smell of pine and more than a month's worth of decaying leaves tickles her nose. The taste of coming rain lights on her tongue.

Tears spring to her eyes. All of the sensory overload is almost too much.

Ella breaks through her jumbled thoughts. "You gonna get stuff, Jenni?"

Jenni nods, vision blurry. "Sure am." She turns, looking at the mother-daughter pair inside the car.

Her heart constricts painfully. "Stay here, no matter what."

Devin nods.

Satisfied, she revolves fully, sighting the elevator.

Jenni grins, sprinting up the entire four flights of steps instead.

* * *

JENNI LEAVES the bigger items like furniture and most of her clothes in the condo, but her pack is full of the essentials. The solid weight of the pack feels as though it weighs nothing.

Thanks to her new bod.

A single photo of her parents, taken during their trip to Point Defiance when she was an awkward teenager, is inside the top pocket of her pack. She could never leave it behind.

The rest of her stuff can stay. She'll come home someday and collect her other things. Having toiletries, that precious photo and enough underwear to last her— she doesn't know—*forever*, is critical. Her sheepish smile can't be helped.

A werewolf living in a condo. Hilarious.

Jenni's nostrils flare with a sudden familiar smell. Something metallic. She'd know it anywhere. *Blood.*

Goosebumps blanket her flesh.

Instantly, her eyes hunt the dark corners of the condo and strike shadows dancing under the front door. Something wet is seeping underneath the door.

Heart beating wildly against her ribcage, Jenni spins in the opposite direction, moving quickly to the sliding glass door. Another bennie of these old condos is generous patios for being outside with a cup of coffee or grilling steaks. She did that with Lance. *Prick.*

I bet the balcony's never been used like this before.

Jenni silently pulls the slider along its aluminum rails. She's grateful for having sprayed silicone on the tracks only last week—the thing had been sticking.

The door retracts smoothly, and Jenni pivots sideways, stepping through the open door and closing it behind her just as someone bursts through the entrance to her condo.

The eyes that meet her through the glass are familiar, yet not.

Bray steps over the body of a uniformed cop in the hall and all kinds of insights hit Jenni at the same time.

Her stomach tightens, threatening to evict the ice cream she ate a couple of hours ago. She can smell Bray through the glass, *sans* drugs—and he's like her.

A werewolf.

He's also killed a cop. And the final *ah-huh* fact: he's coming for her.

Jenni only has time to look over the rail at her car below, her lips moving in a silent prayer that Devin stayed put.

Then her hands are hitting the cold metal baluster that tops the cheap metal on the narrow, wide balcony as she leaps over the edge.

The fall would kill a human.

But Jenni's not that anymore.

Glass shatters, falling over her like hard, sharp rain, and she lands, her knees taking the brunt of the fall, and springs off the lawn easily.

Jenni runs.

Devin screams at something behind her.

Take a guess at who that is.

She doesn't turn, hitting the door handle and leaping inside. The car's engine is already running, or they wouldn't stand a chance.

Jenni shifts into reverse and floors it.

Something lands on the hood, and Jenny's face jerks up from the steering column. Bray's slowly spinning green eyes lock with hers from only two feet away, his talons having pierced the hood of her car.

Fuck *this.*

Cranking the wheel to the left, she almost upends his ass, but one talon stays embedded in the metal.

The car spins out with her foot rammed against the floorboard and her arms spinning the wheel.

Solid German engineering, Jenni has time to think before the momentum flings Bray far and wide from the hood, tumbling in a spinning arc before landing on the asphalt.

Ella screams.

"Not now, Boo!" Devin screams back.

Bray stands in a jerking, zombie-like lurch.

Holy crow.

Jenni suppresses a hysterical giggle, slamming the gearshift into drive while simultaneously depressing the accelerator. The engine roars in response, leaping forward like a coked-up frog. When the car has sped ahead Jenni yells, "Is he following us?"

She can't feel her fingers and loosens her grip on the wheel.

"Yes!" Devin shouts.

She tightens her fingers again.

"No," Ella says, and Jenni can hear her twisting in her belt to look.

"Which is it?" Jenni asks, frantic.

"The bad man is far away," Ella says.

Devin's clinging to the grip handle against the passenger door. "Don't stop, Jenni."

Her jaw aches from clenching her teeth so hard. "Hell no."

Ella doesn't correct their language, and Jenni doesn't stop the car until the low-fuel light comes on over two hours later, her body stiff from holding herself rigid for so long.

A neon sign, creepily blinking like a sleepy eye, has all the letters to spell *Gas* but reads *as* instead.

Jenny hops the steep incline leading up into the archaic gas station and slows the rabbit to a crawl by the pair of forty-year-old pumps. Looking more closely at the sign, she sees it's actually *Olalla Gas.*

A crooked open sign swings in the chilly breeze of late October. Olalla is just a hop skip and a jump from Tacoma. She doesn't like the in-between towns.

Jenni swings the driver's-side door wide, narrowly missing the pumps. She turns around to tell Devin to stay put again and she depresses her thumb on the auto locks. They snap into place, locking the car from the inside.

Good.

She studies the old-fashioned pumps and flicks up a lever. Leaving the tank to fill up, she turns her attention to the convenience part of Olalla Gas and walks toward the storefront.

Without meeting the eyes of the pimply clerk, Jenny grabs twenty bucks' worth of food, three liters of water, pays, and walks back outside.

The nozzle clicks off with a loud snap. She removes her debit card from the pay slot and sticks the nozzle back into the gas pump cradle.

The interior of the car is like a tomb. Ella is asleep, and Devin's in some stage of shock.

Jenni's not sure which, because she's in shock, too. They sit at the pumps for a full minute.

Finally, Jenni dumps the bag of food on the floor and takes out a water. She chugs half then wipes her mouth with a hand that hardly shakes.

"Jenni?" Devin speaks for the first time.

"Yeah." Jenni is staring in the rearview mirror, expecting to see more werewolves chasing them—because this has been a hell of a last twenty-four hours, and that would fit right in.

"I'm sorry."

They look at each other as Jenni hits her blinker, signaling a right-hand turn.

Click, click, click.

"I didn't know Bray was a werewolf."

Jenni looks both ways before pulling out onto Highway 101, saying nothing about the tears streaking down Devin's cheeks.

"The world's full of surprises," Jenni finally remarks.

"*Ella.*" Devin's voice is filled with the fear of enlightenment.

Jenni's eyes flick to the little girl sleeping peacefully in the backseat.

A girl who they both realize, might be half-werewolf.

CHAPTER 22

ADI

"*T*hat was the grossest thing I've ever seen."

Slash grunts, licking each finger clean of the succulent meat—the first *real* meat Adi knows he's eaten since the chicken that Cyn gave him at the Singer compound.

The surprise appearance of his wolf, three days from the full moon was a painful, brutal change, but as a Red, he recovers like a champion.

Adi shakes her head at her mate's ginormous appetite. It's pretty impressive, really. This is the third whole chicken he's consumed since the trolls beat Della into the ground. Adi's had her fill, and her stomach doesn't feel that hot. What with the whole TV screen of Della getting pummeled—and she supposes, the new reality of pregnancy—she's a little squeamish.

Slash hesitates in picking up the last drumstick, and Adi's sure by his suddenly somber expression he's remembering the trolls' grief as they buried the one who sacrificed himself for Adi.

Guilt floods her even as her hand covers her stomach. *I'm so grateful to be alive.* And that their whelp is safe, even *with* all the chaotic bullshit going on around them.

Now they're indebted to the trolls.

"I didn't know there *were* trolls." Adi watches bright embers from the fire kick up toward the sky like haphazard fireflies.

Slash gives a low laugh. "I've been alive nearly three centuries, and they were underneath our noses all this time." He shakes his head.

Adi cups her palm around her lips to keep her words for him alone. "Shouldn't we have smelled them?" *Because, boy, do they reek.*

Not that she would say.

Trolls are a supernatural species that have some weird shit going on. Like, how they could be violent one minute, but gentle the next? They're seriously the homeliest creatures Adi's ever laid eyes on, but as she's gotten to know them, their looks melt into the background.

Kiern, their leader, explained Della's history, and what really interested Adi was how there really was a Hansel and Gretel.

Della killed the witch from the story.

But according to the trolls, Della was even worse than the last witch.

Kiern strides toward them, and Adi sits up straighter in her makeshift stump chair. She can't help but respond that way when he's around. He's got a presence, a commanding air around him.

He's a good troll, Kiern told them.

Like Adi would know the difference.

"Red. Female." He nods first to Slash then to Adi. "Della will soon be ash, to fertilize our great woods." His expressive eyes light on the greenery surrounding them.

Adi squints through the smoke at the elevated pyre. Della's body is a charred, smoldering mass on top. The goop of her body is still sinking into the wood pilings that hold her up and the stones stacked underneath her body.

Burn, baby, burn. Adi shudders.

Kiern smiles at the trolls' handiwork and the expression is a horror of twisted, meaty lips and square yellowish teeth. Although he is gentle, Adi can still close her eyes and see the clubs driving up and down like engine pistons on Della's body until they became bloody stumps of battered wood and what was left of the witch was a mangled, unrecognizable mass.

Her stench fills the forest, but the trolls' magic exits the vapors of her remains in a direct pipeline through the trees, sucking up the residual smoke that lingers like a vacuum into the sky.

"So she stole your magic *and* kept you prisoner here?"

Kiern nods. "I am sure your male has explained the oddity that no other nose-driven species is aware of our existence?"

Slash pushes away the handhewn wooden bowl, dark from a thousand meals and smooth from a thousand spoons, and leans back in a hacked-out tree trunk that's now a chair—a loose match to the one Adi sits on.

"I did mention how odd it was to Adi."

Kiern folds his beefy arms, covered in a downy coating of hair almost resembling the wolfen form of their males. He studies the two of them for a few seconds. "To effectively keep us prisoners in our own woods, she needed to hide our presence. Della possessed powerful spells, but she was trapped in a crone's body—forever—unable to venture from these woods. And she is not the only witch who seeks out Troll dens. Our magic is powerful, and they aren't especially worried with what they must do to suppress us."

"Or butchering parents to take their kids."

Kiern nods, leveling his gaze at Adi. She's mesmerized by his brilliant eyes. Though they're a deep, rich emerald, they glow as if they possess their own light. "Yes. And that would have released her to do far more damage. But because of your bravery, she could not."

Heat covers Adi's face, and she self-consciously places her hands on her hot cheeks. "I thought I'd nailed her, but she's some kind of zombie or something."

Slash laughs, touching her thigh briefly before moving his hand away.

"There is no such thing as living dead. A human fable." A dark chuckle escapes him. "A silly one at that." He meets their eyes. "A powerful sorceress must be ended by fire to be well and truly dead. Until that occurred, a part of her still lived." His heavy knuckles pass over his chin, rasping at a square jaw loaded with dark stubble. He inclines his head in Adi's direction. "It's not your fault. You couldn't have known."

That doesn't stop Adi from feeling like she wasn't thorough enough.

"Or taking her head."

She and Slash look at Kiern. His solemn expression tells her all she needs to know.

"I don't think I was up to *that*." Adi scoops her wet hair back then lets it fall behind her with a dull thump at her back. Her hand falls to her rolling stomach again.

She's taken two showers in one day. Thanks to Slash and his insta-change, she has a bruise on her ass and was knee-deep in the human layer he sloughed off with his rapid-fire shift. Adi was forced to go into the bitch's house again and to wash off all the yuck.

Her fingers tighten on her unicorn backpack. She'll be damn glad to get the hell out of here.

A huge thundering crash has them jumping out of their stump chairs. Adi's eyes dance over everything, coming to a screeching halt at Della's cottage.

It's caving in on itself.

With a wildly beating heart, Adi frowns.

Kiern grins.

Slash moves closer to her until their bodies touch.

As Adi watches, the wood roof, covered in moss and forest debris, folds and falls into a giant hole that's opened below the foundation like a huge mouth.

The gross contents of the cellar where Slash had hung like a slab of meat erupt, pouring eyeballs, organs, and the random brain out of the hole like a slow-moving geyser of bloody sludge.

Adi clutches her stomach, slapping her other hand over her mouth to keep from upchucking.

A moment later, the soup from within the cellar is a swamp of decay from which a great tree begins to rise.

All the things that made it a house turn into something else. Something natural.

Adi licks suddenly dry lips, her hands slowly falling to her sides.

The black pot-bellied stove that had a screaming tea kettle on its top cants to one side then falls over onto the forest floor at the base of the massive tree. Thickening and deeply furrowed bark beginning to carve up the sides of the massive trunk like brown water streaking upward.

The iron door of the stove flops open on squeaking hinges. The dark, cavernous insides reek of burnt logs.

The stove sinks into the ground as though it's fallen in quicksand, and the forest topography rolls over it like a giant emerald hand that scoops the stove from the surface, then a living shroud of lichen, moss, leaves, and needles remove it from sight. Where the stove landed, elegant, lime-green stems spear the ground as they rise, slowly opening to reveal deep blooming throats of pure black, gleaming like dark, sightless oblong eyes in the woods.

"Oh, my Moon," Adi breathes.

"It's beautiful, isn't it?" Kiern says in his melodious voice.

Adi nods, turning to him. "Why is this happening?" Not that she misses that horrible cottage.

"Her magic fades, daughter of the moon."

She blinks. "I've never heard that expression." She thinks it's beautiful, poetic.

Kiern's smile is wistful. "You are young."

"That's what he says." Adi jerks a thumb at Slash, who chuckles.

"Laugh it up, guys."

Kiern lifts a hand, but Adi only sees it in the periphery

because she's utterly transfixed by Della's house giving way to the spectacular tree.

"What is this... becoming?" Her eyes go everywhere—there's so much to look at.

Kiern has come to stand beside Slash. "This is our home."

The giant tree continues to grow and fill out in both size and detailing.

Adi giggles as the ground swallows a white toaster expelled from the soupy hole. In the next breath, star jasmine rises from the spot, twining up the base of the tree. Its petite flowers burst open along the swirling vine, filling the forest with sweet fragrance.

Adi shakes her head in wonder. "I don't know what's real and what's fake."

Slash squeezes her against him. "What does your nose tell you?"

"My nose told me all kinds of crap about Della, too, and I couldn't have been more wrong."

Slash tucks her head beneath his chin. "We both were. Della was like a spider, Adrianna, and we were caught in her web."

"Consider yourselves fortunate. There've been many before you, many who did not love as you do, did not have just the exact combination of circumstances to cause Della to put her plan into motion."

Adi gazes up at the tree, which is nearly as high as the tops of the other trees.

Finally, she has to step back because the trunk has expanded to where they stand.

Kiern gives a delighted laugh that is really strange coming from a troll.

"What?" Adi's awestruck.

She's never heard laughter so light, so free, so happy. But his is all of that.

The other trolls gather around, many with their faces streaked by tears of happiness.

"How long has it been since Della made you prisoner in your own woods?" Slash asks quietly.

The top of the tree shoots through the gap in the forest as though the space were custom-made for it.

The apex of the trunk appears to shimmer like a mirage of brown, tripling as green leaves burst from all sides with a crisp, whistling hiss, like knives of emerald released from their sheaths.

"Beautiful," Adi says softly, having the sudden urge to reach up and touch the new bright-green growth.

Slash nods, but sweeps her backward with a strong arm just as a massive root erupts from the undulating ground beneath them.

"For one thousand years, we've been prisoners."

Adi gasps, turning to the much-taller troll. His eyes don't spin like a Were's, but they're no less captivating. The ethereal shade of blue that outlines green irises stares inquisitively from a brutally fashioned face.

She swallows, suddenly aware that a magical tree is growing in a forest where a killer witch once lived—and Adi's standing next to the first troll she's ever seen in her life.

A violent troll.

His gnarled brows knot as he watches expressions morph on her face. "Don't be afraid."

"I'm okay." She takes a deep, stabilizing breath. *Slash is with me.*

They turn their attention back to the tree.

A roughly rectangular door has formed at the base. It is integral to the tree itself, standing at a height and width Adi thinks would be perfect to accommodate a troll.

"She cut this tree down with her magic. But that is the trouble with magics that alter the natural order. Once they depart, that which was before, returns."

"A thousand years," Slash repeats in a quiet voice. Adi can hear the ring of grief in his tone. To be a natural creature here and have your home stolen by some whacko?

"We will celebrate," Kiern says, breaking into Adi's thoughts and clapping Slash on the back.

He stumbles forward and turns, wearing the first real smile she's seen since the Della mess.

"We want to be a part of your... celebrations," Slash hesitates, and Adi fills the void with "We'd love to."

She gives Kiern a big smile and discreetly elbows Slash.

He frowns, and she turns her smile to him, which she knows damn well is a baring of teeth.

"Yes, all right."

Kiern gives another whack on Slash's back. "I don't think they know their own strength," he mutters as soon as Kiern moves toward the tight cluster of trolls gazing at the tree.

Adi shakes her head. "Nope. But they're good." Her

hands skate up and down her bare arms, trying to warm them. "They killed Della."

Slash nods.

"We can stay and be polite, but I will say that it's a pretense. They killed our enemy, and they want us to share in their happiness." He turns Adi to face him. "However, I will be traveling the nearly seventy miles to the Northwestern pack. Tonight. With my mate at my side."

Adi opens her mouth, and he kisses her softly, saying against her lips, "No arguments. You carry our whelp. I will protect my family."

Slash covers her stomach with his palm. And Adi lays her head against his chest. "Okay, ya boss."

He kisses the top of her head. "They've fed us, and you showered."

"I smell pretty good for an illusion," she quips.

Slash tilts her chin upward, caressing her lower back with his fingers, and Adi tries to ignore the smell and sights of the tree continuing to grow all around them.

"That's the thing. I believe every bit of the witch's illusion to lure supernaturals to her dwelling was real."

Adi feels her frown, pulling slightly away from Slash and searching his stern face. "Then why can her house just disintegrate, and the trolls magic takes over?"

"I don't know." Slash's scar is bright-red today. Adi has noticed that after a shift, it seems freshly made, as if it has to heal again for the very first time.

"But I know I don't want to stay here any longer than we must, Adrianna."

"Fine. But they killed Della."

His lips pull at the corners. "You keep mentioning that."

She crosses her arms. "Well, they get a pass for like... forever. She was a nasty skank ho bitch."

Slash laughs, wrapping his arm around her.

"What?" she asks, lightly punching his side. "You're not going to hassle me about my expression or about how *young* I am?"

He squeezes her shoulder once. "No."

"Why not?"

Slash leans over her as they walk slowly toward the newly formed tree. "Because I heartily agree."

"You 'heartily agree'?" Adi laughs. "Oh Slash. And you tell me *my* expressions are weird."

He doesn't reply, but Adi loves the smile that creeps over his face. A rare occurrence.

CHAPTER 23

TESSA

"*I*s this the last of our gear?" Tessa asks, cataloging the pathetic little bit they still have with a single sweep of her eyes.

After the Suburban 4x4-ing through the rainforest and getting stuck in the river then being hauled, beaten, tied, and thoroughly soaked, Tessa has a backpack with maybe three outfits and zero cash.

Things aren't looking up. "Dammit," Tessa mutters, dropping her ass into the nearest chair and flinging her long legs out.

"I don't know," Laz replies casually, "I still have my human costumes."

Tessa sits up straighter in the plush chair and frowns. "Human clothes?"

"Yes," Laz replies, running a finger over the neat pile of jeans and T-shirts. Each one has been precisely folded, and he plucks the entire pile from the same place Tessa had gotten hers, a low table by the front door to the cabin.

"Are you saying..." Tessa closes her mouth then opens

it again. "Are you saying you *didn't* wear clothes in Hades?"

Laz faces her. "No. Clothing is unnecessary." His expression goes far away.

Tessa laughs. *He's got to be kidding.* Then she remembers how he always seems to eventually run around without clothes. Somehow. With all that they'd gone through, the reason for his random nudity hadn't occurred to her. It gives new meaning to "being comfortable in your own skin." She smirks.

"It is very warm."

Her smile grows wider. "Clearly—it's hell."

"Yes." A ghost of a smile plays over his full lips, and his skin darkens to that lightly sunburned look that seems to follow the varied range of his emotions.

"You know, Laz?"

"Hmm?" His eyes peg her like a moth to a board, and matching heat rises between her legs, at her core. From her heart. That last steals her breath more than anything before it ever could.

She has protected herself without fail. And in many ways, more than the physical. Tessa figured there would never be a male for her.

Now there is. And what a male he is: Funny. Hot —protective.

A demon.

She frowns. Then finishes her observation. "You're not a subtle guy. I can tell when you're all lusty—I can *see* when you're emotional."

He nods, unperturbed by her insights.

Tessa crosses her arms, flopping backward in the chair

again.

Laz's eyes hood, never leaving her form. "The demonic do not have need of subtlety. What we need, we take. What we want, we claim."

The slits of his eyes darken further.

"Is that so?" Tessa asks coyly, widening her knees.

Laz's skin flushes red, his eyes widening and flipping to inky discs. "Yes," he hisses, and his forked tongue flicks out.

Her breath quickens, and they move at the same time, crashing against each other in a tangle of body parts. His fingers thread her still-damp hair, jerking her so tightly against his body that she can't breathe—or move. She doesn't want to. His tongue plunges inside her mouth, and Tessa moans, grinding her pelvis against his, feeling his hard length—and his need for her.

Laz caresses her with his tongue, causing her to shiver at the delicate, erotic stroke of wet heat.

A loud rapping sounds at the door.

Breathlessly, Tessa pulls away with a groan. "Maybe they'll go away."

Lazy spirals of steam leak from Laz's mouth as he chuckles. "Not without special encouragement."

"No, you don't," she says, poking a finger in his tight abs.

He smiles, and his eyes pale to glacial blue, like an iceberg getting ready to calve. Laz's beautiful gaze sweeps her as though he's starving and Tessa's a tasty morsel.

"I have clothes on now. They should consider themselves fortunate," Laz chimes from behind her as she charges toward the door and places her hand on the cold bronze of the lever.

Their eyes lock.

He slaps his palm on the door just as she would open it, and Tessa gazes up at him from beneath a heavily muscled arm, core throbbing from their unfinished business.

"Maybe it is that Lanarre bastard, Neil?"

That's cold water on her libido. *Neil.*

"I heard that, foul demonic!" Neil says from outside the door.

A slashing grin appears on his face. "Then be appraised of my desire to have an excuse to end you." Laz covers the door handle, and Tessa releases the knob as he jerks it wide, whipping her behind him as he does.

"Laz!" Tessa almost stumbles.

"As though my Redemptive would face an unknown foe."

Moon.

Drek fills the doorway, staring at them as if they're apparitions.

"Hi," Tessa says, trying to tramp down on whatever residual lust might be scented. But she gives up immediately. Too much to get rid of. Drek will just have to scent it.

Laz remains ominously silent, fingers clinging to the top of the wood casement that surrounds the door.

Drek's eyes hover over Laz's casual stance of hanging around the threshold as though meeting old friends.

"We need to discuss some things."

Laz swings backward, gifting Neil with an expression

filled with warning. Steam erupts from his mouth, nose, and ears.

"Laz," Tessa says.

He grabs her hand and hauls her backward, pushing her safely behind the protection of his body.

Drek enters, followed by Bowen—if Tessa remembers the name of his right-hand wolf correctly.

Bowen moves through the threshold, closing the door in Neil's face, Tessa's happy to note.

Laz notices, giving a slight smile to the other male.

"Let's sit down."

Tessa's nerves flare. Drek had promised they could go, that he was working on a solution. *Sitting down* sounds like *delay* to her.

Being sexually frustrated while scared out of her wits isn't a good frame of mind to be in, either. But she follows Laz, plopping down on a sectional couch in the center of the room.

"Where are we?" The idea suddenly occurs to Tessa that they've been in this cabin from the beginning.

"It is a courtship cabin."

Tessa blanches. "*This* is where Tahlia was supposed to stay?"

Drek gives a curt nod of confirmation.

"Where is Tahlia?" Tessa's brows pull together. If it's possible for a Were to pale, Drek's doing a stand-up job.

"That is what I have come with. In part," Drek admits.

Tessa wipes suddenly damp palms on her black form-fitting pants. "Huh. You're making me nervous, Drek."

"Tahlia is my chosen, my intended."

Tessa doesn't tell him there was hardly anything about

the way Tahlia was treated that would have allowed her to feel that way.

She can't enlighten him now. Tahlia's gone, Tessa can't help her, and she especially can't do squat holed up with the Hoh pack.

"Okay?" Tessa asks, and Laz looks at her. *I guess I'm rude.* "I mean, I feel bad for Tahlia, too. I want her safe, but our situation sucks. Laz and I want to go."

"I want you to go, too. Believe me." Drek gives them hard eyes. "But I must do something before you go, or I cannot take after Tahlia."

Laz tenses.

This is so not good. "What?" Tessa asks, but the word drops out of her mouth as a thread of her normal voice.

"Laz must partake in blood sacrifice."

Tessa jumps to her feet, upending the side table. Bowen reactively reaches for her and Laz slaps his chest, sending Bowen flying six feet backward. He lands on his ass, sliding across the polished floor toward the door.

"No—you took a blood oath!" Tessa screams.

Bowen flips over to his hands and knees, raises his chin, and sights Laz.

He goes wolfen.

Fuck. Tessa quarter-changes without a thought.

"Stop this," Drek commands.

"Lycan power does not move me." Laz inserts his body protectively in front of Tessa, and she lays her head between his shoulder blades, careful not to constrain him with further touching.

"They mean to drain you of all your blood, Laz. Short of death, but it's a barbaric torture."

"I am demonic."

Her voice shakes, but she forces the reply from between her lips. "And they are Lanarre. They'll kill you."

Bowen comes at Laz, and Drek checks him with a swift clothesline to the torso. His teeth snap, and spittle flies from his gnashing and growling, but Laz remains unmoved.

"Why does Laz receive our worst punishment?" Tessa pleads. "He is not a criminal—he saved you."

Bowen's face shortens, his teeth receding until every bit of him is back to his human form. The display of control is impressive, and Tessa wonders briefly if he has royal blood, as well.

Still, his eyes remain silver as they narrow to razors at Laz. "That's quite a punch, demonic."

Laz nods. "We are strong. But I am stronger still, when defending my Redemptive."

The Lanarre just stare at him like he grew a second head.

"Laz," Tessa begins as gently as possible, "they don't care about me being your Redemptive. The Hoh pack want you to hurt for what happened. Someone has to be held accountable, and because you're demonic..." Tessa bites her lip, her vision blurring with unshed tears.

"If I don't punish him, it will look as though any outsider could gain entry, kill our people, and get off without a consequence. That kind of action, or inaction, would have me defending my throne to all comers. He will not be killed, obviously. I have sworn a blood oath."

No one would want the Moon herself to call blood debt.

Tessa doesn't realize she'd closed her eyes. She opens them, lasering a stare of stark disdain on Drek. "So let me get this straight. The Blood Sacrifice is because you're worried about your power base getting fucked?" With all her restraint, she barely resists the urge to pull her hair out.

Drek rubs a hand over his face. "Not exactly. It's about me not wanting to hunt down Tahlia and come back to…" He jerks his head toward the closed door.

"Oh." *Anarchy.* Her eyes shift to the door where Neil "stands guard" just outside. She shifts her weight, looking between Drek and Bowen.

Drek opens his palms in supplication. "I must do this to save the pack, Tessa. In the end, it is not about me, but about all of us."

"Even the bitch, Tanya?" Tessa knows she's baiting Drek, but can't seem to help herself.

And, Tessa's still on Team Tahlia.

Drek's exhale is weary. "Even her."

"Okay. Say Laz agrees to let every Lanarre Were take a bite out of him? What happens next?" Tears boil over, hot lines of wet anger streaming down her face.

Tessa doesn't know how Laz senses her despair, but he pulls her from behind himself and cups her head, sucking her against his body.

Some horrible, tight knot hitches in her throat, then she's sobbing. Helpless wracking shakes her, and Tessa clutches Laz around his hard flanks. "I don't want you hurt. I've just found you," she chokes out.

"I will prevail, my Redemptive."

She tips her head back, searching eyes gone to the

color of azure seas. "I don't want you to be hurt, Laz—I love you."

She covers her mouth with the admission, and ignoring Bowen and Drek, he pulls her hand away, moving his fingertips to each side of her face. "I am demonic. It takes much to truly harm us."

She searches his eyes like an archeologist at the perfect dig and manages to gasp, "Don't you die."

Laz shakes his head, thumbing away her remaining tears.

But Tessa's stomach drops at the fleeting expression that's washing across his eyes.

Uncertainty.

CHAPTER 24

JENNI

"Now what?" Devin asks in a subdued voice. Jenni has the windshield wipers on max. Water droplets fling away in a torrent as the skinny blades flip back and forth over the slick glass.

She flicks her eyes at Devin then back to the road. Devin is slouched low in the seat, while Ella's gentle snoring lulls them both into semi-dazed, surreal complacency.

But Jenni knows she doesn't have the luxury of succumbing to that. Something deep inside tells her she doesn't have much time.

What she's become will want to get out. *To be.*

A single tear slips up and over the bottom of her eyelid, and she battens down the emotional hatches. Jenni doesn't have time for the pity party she wants to throw for herself.

Her eyes shift to the rearview mirror. In the backseat, a tiny cherub face sleeps. Dusty rose colors her chubby cheeks, and Ella's little hands are curled around Tiki, the Cabbage Patch doll.

"I guess we just get some distance."

"Then what?" Devin asks.

"I don't know," Jenni admits. "But the little I do know tells me that Bray's going to be a huge problem."

Jenni can sense Devin's emotions. It might be a scenting thing—she just doesn't know.

Dammit, Adi.

She shouldn't curse the girl that gave her a second chance, but Jenni doesn't know what the fuck she's doing. Yesterday, Jenni was saving lives while her own ebbed away.

Today she's running *for* her life. Along with a couple she's towed along.

"I have enough money," she says, swinging her gaze to Devin.

Devin's bloodshot eyes look back at her without an ounce of excitement. "Okay."

"Did Bray see Ella?"

"I don't think so."

Jenni bites her lip, using the right lane, she keeps the speedometer at a steady sixty miles per hour. That's all she needs: a cop to notice her and pull them over.

Devin turns toward her, the faux-leather upholstery crinkling with the motion. "What are you thinking?"

Jenni decides to tell Devin her speculations, even though they're sort of awful. "I can smell everything now." She looks at Devin, and their eyes lock. Then driving forces her to face the road again. "I'm betting that means Bray the Bully can, too."

Devin doesn't laugh. "Does that mean he smelled Ella —through the closed car?" A note of hysteria creeps into the edges of her voice. "I don't know about that. Say he could smell her—so what?"

Jenni really doesn't want to tell her this next part but forces herself to. "I knew that you and Ella were related."

Devin's eyes widen. "How?"

Jenni grips the steering wheel harder. "Because there's an undertone." Her exhale is a frustrated huff. "Like a familial connection for lack of a better term. And when I met Bray this second time, I *knew* he was the dad."

"Okay," Devin begins slowly, "say he *could* smell her. Then he'd know he's a dad?" Disbelief is thick in her voice.

"Yeah. Ella's dad."

"I have a daddy?"

Jenni's shoulders slump.

Devin turns around, straddling the section separating the driver's and passenger's sides. "Yes, baby. You couldn't be here without a mama *and* a daddy."

"I wanna see 'im." She rubs her eyes with fists that still have the baby she used to be at the edges.

"Hands outta your eyes, Boo."

Big sigh.

Jenni smiles. Despite the stressful circumstances, there's something about a child that makes her feel lighter. Of course, that thought brings the next one: she's responsible for Devin and Ella. There's no amount of justification that takes that feeling from her shoulders.

"So what does that mean—for us?" Devin asks, voice quivering.

"It means we ditch this car and find a place that makes it tough for Bray to get us—you."

"But why not be with Daddy?" Ella asks in a tiny voice.

"Because he's a bad man," Devin replies loudly. And Jenni knows fear is the strength behind the statement. Fear for her child.

Ella's brown eyes meet Jenni's in the rearview. "Is my daddy a bad man, Jenni?"

Tough truths today. "Yes, he was the man who chased me, remember?"

"When we got your stuff at the canda?"

"Condo, baby."

"Uh-huh."

Jenni keeps her eyes fixed on the road. "Yes, that was him."

"Why?"

Devin turns, facing Jenni, and laughs. "It's not the terrible twos, by the way. Somebody got that wrong. Dead wrong."

She laughs. "I think there's probably plenty of challenging ages for kids." Her smile fades. Jenni can't have kids. All that radiation killed her female machinery. Oh well, there's no guy. And she's going to be howling at a moon shortly anyway.

God.

"You look sad, Jen-Jen."

"I am," she says. And as if admitting the emotion makes it worse, the tears begin to flow.

Damn, damn, damn.

A sign off the highway says Gig Harbor in reflective white font with a green background.

Jenni's got to rest. They've been driving for a couple of hours, and she's exhausted. She throws on the blinker and guides the car to an on ramp. The gentle incline moves to an overpass, and she catches sight of a Little Oscar's pizza place.

"Hot and fast," it says.

Good enough for me.

* * *

"I KNOW this is super tacky, but can I just say food tastes better when you don't pay for it?" Devin groans, pulling a piece of cheese that's stretched between the thick square of pizza and tipping her head back to catch the entire steaming wad on her tongue.

Jenni doesn't answer for a second because she'd too busy licking grease off her fingers then hunting around for the napkins.

Devin pops the glove box, and about a hundred bounce out in a flutter of white paper.

"Yummy!" Ella says, as slurping pipes through from the back seat. "Mama gives me pop."

"Don't get used to it, kiddo," Devin says from the front, mumbling around a mouthful of food. She glances at Jenni's empty box.

Yeah, that's right.

Jenni consumed the entire pizza. Of course, she ordered four, plus bread sticks with plenty of that marinara sauce.

She digs into the second box.

"Leave some for the pigs," Devin exclaims with a laugh.

Jenni ignores her, swigging icy Coke down the hatch and attacking her pizza again. She can't remember needing food this badly since—hell—her growth spurt at twelve years old.

Her parents said she was a five-feet-tall locust. Jenni smiles around a folded half slice crammed into her mouth.

"Oh, my God—are you *okay?*" Devin sounds worried.

She turns. "Yeah." Jenni's cheeks are distended, but she manages to belt out the answer, swallow the entire load down, and take another guzzle of pop.

Ella slings her arms over the seat between them. "Mama called you a hog." She makes the pig sound. *Oink-oink.*

Out of the mouths of babes.

Unable to refute the observation, Jenni laughs. "Yes, I guess I am." She picks up another piece, making short work of box number two.

"You're not seriously gonna have another slice, Jenni."

"Jen-Jen needs to eat a lot a food. Because she's a woof, too." Ella smiles.

Jenni smiles back. It's official—she loves Ella. Devin's not too bad, either.

Now, if they can just elude Bray.

* * *

"THAT WAS DELICIOUS," Jenni says, tapping her belly. She's not hungry anymore, but she can't say she's *full* exactly.

A burp erupts. One of the kind boys did in middle school.

Oops.

"Gross, Jen-Jen!"

Yes, *gross.* A silly grin spreads over her face. "Excuse me," she says demurely, giving a sheepish dip of her chin.

Devin can't stop grinning, either. "I don't think I've ever seen anyone consume almost three pizzas at one time. It's a *thing.*"

Jenni meets Devin's eyes. "Yeah," she replies softly, thinking back to all the weight she lost during chemo. Jenni swears the treatment made her sicker than the cancer. Doesn't seem possible.

But it was the reality.

Jenni looks around at people going in and out of the strip mall where the Little Caesar's pizza dive is at the corner.

The neon sign still says open, but it's getting later, and even Ella, who is draped over the middle, swings her little arms as her eyes droop.

"Ready to find a place to camp out?"

Ella sits up straight. "Yes, yes!" she bounces, reenergized.

Jenni turns the engine over and backs out of the parking space.

"Toss these empty boxes, Devin." She pulls up at a dumpster partially hidden by a copse of trees. Devin opens the door and slides out then tosses the empty boxes inside.

"That's a lot of pizza," Ella says.

"I'm a hungry wolf."

Ella gives her a speculative glance. "When do you make a furry?"

Too soon. Out loud, Jenni admits, "Not sure but if all those stories are true, probably at the full moon."

Ella looks up at the sky, twilight a promise. "Don't see any moon."

"Clouds, rain, and all that stuff sometimes hide the moon."

Jenni can feel the moon like a dull pulse at the back of her head. *Thump, thump, thump.*

Devin hops back in, shuts the door, and hits the lock with a decisive smack of the metal knob.

"That gonna matter, if the moon's hiding?" Ella asks.

"What?" Devin asks, looking between the two of them.

"No," Jenni says, her stomach tightening, "I don't think it will matter if the moon is hiding or not."

Jenni thinks the moon being full is probably all it will take. She has to take measures. Measures to protect these innocent girls.

"Let's get," Jenni says. Spying a sign for gas, she takes a right-hand turn, heading toward a promised convenience store.

"Arletta 3 miles," the sign says.

Strange name.

* * *

A SIGN SWINGS in the breeze, night nipping at the heels of day.

It once said Arletta, but one of the letters has faded so badly, it's fancy guesswork to make it out.

Jenni steps out of the car and stretches until all the bones of her spine pop. Landing on her heels, she asks

Devin to gas up and walks toward the convenience store door.

It's a squat building, probably dating to the 1950s. It's tired, but as the bell tinkles while she struggles through a glass swinging door that sticks, a middle-aged gal sits up straighter and has a ready smile. Becky, her nametag reads. Slim, with weathered dark-blond hair, she's smoking a cigarette. To Jenni's senses, the acrid vapor is an insult, and she gives a thin smile. It's about all she has in her at the moment.

"What can I do for ya?"

"Just gassing up," Jenni flicks a thumb behind her, vaguely indicating her car and hidden passengers.

"Right," she goes back to working on a crossword. Jenni takes in the obvious personal touches, such as a glass lamp filled with seashells.

Her gaze roams the indistinct creams, whites, and ivories of found beach treasures, and an instant idea forms. "Pretty shells."

Becky looks up, and Jenni sees her eyes are her best feature, a pure, rich hazel green. Big flakes of brown are sprinkled throughout rich green irises. Reminds her a little of Adi.

"Yeah." She smiles again. "They're local. Me and the kids—well, when the kids were small anyways—collected all those. Love 'em." She leans as far as she can reach and turns the switch on for the lamp. A dim LED bulb brightens the interior of the store and stands like a small beacon in the window.

"Ya got lucky, I was just gonna shut 'er down before you came. We close early here outside of town."

Right, Gig Harbor.

"Where was the beach you found these shells at?"

"Oh, Forest Beach. Horsehead Bay area," she says with a dismissive wave.

Jenni smiles politely. She'll GPS that later. Where there's a beach, there might be public restrooms and a remote place to camp out. Thank God Devin brought blankets and a Disney Princess sleeping bag for Ella.

"That's great," Jenni says, then easily lies, though she's always been a scrupulously honest person. Before. "My niece is with me, thought I'd take her and my sister there tomorrow."

Becky smiles.

Jenni shifts her gaze away, quickly locating the candy, beef jerky, and tons of other snacks that the fifth and sixth pizza she went back in and bought won't cover tomorrow.

She pays for the supplies and gas and is turning to leave when Becky calls out.

"Hey."

"Yes?" Jenni asks, hand on the solid metal bar bisecting the glass door.

"You from around here?"

Jenni's heart begins to pound for no reason at all. For every reason. "No."

"I didn't think so." Becky smiles again.

Why does it look like her teeth are a little too *sharp?*

Jenni walks out without looking back, ignoring the tinkling bell, and strides to the car. She pops the latch on the trunk and carefully puts her haul inside before closing the lid securely.

She rounds the car, eyes stumbling over the gouges in

the hood for a long second, then scoots behind the wheel, heartbeat thumping erratically.

Jenni feels ridiculous. It's like she's seeing a monster around every corner.

Get a grip.

Devin looks at her. "You look like a ghost walked over your grave."

"Kinda," Jenni says, but doesn't elaborate.

"We got a plan?" Devin's dark-blond eyebrows lift, a startling contrast to the faded black dye job on her head.

Jenni nods. "We're going to camp out at a beach. Regroup."

She doesn't say anything about the wolfish grin from Becky inside the convenience store.

Devin nods, and Jenni checks on Ella, who's pretending with her dolly, telling her how the werewolves come even when the moon hides.

Jenni's hiding from the werewolves who chase her, Devin, and Ella. She's hiding from the moon.

Just hiding.

CHAPTER 25

SLASH

*T*here's not a snowball's chance in hell that they're following the good trolls into their new, magic tree.

Not one.

Every sense Slash possesses flares to life, begging him to run in the opposite direction, but he has put on a smooth front. He's broken bread with their "saviors," done everything he could so that the element of surprise would be the one thing he could pin his hopes of survival on.

Kiern waves at them from the entrance, and Slash nods, lifting his hand in a wave at the same time he says to Adrianna like a ventriloquist, "Do you trust me?"

Adrianna swings her face to his, unconsciously flicking her right shoulder back to resettle the unicorn pack.

The tip of one horn sparkles in the dying light still filtering through the high canopy of the forest, as though they're lost pieces from the sun. Faded and ethereal, the forest glows with the last breath of day before twilight chokes it out.

"Yes," she says quietly, thick worry saturating her voice.

"Piggyback, Adrianna."

Slash utters a prayer to the moon then pivots in a blur, crouching, and hikes Adrianna onto his back.

He doesn't tell his mate to hang on. She chokes him with her hold.

Slash goes wolfen, and her stranglehold stops mattering. Slash churns the dirt as his boots blast off his feet. His shirt splits, and the athletic pants he wears when traveling max out at the waistband, but Slash is already moving.

The air shimmers in the distance, another vision replacing the realty of their environment.

Women appear as though he's seeing them through rain sheeting over glass.

But Slash is moving, following his nose and nothing else.

A roar like a hundred unleashed lions stomps his eardrums as the thunder of the trolls' footsteps charge after him, shaking the ground.

Green leaves fall like fresh, soft rain and Slash feels Adrianna's tears on his neck where she clings to his back.

Slash races toward that shimmering mirage. He can smell the trolls as they gain.

He thrashes through undergrowth, missing trees by inches. Small saplings snap as the trolls plow through what he avoided twenty paces before.

Space folds, and Slash feels the brush of something bearing down on them.

The fine hairs all over this form rise.

"Slash!" Adrianna screams, and Slash leaps, tossing his arms out to catch whatever hangs.

As luck would have it, a low branch accepts their weight, and he swivels to the right, praying to avoid anything that's grabbing for Adrianna.

He swings back, catching the branch with both hands, and meets the eyes of Kiern.

The troll opens his mouth and roars, tendons at his throat standing out like cords of rope.

The group of trolls do not move forward.

Kiern swipes toward Slash and Adrianna hanging above the steep gully, tantalizingly near, in obvious frustration, but ten feet separate them.

The trolls seem unwilling to breach that distance for reasons Slash can't fathom.

"Jump!" an unrecognized voice says from behind Slash.

He doesn't dare to take his eyes off the trolls to see who is speaking.

Slash can't go back the way he came. Twenty enraged trolls pile up behind their leader. Spittle drips from their mouths and clubs stained red from prior use are ready in their mighty fists.

He can't protect Adrianna from all of them.

Thank the moon he sensed the trolls meant them harm, or their fate would already be sealed.

"Adrianna."

Her hold tightens. "Get us out of here!"

"Listen—look behind us."

"O-Okay."

A moment that seems like eternity passes, and finally she says, "Three women are about twenty feet behind us."

"Who?"

She whispers, "They smell like Della."

Slash fights closing his eyes in misery. Somehow, he and Adrianna stumbled on some kind of witch-troll feud, and they are dead center in the middle. Exactly where they need not to be.

The trolls mean them harm. Every inch of him feels it.

"Slash," Adrianna says in a low, miserable voice.

Making a split-second decision where there really is not one to be made, he swivels, arcing his body, and tossing himself and Adrianna toward the witches.

Kiern lunges just as Slash lands in a crouch, Adrianna tucking herself tightly against his back.

Slash turns back just in time to see Kiern's nose sheared off as though an invisible blade hacked at the end.

His hand drops next, and disembodied fingers twitch as it flops on the forest floor.

The troll leader bellows, clutching the stump of wrist as he attempts to roll back in the direction he came. Instead, gravity pulls him forward, dragging him down the slope toward Slash.

Slash digs his talons into the steep ravine, pushing hard, and leap frogs up the side, bringing them farther away from the rolling troll.

He turns a second time, surveying the trolls.

None go where their leader hazarded.

Kiern groans, cursing them as part of his small toe and a kneecap join his other dismembered body parts.

The bits and pieces of the troll smolder close to where he writhes against the undergrowth as an unseen force acts as both knife and barricade.

As Slash watches, another bit of Kiern's flailing arm flies off.

Slash runs his eyes over every inch that stands between them. Kiern screams in agony as he attempts to roll over, and half his buttocks is shaved off in the process.

White fresh skin glows for a horrible handful of seconds and begins to fill with blood.

Slash backs away from the sight.

The trolls will not be following them. Somehow, he and Adrianna passed through the invisible obstruction unharmed.

"Slash," Adrianna calls out. He reaches around, securing her at the same time as he offers his reassurance.

He rotates slowly, arm still on Adrianna, and faces the women.

"Talk now, or I'll attack." His arm falls away from his mate, and he plants his feet wide in readiness, staring the three women down.

Their eyes widen. "We are witches."

"Wrong answer," Adrianna says in a dry voice, and Slash can't help the curling of his lips.

He is blessed with a resilient mate. With trolls at their backs and witches at their front, Adrianna jokes.

Moon, how I love her.

"We have already encountered one of your kind." His gaze fields them together, marking them for the wounds he will inflict, when a tall woman steps from the knot of three. "Della is insane. She was our best guard of the trolls, and when we lost contact, we knew all hope was lost."

Slash contains his surprise of their foreknowledge.

"Guardian of the trolls?" Adrianna slips off his back, but maintains a touch on his body with her hand. He draws her against his side, subtly turning his body to keep the trolls in his peripheral vision while also keeping the witches within view.

The tall witch nods. "We came to this country from Europe long ago—centuries. The trolls have always required guardians, a debt tasked to us. They are too dangerous to live freely."

Adrianna snorts. "We thought they were good."

The witch's eyes, like gleaming seawater, look beyond them at the trolls still wailing and gnashing their teeth. "Their magic is deep. There would be much they could gain from a Lycan couple in true love. Much."

Adrianna presses against Slash. "That's what Della said about us."

"She should have been relieved by another. By the time we found there was a problem, we had to curse her, locking her in with her own magic—she and the trolls both."

The witch at the woman's left—Slash has a difficult time telling between the three because they look so similar—comes forward. "To live too long amongst the trolls is to go crazy."

"Yeah," Adrianna comments.

Slash squeezes her lightly, and she doesn't say more.

"We want safe passage. And my patience is gone. Della tried to kill me and poison Adrianna, for the child she bears."

The witches' eyes widen. "She was more lost than we could imagine." She gives Adrianna a gaze of unfiltered sadness.

But Slash isn't buying any of it. The supernaturals of this area have done nothing but attempt to dupe them the entire time. He'll trust himself and no one else. Like he's always done.

"You're not baby killers?" Adrianna says.

Slash growls.

The tall witch gives a solemn shake of her head, black hair slithering over her narrow shoulders encased in a deep scarlet cape. "No. We are Druid. We come from ancient sorcery bloodlines. We are the protectors of life—not the takers."

"Della didn't get the memo."

"Adrianna."

She takes a step forward. "Let us help you. We owe you that."

Slash shakes his head, his talons flashing without a command. "I've had about enough help as I can stand."

Her eyes tighten at the sight of the weapons that sprout from the end of his fingers. Of course his physicality is not proof against magic, but Slash can still inflict grave injuries quickly.

And these witches appear wandless.

Slash chances a glance at the trolls, some of which are carefully making their way down the path to their fallen leader, presumably attempting to pull him to safety.

"It was your feelings for each other and supernatural status that allowed you entry. A fluke," she continues.

"I don't care if it was a meteor strike. Adrianna and I will leave this place." Slash feels his brows drop. "Or I will kill you." His gaze runs over the three, including them all in his proclamation.

The youngest looking of the three eyes the trolls, gives an exhale of pronounced defeat, and begins a slow trudge to where the trolls are.

"What's she doing?" Adrianna asks.

Slash keeps his eyes on the witches, watching the youngest.

"Dying," the other two say in eerie unison.

"What?" Adrianna says, clearly alarmed.

"Stay out of it, mate."

"Eff that, Slash."

He holds her against him in case she becomes foolhardy and tries to rescue someone who might be their enemy.

The youngest witch continues her short trek then passes the invisible line. Tears streak her face like liquid gems.

When she gets near the area where Kiern lost his body parts, she reaches out, touching something no one can see directly in front of her. A pulse of color stretches out from the contact, unveiling a wall of light and energy.

The witch's body goes from strong and youthful to withered and old. The wall grows brighter, brighter—brighter still.

When there is nothing but skin and bones and her eye sockets are hollowed holes inside her head, the witch drops in a pile of fabric and skin.

The wall bursts in front of them with brilliant rainbow iridescence, shimmering like fine crystal in sunlight.

Slowly, the appearance of the burning wall begins to soften, growing dull and melting back to air and space, leaving a steep, small ravine and emerald forests between where they stand and where they were.

The trolls raise their faces to the sky, bellowing their rage.

Slash hikes Adrianna against him, and she clings to his neck. Their eyes go to the fallen witch.

"Why did she do that?" Adrianna asks, and Slash feels the thump of her heartbeat against his body.

The two remaining witches have tears staining their faces. "So that another of us would not be sacrificed for the next one thousand years of safeguarding. And losing our minds, possibly hurting or murdering innocents."

They look at the heap of clothing from the fallen witch.

"Deandre gave her essence, her energy, to maintain the veil around the trolls. She strengthened this part of your world that is thin. Keeping them in place. Protecting humans and supernatural, alike."

"Okay, let's go," Adrianna whispers.

Slash doesn't ask permission or speak. He begins to walk away backward—from the dead witch, the clearly evil trolls, and the two Druid witches. They will not take him from behind if they have a mind to.

Their eyes mark Adrianna and Slash's progress.

"We're not the enemy," the tall one says.

Without a reply, Slash keeps walking, watching for them to make chase, cast a spell, or try for his mate.

They don't, but Slash will feel ease only when there's sufficient distance between these plagued woods and Adrianna—and the whelp she carries.

As far as he's concerned, one million miles wouldn't be enough.

Slash heads south, toward the Northwestern, where he and Adrianna might have a chance at a life. A life not filled with strife.

He doesn't know what kind they'll have; he can only hope.

They don't break stride or hesitate until they're almost to the human highway, far from the trolls, witches, and whatever other bewitchery seethes inside the deep woods, waiting like an unsprung trap.

Slash finally turns, giving the witches, who are miles away now, his back.

He runs, taking his new mate with him. Her warm safe presence at his back is a balm to his soul.

They run a course that parallels the human highway but doesn't move too far within the woods.

The ancient forest holds many things. And Slash is not curious to discover what they are.

THE END

Read more

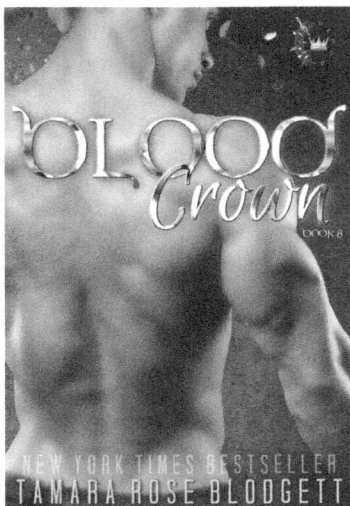

☞ **Your words are powerful.** If you enjoyed REDEMPTIVE, please post your star rating/thoughts **HERE** and help another reader discover a new author. *Thank you!*

Never miss a new release - **Subscribe** below:
SIGN UP TO BE ON THE
♥ MARATA EROS VIP LIST ♥
SIGN UP TO BE ON THE
♥TAMARA ROSE BLODGETT VIP LIST ♥

☞ **Your words are powerful**. If you enjoyed, *Redemptive Blood,* please post your star rating/ thoughts and help another reader discover a new author. *Thank you!*

Other Marata Eros/ TRB novels as follows:

PUNISHED

CLUB ALPHA

BLOOD SINGERS

A HARD LESSON

DEATH WHISPERS

REAPERS

THE REFLECTIVE

NOOSE

HER: A LOVE STORY

THE PEARL SAVAGE

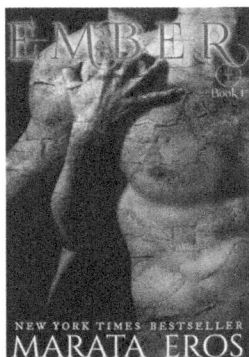

EMBER

PROVOCATION

BROLACH

THROUGH DARK GLASS

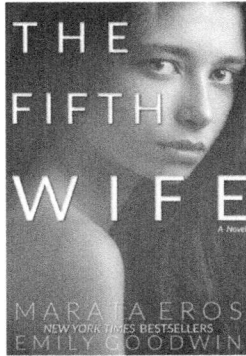

THE FIFTH WIFE

Read on for a bonus chapter from another Marata Eros work ....

PUNISHED

An Alpha Claim World Novel

Book 1

New York Times BESTSELLER
TAMARA ROSE BLODGETT

* * *

Narah

My legs are kicked up on the desk, the toes of my left combat boot stacked on the heel of my right. I lean my feet a couple of inches to the left and look at my boss.

Kinda wish I hadn't.

The tongue-lashing was going to be brutal, and not the fun kind. I just barely hold back a snort of self-serving comedy.

"Narah," Casper leans into the desk, edging a butt cheek on the only part not covered by my assortment of shit. My eyebrow cocks. Perturbed doesn't cover it. If I wanted a butt on my desk, I'd ask.

"What?" I bark with anticipation.

A vein in Casper's forehead throbs and I dial it back some. No need to bring the guy to heart failure.

"What?" I repeat more good-naturedly, though both of us know I'm nothing of the sort.

He sighs, scrubbing a palm over his face. Hair almost as white as swan feathers glows under the LED lighting in my tiny office, and his glacial eyes tighten, fighting for a view of my face over the top of my boot.

I jack my feet down and stuff them underneath my desk. My fingers itch to go to my smart phone. Anything to not commit to this conversation.

"You know we appreciate your skill set."

Blah, blah, stinking-blah.

"But we can't have you pulling firearms on all your bounties."

My bottom lip pops out in a pout. "It was a very small gun, Casper." I put my index and thumb almost touching.

"Using manstopper ammunition?"

He might have a small point.

"Outlawed in 1898," Casper adds.

I shrug a bare shoulder, my tank top skin-tight against my small frame. I find loose clothes are handles to make a bludgeon against me easier. I nail the targets but if there's nothing for them to grab onto, so much the better.

"I like antique weaponry and ammunition," I say with deliberate nonchalance.

"Really?" Casper says and I wince at the sound of his voice. "Let's run down the list of target fatalities."

Hmmm.

"Target 103, lethal stabbing."

I lean back in my chair and cock my neck back, staring at the dingy ceiling. A water stain has spread out from the center in a pattern of copper lines that somehow resemble a flower opening.

It's sort of like watching clouds outside, but inside.

"Narah!"

I sigh, answering the ceiling. "Yeah."

"Target 424, beheading."

Yeah, that'd been messy.

"Again, I was in fear for my life," I say, not sounding defensive.

At. All.

"Thirteen times?" Casper asks softly.

My chin snaps down and I meet his eyes. Mine are big and golden hazel like a cat's, and that's why I hide them behind my aviator shades. The sun hurts like hell. I've always been sensitive to sunlight.

I shrug. It'll get me nowhere to fight with Casper. Who has the nickname in the office of, The Ghost. No one says it to his face though. I fight a snicker.

"We are the last profession for use of lethal force, you know. It's not goddamned 2015, when everyone thought all physical force was necessary in some capacity."

I'm in the wrong era, I muse with regret.

"We are the last stand against the criminals of our time. When the police can't nail them, then it's up to us. But Narah," Casper scrubs his head, his crewcut bristling from the contact, "we can't have you killing all the targets. They must be brought to justice."

And of course, if I kill a target, Casper doesn't get credits. That's what this is *really* about. I bring in the most targets in our office. I get results and he gets credits for my hard work.

We stare at each other. I won't break and Casper knows it. "You're the finest bounty hunter we have. Your instincts are uncanny, and you never let being a woman get in your way..."

I lunge to my feet and Casper jerks to his, eyeing me warily.

Good, my desk is finally free of his ass.

"Nothing about me being a woman comes into play here."

Casper shoots out an exhale like a cannon. "Everything about it matters. You're smaller, you're vulnerable to things a man could never be."

Rape is the clear inference.

"You think a man can't be raped?" I bark out a laugh. "You think that my looks don't disarm. They do, Cas." My eyes laser down on him and his shift away. "You know I'm a proficient, Level Ten."

"Nothing to sneeze at," he concedes and opens his mouth to add more, perhaps dig his grave a little deeper.

I raise my palm. *Nothing to sneeze at.* I can feel a royal conniption fit brewing. "No. If I've killed while gunning for a target," Casper frowns at my wording which causes me to grin, "then they needed dying. Period."

Casper walks to my office door. "I'm sorry, Narah, I've done what I could, but the law states that there can't be more than ten sanctions in one quarter. You have thirteen. I got the bonus three waived." He whips his palm in the air like he's performing a magic trick. "Now you'll have to go before the magistrate."

Fuck. They'd plug me a second ass after a first class reaming. If—*if* I could even bounty again.

I jerk my leather jacket off the back of my chair and sling it on. A bright headache, a new friend of mine of late, settles into my temples with zeal. I press my fingers against my head.

I hate not having a target. The chase is the one thing that makes my life worth living. No longer an outcast—always in the game.

Now the rules are being threatened.

And all I want to do is play.

* * *

Aselin

Edan jerks a thumb my way, throwing a towel I deftly catch. I dab at the sweat running like a river from my scalp and making its way to the waistband of my work out gear.

"Corcoran's asking for you."

I look at him, narrowing my eyes.

"Hey man, don't kill the messenger," Edan's hands spread away from his body.

He'd look so much more innocent if he had even one spot of bare skin. Edan's tatted from head to toe. Well... that's not entirely accurate. Don't think his feet hold the tats of our species. Or his face.

Turners are required to be marked.

It's grounds for immediate execution to civilian vampires if they touch us. After all, we're the only savior of our dying race. They can't miss our marks. In the human world, tattoos no longer stand out. We hide in plain sight now.

I flick irritated eyes to him. "I'm on leave, Edan."

He shrugs. "You know the drill. If a female comes on the radar, we're all on alert."

I throw the damp towel in the soiled laundry hamper. I'm bone tired. Not physically—mentally. So many scouting expeditions and coming up empty handed has taken its toll. I rub a hand on my nape, trying to make a raw spot. "I've worked a solid quarter—nothing."

My eyes meet his. Edan's looks are unusual for a Turner. Most of the sub-sect of vampire Turners possess dark coloring. Our only unified feature are silver eyes. Edan's are amber. Some kind of genetic throw back. My own hair is a deep chestnut, more red than what is considered fashionable. And if we want to enjoy female vampire company, it matters. They're few and far between. If they can't be our mates, it's only for release. And that's become an empty vessel.

"But what if we have a live one?"

I smirk at his words. "You mean undead, right?"

Edan throws up his hands. He's muscled, like the rest of us. Mandatory training makes our bodies at battle readiness. Last month we'd just missed a female by minutes.

She'd been sterilized. Technically, it'd been on our watch.

The loss had brought the entire team down and morale had not recovered.

Edan spoke my thoughts, "We need this, Aeslin. We need a female. They're so vulnerable to the Hunters..."

I toss my palm up. "We've been over this. It's a race against them. And they got to that female first." I see guilt on his face and know mine looks the same.

"Then why can't you see that every lead should be followed?"

Tired of fucking losing, that's why. Or just tired.

My eyes feel like they're on fire when I glare at Edan, a Turner I've fought shoulder to shoulder beside. "You don't think it haunts my fucking every thought that she could have belonged to one of us?"

"Does it?" Edan asks in soft disbelief.

"Yes," I hiss defensively.

"Then join us."

I don't want another dead end. Another disappointment. "I'm not rested."

"So when has that ever mattered?" he asks.

Since that female was lost, I think but don't say.

* * *

Corcoran stands at the window when I walk into his office and shut the door.

He doesn't turn.

Corcoran is a Noble.

A politically correct word for being in charge of the Turners. But he became a Noble the hard way, having been a Turner first and struggling through the ranks to prove himself invaluable to the cause. Now he rules over the Turners of our region with an iron fist.

Hell, in his day, there was a female turned every month. Now we were lucky to turn one a quarter. However, there was one biological advantage. A human female with vampire blood once turned, was always meant for her biological other half. Lucky bastard. It meant offspring.

A chance at happiness.

With Hunters killing off every vampire they could, our numbers continued to dwindle. In the last half-century, one in two females who possessed enough of the blood of our kind had been sterilized before they could be turned, negating their vampire ancestry and the ability to have children.

A Turners' goals were two-fold. Find the hybrid vampire females before the Hunters did, and determine how they were setting their sights on the rare females.

Easier said than done.

"Aeslin," Corcoran said as greeting.

I remain silent.

Corcoran turns, eyeing me up. "You look rested." He sounds hopeful. We both know I've had only four days respite.

I need a month.

I haven't taken enough blood, had enough sex, slept inside the ground as I should. A lot of *have nots* on the short list of my exhaustion.

I lift my shoulders in an answer that isn't one. It will do no good to rehash the discussion I had with Edan.

Corcoran says something under his breath. It sounds suspiciously like a curse.

"You're the best I have, Aeslin," he says quietly.

"Let Edan take it. Hell—Jaryn could..."

His gaze darkens. Eyes not the common light gray of the Turner are pewter in a face devoid of emotions. Corcoran's gaze is a coming storm.

"I need you on this."

That's just what Edan said. "I mean no disrespect..."

"Yes, you do," he says with the barest bit of humor.

My lips thin. "Yes."

"She's a Turn, Aeslin. I know it." Corcoran closes his fingers into a fist.

My breath leaks out of me in defeat. "Okay."

I simply don't believe anymore. There's been so many dry runs I can't remember the last one that wasn't.

"She's sending out pheromones like a distress signal."

"Who called it?"

His face closes down. "Torin."

Corcoran and Torin don't see eye-to-eye. I say nothing, waiting. I'm not political and won't immerse myself in it now.

Corcoran slams a fist against the wall that bisects the bulletproof windows. "She's bounty."

His frustration gets my attention. Hell, her occupation stalls me and I unlace my fingers and straighten my posture. "What?"

"Damn," he grits through his teeth, knowing full-well the risks of this acquisition.

I tell him anyway. "Too high profile," I state, hands going to my hips.

"She's manifesting."

Dammit.

"Is Torin sure she's a Turn?"

Corcoran exhales in a rush, taking a rough palm down his face, nodding.

I suck in a deep breath. "I'll do it."

Corcoran looks relieved. "You know the risk?"

Hell yes. But another sterilized female? That we don't need. Can't stand.

"Yes," I answer.

If Torin's got a bead on her, then so do the Hunters.

The thought of a female out there and vulnerable tightens my guts. This is the part of my job I hate. However small, the emotion is there in my suppressed emotional makeup. The hardest to squelch, the most damning.

Hope.

* * *

Rio raises the paper in the air. "Right from the top, Matthews!" I snap my head up, my back on the bench as I flick my eyes to Rio then back to the bar. My arms shake from exertion but I can't take my eyes off the weights I'm pressing. Not unless I want my body as a pancake.

"Spot me, asshole," I grit.

"Right! Sorry hoss."

I'd roll my eyes if I wasn't so fucking plowed from fatigue.

Rio appears upside down and above me. His hands hover over the bar, I lift, as I take the last rep by storm. I heave another.

"No clanking," Rio chimes.

Gonna kill his ass.

Beads of sweat roll, burning into my eyes as I gently set the bar on the brackets. It's almost soundless.

Rio smirks.

He whips the paper around and I duck out from underneath the three hundred pound weighted barbell set.

"God *damn*—you're a beast, Matthews!" Rio chortles.

"Give that to me and stop with the verbal diarrhea."

Rio's face tightens. "Fine, fuck. You need to get laid if you're going to get your jock strap in a bunch all the time."

I jerk the paper out of his hand and read the words.

Assignment thirteen.

I smile.

Thirteen is my lucky number.

I give the paper back to Rio. "Gonna save the world, brother."

"On your life."

"I hope not," Rio winks and begins to walk off.

"Specs?" I yell after him.

"Same delivery as usual." I shouldn't ask, it's protocol but I like to hear the words anyway. It makes me uneasy when things are changed. I like routine—crave it.

I sit on the weight bench, thumbing the missive. A thrill races through my body.

I'm a Hunter.

And being a Hunter is bigger than me.

It's for humanity.

People walk the streets; eating, sleeping, shitting and humping. They never realize there's an entire underworld of supernaturals vying for the top of the ecological heap. They're oblivious to the danger that sweeps past them like an unrelenting current.

Hunters have been in place since ancient times. Our opposition have the same sorcerer's blood that we possess.

Druid.

Both sides descend from priests of the highest order.

But instead of exterminating the vermin, they are saviors of those that would harm who we're sworn to protect. They believe in perpetuation, and we believe in sterilization.

The Harborer's are the nemesis of our kind. Brothers by blood, enemies by deed.

The sooner we wipe out the supernaturals, the sooner the threat to mankind will end. And we're making steady progress.

I move through the expansive gym where all Hunters hone their forms, turning sideways to pass between the heavy equipment. I've worked myself so bulky I'm at the point of losing grace. However, no Hunter wants to be distracted by their own lack of strength when they've got an assignment to fulfill.

I'll get the details of my next sanction and be done. Hopefully it's another kill. Nothing gets my rocks off more than nailing one of the fangs myself. A larger threat would be a Harborer showing up for the same assignment. But they are fewer in number than Hunters. Vampires are the greater threat.

Even a skilled Hunter full of quality bloodline magic can find himself in the death embrace of a clever fang and poof—dead meat. The ultimate threat of being turned by one of them hangs over every one of us.

No Hunter wants to deal with that potential. Get in, kill the fuckers, and get the hell out.

Simple.

* * *

I run my high security keycard through the slot and the door to my penthouse suite whispers open. I move through and the door slides closed behind me. The midwestern skyline bleeds a purple and red sunset over downtown Sioux Falls as it colors my floor like beaten fruit.

I stretch and the vertebrae in my back give a satisfying round of pops. I toss my car keys in a low bowl of Mexican pottery that sits on top of a table hugging the jog out in the foyer.

The floor plan is one of my choosing. It's narrow in the entrance and widens to an open living room and kitchen combination.

Not that I do a shit ton of cooking. My lips pull at the thought of cooking as I cruise to my fridge. I open it, and true to form, there's no food, but plenty of beer. I grab one and pop the lid using a sterling band on my right ring finger. It's hell on beer caps.

I take a hard pull, taking the frosty beer to half empty and move to the view seen through my floor to ceiling glass windows.

Philips Street is overrun with tourists enjoying the bronze statues and Native American shops that dot the area. My excellent night vision is not necessary at the moment. Not with twilight promising nighttime. I roll the cool bottle against my forehead as my gaze wanders and sigh.

I have twelve hours before response is required for the sanction.

I set the nearly empty beer on a low thick glass coffee table. A hot shower and catching five hours of sleep is my entire goal before this mission. I'm beat. Chasing down hybrids is a full-time job.

Walking to the wall that rounds to the hall leading to the bathroom, I pass a palm over a glass sculpture that hangs like artwork.

It's not.

A brilliant blue spiderweb of light harmlessly lasers over my skin, reading the unique lines of my hand. A single chime sounds in the silence and the front slides away to reveal a black hole.

I pull out a cylinder that rests inside.

It'll have all the instructions for assignment thirteen. Name, birthdate, location. My sector covers the midwest states. There are twelve of us serving this area.

A vial with a syringe is enclosed in an thick airtight lucite case. My pulse quickens.

It'll be my first.

A woman.

Hunters sanction male hybrids. It's the Hunters' core belief that women should be protected. None of us kill females. I don't allow myself to touch on what happens when a rare hybrid is located and a Hunter won't sterilize. The penalty is severe and immediate for lack of follow through.

Or the disastrous transgression of mating with a hybrid, though rare, it's not unheard of. Those are grounds for a Kill Order.

I set my dark thoughts aside as the specs fall out last, rolled neatly with the traditional black satin ribbon keeping them in a tight circle.

I pop the ribbon and look over the specs, reading them twice.

Occupation: *Bounty Enforcer.*

I whistle low in the back of my throat. I'm all for a challenge.

I slug the rest of my beer back, running a fingertip over the name.

Narah Adrienne.

I crush the specs, having already committed them to memory. I walk over to my fireplace and toss the crumpled parchment inside the firebox. Striking a match on the base of my boot, I throw the lit match inside and watch it burn. A low flame bursts over the ancient paper and renders the message unreadable.

Ash rises up the flu. Ms. Adrienne's fate is not yet set in stone.

I smile at the thought of destiny. *Here I come, sweetheart.*

Read more

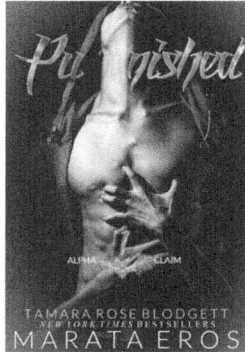

ACKNOWLEDGMENTS

I published both *The Druid* and *Death Series*, in 2011 with the encouragement of my husband, and continued because of you, my Reader. Your faithfulness, through comments, suggestions, spreading the word and ultimately purchasing my work with your hard-earned money gave me the incentive, means and inspiration to continue.

There are no words that are sufficiently adequate to express my thankfulness for your support.

I truly feel connected to my readers. It is obvious to me, but I'll say the words anyway for clarity: a written work is just words on pages if they are not read by my readers. As I write this I get a lump in my throat; your enjoyment of my work affects me that deeply.

You guys are the greatest, each and every one of ya~

Tamara
   xoxo

Special thanks:
You, my reader.
My husband, who is my biggest fan.
Cameren, without who, there would be no books.

Special mention:

Jackie

Dawn

Susan

Erica

Liz

Cherri-Anne

Theresa

Bev

Phyllis

Eric

ABOUT THE AUTHOR

www.tamararoseblodgett.com

<u>**Tamara Rose Blodgett**</u>: happily married mother of four sons. Dark thriller writer. Reader. Dreamer. Beach-combing slave. Tie dye zealot. Digs music.

She is also the *New York Times* bestselling author of <u>*A Terrible Love*</u>, written under the pen name, Marata Eros, and 75+ other novels. Other bestseller accolades include her #1 bestselling **TOKEN** (dark romance), **DRUID** (dark PNR erotica), **ROAD KILL MC** (thriller/top 100) **DEATH** (sci-fi dark fantasy) series. Tamara writes a variety of dark fiction in the genres: erotica, fantasy, horror, romance, sci-fi, suspense and thriller. She splits her time between the Pacific NW and Mazatlán Mexico, spending time with family, friends and a pair of disrespectful dogs.

To be the first to hear about new releases and bargains —from Tamara Rose Blodgett/Marata Eros—sign up below to be on my VIP List. (I swear I won't spam or share your email with anyone!)

SIGN UP TO BE ON THE **MARATA EROS** VIP LIST https://tinyurl.com/SubscribeMarataEros-News

SIGN UP TO BE ON THE **TAMARA ROSE BLODGETT** VIP LIST https://tinyurl.com/SubscribeTRB-News

Connect with Tamara:

Clapper (*a TicTok alternative*)

Rumble (*Free audiobooks/ Tin Foil Crown thoughts*)

Website

YouTube (*Carnivore/Zero Carb eating*)

Follow Marata Eros on Bookbub

Follow Tamara Rose Blodgett on Bookbub

🐦

♥ **Read more titles from this author** ♥

A Terrible Love (NYT & USA Today bestseller)

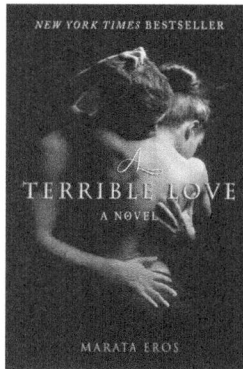

The Reflective – REFLECTION

Punished– ALPHA CLAIM

Death Whispers – DEATH

The Pearl Savage - SAVAGE

Blood Singers– BLOOD

Noose – ROAD KILL MC

Provocation – TOKEN

Ember – SIREN

Brolach – DEMON

Reapers - DRUID

Club Alpha – BILLIONAIRE'S GAME TRILOGY

REDEMPTIVE BLOOD
A Blood World Novel
Book 7

New York Times BESTSELLER
TAMARA ROSE BLODGETT

Made in the USA
Las Vegas, NV
21 January 2025

16725933R00184